SPLIT

C O M E S   I N   T H R E E S   S E R I E S

Three - Way SPLIT

COMES IN THREES SERIES

ELIA WINTERS

Entangled Publishing, LLC
2614 South Timberline Road
Suite 105, PMB 159
Fort Collins, CO 80525
rights@entangledpublishing.com

Scorched is an imprint of Entangled Publishing, LLC.

Edited by Tera Cuskaden
Cover design by Cover Couture
Cover photography by
ChirtsovaNatalia/Shutterstock
lithian/Shutterstock

Manufactured in the United States of America

First Edition August 2018

entangled
scorched

To the A-Team

Chapter One

Hannah sank back into the booth seat, the smooth leather cushioning her with the familiar cradle of a well-known spot, and looked lustfully at the man emerging through the swinging door of the Mapleton Pub kitchen. The burger he was holding was beautiful, but the head chef carrying it was definitely the tastier-looking entrée. With his blond hair, chiseled jaw, and steel-gray eyes, Mitchell Fredericks was so model pretty it was practically a cliché. Add in that body, built like a brick wall, and she would take whatever he was serving her. She smiled at Mitchell as he reached her table, resting her chin on her hand.

"Damn, Mitchell, all that meat for me?"

Mitchell gave her a tight-lipped smile, his favorite kind. "You know it, Hannah." He slid the burger in front of her, giving her the chance to ogle his taut forearms below the rolled-up cuffs of his chef jacket. "And for you, Lori, the fish and chips. Just as fried, just as deadly." He pulled a bottle of malt vinegar out of his jacket pocket and set it down next to her. "And your malt vinegar. Like I could forget."

Across from Hannah, her best friend, Lori, smiled up at Mitchell and accepted her plate. "Ahh, Mitchell, nobody's coming here for the health food. You're not going to sell salads as long as the rest of your menu is so delicious." She shook her head in appreciation, the loose spiral curls of her afro bouncing with the movement. After tapping her fork on the batter of the fish, she made an appreciative noise that sounded obscenely sexual. "That is a beautiful batter."

"Thank you." Mitchell looked between the two women. "Do you ladies need anything else?"

Hannah flashed him another dazzling smile. "I was hoping to make some more inappropriate double entendres about the burger if you wanted to stick around."

Mitchell sighed and shook his head. "I swear you only like me for my food."

Hannah shrugged. "I can't help it. You deliver the meat. Besides, you'd be disappointed if I stopped making lewd comments. What else are you going to think about at night?" She bit into a french fry, still looking up at him through her lashes. Teasing Mitchell was one of her favorite games.

"I'm sure I'd think of something." He put his hands on his hips. "You planning to be at tonight's Chamber of Commerce meeting?"

"You know it." Hannah raised her water. "Some late-breaking news about Fall Festival."

"Yeah, I saw the email." He scratched his jaw, where he always had a light dusting of blond stubble. Hard to tell if he was keeping that on purpose or if he just got lazy about shaving. Probably the latter. He didn't seem to be the type to obsess about his appearance, except for clearly working out on the regular. He kept talking as she poured out some ketchup for her fries. "I want to see if Ben will come tonight. He might want to get involved in the festival."

"Ben?" Hannah hadn't seen Mitchell's best friend at the

Chamber of Commerce meetings in a long time. She seldom saw him in general, even though he and Mitchell were co-owners of the restaurant. "Is he going to sell beer at your booth?"

"I don't know. Regulations have been a pain in the ass in past years. They've always charged a lot more to booths that sell alcohol."

"You should, you know." Lori piped up and lifted her glass of German-style wheat beer. "Sell this stuff at the festival. Even if it costs more. I would cut a bitch to get some."

Mitchell fixed her with a deadpan expression. "If you don't want to get violent, you could just buy some in the shop. Or at the supermarket. We distribute all over western Mass."

"You get your beer wherever you want, Lori. I'll be here every week as long as everything stays so delicious." Hannah winked at Mitchell, who shook his head at her lewd expression.

"Enjoy your lunch." Mitchell took a step back. "Jess will be over to check on you soon."

As soon as he was back in the kitchen, Lori rounded on Hannah. "You are a whore, you know that?"

Hannah laughed. "You're not allowed to call me a whore! You're doing your entire dissertation on alternative sexualities."

"Your only alternative sexuality is flirting shamelessly with that man and never doing anything about it." Lori sighed, turning to peer at the closed kitchen door, then turned back to Hannah. "He is a fine piece of man."

"You want him, you go after him." Hannah took another bite of burger. "You know I don't do relationships."

Lori wrinkled her nose. "I don't know. He's hot and all, but I haven't dated a white guy in a really long time. And I don't think the middle of my PhD dissertation research is the time to get involved with someone new. Plus, he's so serious.

I need someone more lighthearted. Or several someones. I don't know." She used her fork to break apart the flaky fish and batter. "The deeper I get into this dissertation, the more I think that monogamy is fundamentally flawed." She popped the bite into her mouth, then sprinkled some malt vinegar over the entire plate.

"I don't think so." Hannah contemplated her friend across the table. "I know lots of people who are happy with monogamous relationships. Just because I'm not one of them doesn't mean the whole system is a failure." She set the burger down and gestured at Lori with a fry. "You're having sample bias. You've only been talking to nonmonogamous people, and now you think monogamy is terrible."

Lori broke off another piece of fish. "Maybe. But aren't you being hypocritical here? You're always blabbing about how you'll never tie yourself down to one person, one man can never meet all your needs, blah, blah, blah. How is that any different than what I'm saying?"

Hannah picked up her burger and thoughtfully chewed a bite, considering how to answer. "I think most people are happy with just one partner. I'm too independent for that. It wouldn't be fair to put all my desires onto one guy and think he can be everything to me." That, and the idea of being vulnerable and risking heartbreak was not on her to-do list. "My needs are...varied."

Lori snorted. "Kinky as fuck, you mean." She gave Hannah a knowing look, and Hannah grinned in response.

"What can I say? I own a sex-toy store. It's spoiled me for vanilla missionary sex." She ate more of her burger. "God, if I could fuck this burger, I would."

"That's unsanitary and terrifying." Lori sprinkled some more malt vinegar over her plate. "You should fuck the chef instead."

Hannah sighed. "Don't think I haven't considered it.

Nightly, and in a number of detailed ways."

"What's stopping you?"

"Mitchell's a relationship kind of guy. You can just tell."

"How can you just tell?" Lori pressed.

How *couldn't* she just tell? All the conversations she'd had with him, both here in the restaurant and at their monthly Chamber of Commerce meetings—it was obvious.

"It's hard to describe. You spend so long working in a sex shop, you get a feel for people. Who's a freak, who's not. Mitchell's not. He's vanilla. He's monogamous. He's probably looking for a committed relationship. Or maybe he's not looking for any relationship at all. This restaurant probably keeps him pretty busy."

Lori shrugged. "Maybe he's already in a relationship."

"Nah." Hannah paused, looking off toward the closed door, then back at Lori. "You think? I've never seen him with anyone besides Ben, but that makes sense since they live together."

Lori raised both eyebrows but didn't comment.

"No, I don't think so. It's not like that." Hannah shook her head. "They're best friends. Business partners. And Mitchell flirts with me like that all the time. I feel like if he were with someone already, I'd know about it. He'd talk about it, at least."

"Maybe." Lori didn't look convinced, but she also didn't continue to debate the issue with Hannah. Any sort of friendship that lasted so long—in their case, the ten years since college—came with that kind of sixth sense where she felt like she knew Hannah better than Hannah knew herself. Hell, sometimes she probably did.

It was probably Mitchell's loss, though, that she wasn't going to fuck him. She was good in bed—she'd had enough experience to confirm—and her career had taught her a few tricks not known to the more traditionally employed. After all, when you had eight hundred square feet of retail sex shop space plus two hundred square feet of storage, you had a *lot* of sex toys, and a lot of time to learn creative ways people might use them.

"If you're not going to fuck the chef, then who are you fucking?" Lori stopped eating long enough to drink some of her beer. "I know you've got to be fucking somebody. I just keep thinking you're hiding it from me. Like, maybe you're fucking a celebrity and had to sign an NDA."

Hannah snorted in laughter. "Not in over a month. Work has been crazy, and we had inventory last week, and before that, my parents were visiting." She grimaced at the memory. She loved her parents, but having them a few hours away in Maine was much nicer for their relationship than when they were staying in her house. They always found little ways to criticize her, small, well-intentioned comments about how she might be living her life differently that left her on edge by the end of any visit.

"How are you even coping without sex?" Lori's smile was teasing, a flash of white teeth.

Hannah shrugged. "I don't *need* sex, Lori, I just like it." She had always been the most sexually adventurous of her friends, quickest to invite a potential partner to bed, unable to wrap her mind around the shame that others seemed to feel about the act. "Good sex is like good food. It's one of the most beautiful pleasures in life." She held the mostly eaten burger up for emphasis. "It's like this burger. You get a burger this good, you savor it. You don't worry about calories, or carbs, or whatever. You live in the moment; you don't ruin it by trying to make it be more or different than it is." She set it down and picked up a french fry. "But you can't live on burgers."

"You'd die of a heart attack, for one." Lori ate some of her own fries.

"Well, right. But you won't get a heart attack from good sex." Hannah paused. "Maybe from *really* good sex."

"I'll drink to that." Lori clinked her glass with Hannah's.

Hannah took a drink of her water. "Truthfully, though, I'm thinking about giving up one-night stands." She set the glass down. "When I don't know a guy well, he doesn't fuck me well. I don't have the time to teach him what I like." Her most recent date came to mind, an app-generated hookup with a local grad student. "The last guy I slept with, really nice guy, but he was probably in his midtwenties, and he just didn't know enough about how to please a woman yet. I taught him a few things, but Lori, I'm almost thirty. I don't have time to teach college boys how to fuck."

"That doesn't sound like a one-night-stand problem. That sounds like a young-guys problem."

"Maybe, but my two hookups before that were my age, and they weren't any better. I guess my clit just has a steep learning curve." Hannah sighed. "The fuck buddies thing was working well for a while, but Jalen moved away, and now Tim's gotten serious with Deborah." She rested her chin on her hand. "I need somebody I can fuck around with on an ongoing basis and have it not be serious."

Mitchell walked past them carrying plates of food for another table, and Hannah watched him go, absentmindedly turning to check out the flex of his ass in his slacks as he passed by. When she turned back forward again, Lori was giving Hannah the biggest "are you fucking kidding me?" face.

"What?" Hannah couldn't help how defensive she sounded, nor the red flush that crept up into her cheeks. "It's like looking at beautiful art."

Lori snorted. "Beautiful art that you want to ride like a pony."

"Shut up." Hannah smiled anyway. "No harm in looking."

"What's up for the Mapleton Fall Festival this year?" Lori drank some of her beer. "You get a booth? It's been a few years since you've done it."

"Not this year." The festival was such a blessing and a curse all at once. "It's always the same situation. It's a family-friendly event. I can't sell toys. I have to sell the tamest stuff I have, like the massage bars, and the candles, and those stupid love coupons. I barely break even. Sometimes I lose money. I wish there were a way to sell my actual products, but the chamber would never go for it."

"Why not? Can't you just card people? They do it at the booths that sell beer."

"They don't want underage people to even be able to *see* my products." Hannah grimaced. "I suggested a curtained-off space with ID check, and they still wouldn't go for it, worried kids might run in and accidentally see a dildo. There was a lot of pearl clutching at the idea." Sometimes Mapleton wasn't nearly as progressive as they wanted everyone to think they were. "The chamber sent out some surveys over the summer asking for suggestions, and I've been pushing for an adults-only night event." She gestured toward where Mitchell had been, like he was still standing there. "But it's also like Mitchell said. Even if they give me the go-ahead, it's pricey. I haven't been able to afford the space in, like, three years now."

"It's a good event, though. Builds visibility. You spent all that money on marketing earlier this year. Seems like this would be more good marketing."

"I know." Hannah picked at her fries, drawing patterns in the ketchup on her plate. She did like the spirit of the festival, when the entire town essentially shut down to celebrate their community and local businesses. "It's good for community spirit. The problem is that community spirit is going to drain me dry."

"Meh, it's an investment." Lori shrugged. "And you always have a good time."

"You know how hard it's been for me since the new property owner bought the building last year and raised my rent. I can't take any financial risks right now." Hannah hated talking about this shit out loud. Lori might be her best friend, but it was also hard not to envy her professional competence. Lori was juggling so many responsibilities: writing for the *Valley Voice* paper, interning in the community, teaching a class, and writing a doctoral dissertation. Hannah was struggling to keep one simple business operational. It was pretty damn embarrassing.

"But a boost in sales wouldn't hurt." Lori tapped a fry against her lips, then ate it. "You've been saying for months that if you got a sudden cash boost, you could turn the tide before the holidays."

Lori had a point, but Hannah had run the numbers. The financial burden was still too great. "I didn't send in a vendor application, so I think that ship has sailed." Hannah rested her chin on her hand. "But I don't know. The email they sent us was really cryptic, something about last-minute changes to the event. Maybe they'll make all the booths suddenly free." She forced a laugh.

Conversation drifted to Lori's ridiculous schedule, and thank goodness they had moved on to talking about something other than her. Even best friends like Lori got a little intense sometimes. She didn't want to admit it, but Lori always asked the questions she didn't want to ask herself. Why didn't she ever ask Mitchell out? Was it really because she thought he was a committed-relationship kind of guy, or because she wasn't sure he was really into her?

All this time flirting with him, over a year of eating regularly at the Mapleton Pub, and he never progressed past flirtation. He never seemed bothered or uncomfortable about it, but he didn't return her affections, teasing as they may be. Even if she wanted to fuck him, she wasn't entirely sure he was interested. Normally, that sort of thing didn't matter. She could handle rejection when it came to sex. She wasn't everybody's type. With Mitchell, though, something seemed different. Getting rejected by Mitchell would feel like a deeper rejection. Somehow, she'd come to care what he thought about her.

She watched him pass by on his way to deliver another table's food, and as he caught her eye, he gave her a quick smile, which she returned. No, Mitchell was good to flirt with, but she wasn't going to take that any further. She could find a fuck buddy, or she could entertain herself.

Chapter Two

Mitchell flicked on the lights in the living room as he passed through, already itching to strip his clothes off. Everything he wore smelled like food. He was nose-blind to it, but that didn't mean he didn't *know*, and he couldn't wait to shower and change. Tonight was the monthly Chamber of Commerce meeting, and he didn't want to smell like the kitchen at the Mapleton Pub. This meeting was one of the only places he saw Hannah outside the restaurant, and it would be nice to remind her that he was more than just a chef.

Except in all the ways that he was *not* more than just a chef, like how his restaurant had subsumed almost all meaningful relationships in his life. Still. Hannah didn't need to know that. At the Chamber of Commerce meeting, he could wear normal clothes, approach her without carrying plates of food, and…talk about the restaurant. Yeah. Super exciting.

Thinking about Hannah while standing under the hot stream of water was always a quick journey to half hard in no time. It always started innocently enough—picturing her mischievous smile, those dimples, the way she laughed…

maybe laughing at one of his jokes. But imagining her smile always led to him imagining other expressions she made, like the way her eyelids fell half closed and her lips parted in bliss after a bite of dessert. Studying her like that, as he sometimes did, he could easily picture that expression in other situations. Perhaps her mouth would fall open in the same way as he kissed her collarbone, or rolled her nipples between his fingers, or dipped his tongue into the wet heat between her legs...

"Hey!" Ben's excited voice boomed in the small space of the bathroom.

Mitchell lost his footing in the tub in surprise, banging his funny bone hard on the shower rack.

"What the fuck, man?" He rubbed his elbow, the pain wilting his erection down to half-mast. His fantasy evaporated. Nope, here was the only meaningful relationship he had in his life right now: Ben Harrington, the man with terrible timing and no sense of personal space, his business partner and roommate, and—for over two years now—his fuck buddy.

"Did I scare you? Sorry. You've gotta try this." A large hand was suddenly thrust into the shower, holding a pint glass half full of beer. Mitchell's erection withered the rest of the way.

"This can't wait until I'm done showering?" Mitchell pulled back the curtain and glared at Ben, who was grinning like an idiot. Ben always looked younger when he got completely immersed in his projects. Even his full beard and six-foot-five stature—a height that should probably qualify him for giant status, in Mitchell's opinion—didn't take away from his childlike wonder. It was hard to believe that, like Mitchell, he was already in his thirties. Maybe Mitchell carried his stress more visibly, because compared to Ben, he always looked much older than his age.

"What? Your showers take forever." Ben gestured with the beer again. "I didn't want to wait for you to spend a half hour jerking off. Try this beer." He lifted the glass again, shoving it into Mitchell's face. "This is the newest ale. It's the first barrel with that malt I special ordered."

Oh yeah, Ben had been babbling about different varieties of malted barley a few weeks ago. When Ben got like this, he was better off just giving in, even if that meant drinking half a glass of beer while standing soaking wet in the shower. He wrapped the shower curtain around himself for an extra measure of modesty.

"Come on. It's not like I don't see you naked all the time." Ben gestured at the curtain and the area where Mitchell's cock was now draped in opaque plastic sheeting.

Ignoring that comment, Mitchell took a sip of the beer. "It's good."

Ben waited expectantly for more. Mitchell took another sip, trying to be more specific. He had an excellent palate from his culinary training, but he wasn't as good at beer as Ben. "It's...smooth. Notes of chocolate?" He sniffed it, then took another sip. "It's not that hoppy."

"Right? Mostly malt, fewer hops." Ben nodded. "You want to finish it?"

"I want to finish my shower." Mitchell handed the glass to Ben and pulled the curtain closed. The water was starting to run colder. "I'm losing all my hot water."

"Nobody wants that." Ben's voice sounded muffled, like he was speaking through fabric. Mitchell heard the telltale sound of a zipper, another shuffle of fabric, and then the shower curtain was ripped back as a fully naked Ben stepped into the shower with him.

"Fucking hell." Mitchell stepped back under the water, laughing despite his protests. "I've told you before, our shower is not big enough for this." Ben's large frame crowded him against the wall, and his body responded even as he gave lip service to refusing. He couldn't help the way his heart rate quickened at Ben's proximity, thoughts running fuzzy as his cock twitched.

"You say that every time, and every time you stop complaining when I get my hands on your cock." Ben's hand closed around Mitchell's dick and, with one smooth stroke, brought him all the way to hardness. Lust slammed into him full force, his toes curling.

"It's the—" Mitchell lost his words in a gasp as Ben started to stroke him in earnest, large hand pulling steadily at his erection. Jesus, he was trying to *say* something.

"What? Hmm? The what?" Ben was grinning. Yeah, he could laugh—he wasn't the one who was dissolving into incoherence. "What is it?"

Ah, fucking hell. This was the only way Ben could get the upper hand, and he knew it. Not that Mitchell really *minded* getting topped now and then, that breathless overwhelming feeling crashing through his senses, but damn, he was gonna get even. Ben twisted his wrist at the top of the stroke, and Mitchell's only response was a groan, slamming one hand on the wall behind him to keep his knees from buckling. Ben knew he couldn't resist, knew just what to do to turn him from focused to desperate. Mitchell screwed his eyes shut, trying not to thrust into Ben's hand, trying to keep some control over this moment and failing miserably as his hips stuttered forward.

Ben leaned in closer, his mouth nipping at the sensitive skin of Mitchell's earlobe. His hot breath against wet skin was a shock of contrast, and Mitchell couldn't stop the needy noises coming from his mouth.

"Fuck, yeah, that's right. Give it up for me." He leaned in for a kiss.

All right, yeah, he loved this. Mitchell kissed him back,

letting all his control fall away—just for now, just for this moment—and thrusting into Ben's tight, perfect fist around his erection. With Ben, he could come apart like this, didn't have to worry about anything but the all-consuming, breathless pleasure that fuzzed out his brain. Ben had discovered this power over two years ago, when he first propositioned Mitchell to take his mind off an upcoming restaurant inspection. Fucking Ben was the best antidote to stress he could have imagined.

Mitchell's breath hitched, and Ben pulled back to look into Mitchell's eyes. Mitchell couldn't look away. The intimacy was too much, and he couldn't fight it, could only give in to the pressure in his body and Ben's deep, searching gaze. He seized up, his orgasm roaring through him like a tidal wave, pulled from the depths of his body and whiting out all the thoughts in his head except for how incredibly good it felt. He was lost, coming all over Ben, who stroked his cock all the way through it until Mitchell was too twitchy and sensitive, and he pulled back.

"Fucking hell." Mitchell wiped an arm across his forehead, panting, reality returning as Ben rinsed his hands off under the water with a smug expression on his face. "What was that for?"

"It seemed like a good idea." Ben leaned in to kiss Mitchell, sweeter and more gentle than his words. Moments like this, Ben was tender, hinting at a desire for some intimacy beyond the intensity of their frequent sex. Then it faded, and all that sweetness was replaced by an impish grin. "Now, get out. There's almost no hot water left."

"Fuck no. It's your turn, you asshole." He reached for Ben, whose erection jutted out almost obscenely, and wrapped his hand around Ben's thick cock, which was proportionately appropriate for his giant body.

"We're running out of hot water," Ben protested, but it

was a weak protest.

"You just want me to make you take it."

Ben's answering grin gave him away.

"Yeah, that's what you're waiting for." Mitchell smiled. "Tease me, wait for me to get my revenge. Make you give in. Hmm?" He let his voice drop low. "Jerk you off like this so you can't get away?" This side of himself was always a surprise, this bossy, dominant tendency that he exhibited in the kitchen and also in bed. It worked for Ben, too, who let his smile slide in favor of a gasp. Mitchell was working him over hard, rough, probably almost too much, and Ben was fucking loving it. His mouth had fallen open, all laughter gone as he sucked in breath after breath. He was so sexy like this, and if it were possible for Mitchell to get it up again so soon, he would have.

"Fuck yes. You want it so bad."

It was such a rush ordering Ben around, directing this man who was so much larger than he was, and then watching Ben obey. They'd fallen into this dynamic, and after so long, they barely deviated from it, even if he might sometimes want something different. When Ben reached for his own dick to help, Mitchell swatted him away again.

"Hands behind your back."

Ben did as he was told, leaning back against the wall of the shower with his hands pinned behind him. Mitchell wrapped both hands around Ben's dick and began to stroke, steady and firm, the exact way that Ben liked it. Taking him to the edge like this was satisfying, a steady burn of pride in his gut, the power of making someone else feel this kind of pleasure. He and Ben had always felt this tension between them, and once they gave in to it, they were able to have some of the hottest sex he'd imagined, without even worrying about feelings getting in the way.

Even if Mitchell might sometimes want feelings to get in

the way.

The water was fading, lukewarm to downright cold, and Ben's expression changed with mingling discomfort and arousal. His ensuing climax kept him motionless even as the water ran colder and colder over his erection, and perverse satisfaction tingled across Mitchell's skin. The cold water would delay Ben's orgasm but not prevent it, and the temperature shock would make the moment more intense. The paradox was evident in each shift of Ben's body, wanting to pull away from the stream of water but also push into Mitchell's hands, and Mitchell couldn't look away from his face, fascinated. This kind of control, freely given, coursed through him like a drug.

"Fuck," Ben groaned, wincing, his open mouth turning into a grimace. Mitchell knew that look. He kept up the intensity, one hand twisting at the head of Ben's cock, the other running along the shaft in firm, insistent strokes, dragging Ben over the edge, and he came with a shout. Power ran through him, that mix of pleasure and sadism along with the cold water like needles on his sensitive skin. Mitchell let him go and rinsed his hands in the icy-cold water. At least an unexpected benefit of the cold water was it helped him fight off the urge for tenderness.

"You fucking asshole." Ben leaned heavily against the shower wall, his knees clearly shaking, smiling despite his words. "I'm fucking freezing. Let me out of here."

After getting dressed, Mitchell joined Ben in the kitchen, where he was sitting at the kitchen table with some beer bottles lined up in front of him. He gave Mitchell a grin. "You're a fucking sadist, you know. You probably take cold showers all the time."

"It's good for my muscles, yeah." Crossfit made him sore, and cold showers were one of the ways he'd learned to ease some of the soreness. Plus, cold showers were bracing. Taking a cold shower, he could conquer anything, his body completely under his control. When so many things felt out of his control, ownership of his physical body was empowerment. Mitchell opened the fridge and peered inside. Damn, they needed to get groceries soon. He was running out of everything. "So, before I was rudely interrupted in the shower, I was trying to ask if you were coming to the Chamber of Commerce meeting tonight."

"Yeah, I think I'll go. Still figuring out what I want to feature at the booth. I've got a few new flavors that I think would make out there. I'm going to try and write a few of these descriptions before tonight." Ben took a sip of one beer, stared off into space for a moment, then started scribbling in a notebook.

The kitchen stayed silent except for the scratching of Ben's pen as Mitchell started poking in the fridge again. Pasta would have to do for dinner. He pulled out a couple of the birds' nests of pasta that he'd made yesterday after work, then started scrounging around for the ingredients he'd need to make sauce. He didn't have time to prepare tomato sauce from scratch, but he could doctor up some canned sauce so it didn't taste so processed.

Ben didn't look up until the sauce was on the stove simmering away, and then he came to like a man being startled awake. He looked around, blinking in surprise like he'd forgotten where he was. "You're making dinner?"

"Yeah, I'm making us pasta. I have to use canned sauce, though."

"You know I can't tell the difference." Ben set his pen down and leaned back in the kitchen chair. "You want some help?"

"Nah, I'm good." This wasn't the kind of cooking Mitchell enjoyed, since canned sauce was barely a step above drive-through. Even in this limited form, though, he liked the process of preparing food for someone else. Somehow, running a restaurant hadn't cost him his love of cooking, and he hummed to himself as he salted the water for the pasta.

"How can you tell the difference between thirty types of hops and you can't tell between canned sauce and fresh sauce? I don't know why I bother with you sometimes."

Ben smiled, the infectious, charismatic grin that no one could ever say no to, including him. If Ben set his sights on a beautiful person, it was only a matter of time before they ended up in his bed. He hadn't had any company other than Mitchell in a while, but it was probably only a matter of time. There were no expectations of exclusivity, no strings attached, and Mitchell was able to get off with another person instead of alone. Maybe things would be different for Mitchell if he started dating again, but he hadn't been willing to step into that minefield for some time.

As the bubbles began to bead on the bottom of the pot, Mitchell's thoughts wandered. Ben's kind of charm must be nice. His own dry sarcasm didn't seem to have the same effect. Ben would probably have asked Hannah out by now. He snorted quietly to himself at the thought. It had been far too long since he'd dated anyone. Starting with someone like Hannah, who challenged him and brought out all of his most intense feelings? Probably too much for both of them to handle.

"Hmm?" Ben was poking in the fridge and glanced up at the noise Mitchell made.

Mitchell shook his head. "Nothing. Grab me a beer while you're in there?"

If he were honest with himself, which he tried to be, his reasons for not asking Hannah out didn't have anything to do with his personality. He knew they'd get along. But how was he supposed to commit to one person with a job that took up so much of his time? He could imagine *that* conversation.

"Hey, I don't have time for a meaningful relationship with you because I run a restaurant, but I jerk off to you a lot, so maybe we could date a few times anyway"? Fat chance. Between what more than one girlfriend had called his "emotional intensity" and his crazy work schedule at the restaurant, relationships weren't really his thing. Whatever this thing was with Ben, it was right for now.

Even if Ben wasn't interested in a true emotional connection.

Hannah was busy, too, though, a small voice reminded him. But maybe they could eke out some time for each other...

No, that was ridiculous, too. He couldn't provide the kind of emotional stability a romantic partner needed. He couldn't promise to be there for her in every way she might want. The prospect of being everything she needed, whenever she needed it? Christ, who could live up to that? But it was such a treat when she came to the restaurant alone, eagerly expectant and peering toward the kitchen door every time he came through it. He smiled just thinking about it. Seeing her eyes light up when she looked at him was the highlight of his work shift on those days. Or at least it made work a little more pleasurable. He'd been seeing her so much and they had hardly had a long conversation. They'd talked casually, but none of the deep, soul-searching conversations you were supposed to have when getting to know someone.

Maybe that was for the best. He was intense, and that intensity tended to drive people away.

With the water boiling and the sauce ready to go, he dropped the two nests of pasta in and gave them a stir, watching the noodles separate. Behind him, he could hear Ben setting the table. This was all the domesticity he needed; at least it was something.

Eating together felt like the early days of when they moved in, each rootless for different reasons. That was, what?

Six years ago? Six and a half years. It would be seven years this coming March. Somehow they'd kept out of each other's beds for most of those years, until that night Ben had come to Mitchell's room, casually leaned against the doorjamb, and asked if Mitchell was going to freak out about the restaurant inspection all night or if he wanted to fuck instead.

Thinking about that night still sent chills down Mitchell's spine. The switch had flipped inside him, no longer dancing around what they had been avoiding for years. Wrapping his hand around Ben's cock for the first time had felt like a benediction, everything he never knew he always wanted. Nobody he'd been with before that, no girls or guys, had ever let him take control the way Ben did. Ben just yielded, letting Mitchell push him down on the bed, groaning at Mitchell's strong touch. Their kisses were hot and passionate, the sex like an explosion. Afterward, though, when Mitchell had leaned in for comfort, Ben had clearly and politely drawn a line.

"You're not a cuddler, are you?" he'd joked, smiling.

Now Mitchell knew his limits. Across the table, Ben was eating the pasta with all the focus he usually attributed to the chemistry of brewing.

"This is really good." Ben gestured with his fork to the pasta. "You said this is canned sauce?"

"And some extras." It was always nice to have his food complimented. "You want to walk to the meeting tonight? Or is it still hot as balls outside?"

"Shit, man, I don't know. I spent the whole day in the brewery." Situated in the basement below the restaurant, the brewery was always cool no matter what the temperature outside.

"You walked home."

Ben tipped his head to the side, thinking. "Right." His eyes got that faraway look they always held when he was remembering, shifting through his near-photographic memory for moments and experiences from the past. It was disconcerting most of the time, but damn, there were pluses to having a fuck buddy who literally remembered every single thing that had ever made you come like a freight train. "Yeah. It's still hot outside."

"I think I'd still like to walk." He hadn't worked out that day, and his muscles felt tight.

"Me too. I want to take a little more time with the beer descriptions, though. You go ahead and I'll catch up." Ben finished the last of his pasta. "Bet everyone will be surprised to see me there. I don't think I've been to one of those meetings in over a year. Anybody still ask about me?"

"Not that I can think of." Mitchell thought back to his day. "I mentioned to Hannah that you might come tonight."

Ben's vision went distant again, probably trying to recall Hannah. Mitchell could tell the moment he alighted on the correct person. "Oh! Right. Where did you see her?"

"She comes into the pub every week or so. Usually she just gets a beer, but sometimes she gets food." Mitchell reached out for Ben's dish to clear it away, but Ben was faster, scooping up both plates and heading to the sink. Relief washed over him: Ben barely remembered Hannah. That relief was immediately offset by guilt. Obviously, if Ben set his sights on Hannah, then he, Mitchell, would never have a shot. Did Ben and Hannah have any contact other than the Chamber of Commerce meetings? Ben was hardly ever in the restaurant, but Hannah did run that sex shop. He'd never thought to ask Ben if he went in there. He'd thought about shopping there a few times but never got around to it. He should make a trip sometime.

A damp dish towel across the face brought him back to the present. "Hey!" He came to with a start to see Ben laughing. He rubbed his stinging cheek. "That hurt, you asshole."

"Well, stop staring into space like a zombie. You've got to head out in a few minutes." Ben snapped the towel at Mitchell again, this time at his ass, but Mitchell deftly avoided it. "I know how much you hate being late."

• • •

Ben scanned the twenty or so people gathered inside the main meeting room at the town hall and looked for familiar faces. One of the many blessings of a nearly eidetic memory was his ability to remember names to go with these faces, even after having not seen them in over a year, and he recognized almost everyone in the room.

Schmoozing definitely played to his strengths. In the twenty minutes before the meeting began, he managed to say hello to most people and introduce himself to those who were new since his last appearance. He had just finished a jovial conversation with the owner of a local bookstore when he spotted Mitchell over near the snacks table, looking pained and disgruntled. In other words, one of Mitchell's usual looks.

"Do you always just stay here by the snacks and avoid everyone?" Joining him, Ben poured himself a glass of water from one of the carafes. "You know it's a social event, right?"

Mitchell made a humph noise. "You're the one who can make everyone love you in a minute." He scooped some ranch dip onto his plate with a plastic spoon, then gestured at Ben with a carrot stick. "It's not really fair for you to be a genius and an extrovert. It makes the rest of us look bad."

Ben chuckled, self-consciousness brushing the back of his mind. Mitchell liked to drop lines like that out of the blue, lines about his intelligence and charm. Before he could respond, though, he was distracted by movement near his right shoulder. Hannah Stewart had joined them at the snack table and was using a toothpick to spear cheese cubes onto her plate with surprising viciousness.

He remembered Hannah, of course. She was a hard person to forget, even for looks alone. Some women with long hair let it hang straight and flat, but Hannah's dark brown locks looked styled, layers flipping up at the ends like she had it professionally done or something. He was far from an expert on women's hair, but hers looked nice, and he wouldn't mind running his hands through it. She also wore these adorable square-framed librarian glasses, which were sexy in a dorky way. What he always noticed about her, though, was her pout: those full, rich lips turned slightly down in dismay at the assortment of cheeses that she was attacking as if they personally wronged her.

"Maybe you should give those cheese cubes a chance to fight back."

At the sound of his voice, Hannah looked up, her eyes going wide in surprise. In this light, it was hard to tell if they were green or gray. True hazel eyes were rare, and hers seemed to shift in color even as he looked into them.

"Hi, Ben. I didn't see you there." She brushed her hair back over her shoulder. "I had to close late and didn't get time to run home for dinner. Looks like it's cheese cubes tonight." She sighed. "I can't even get mad, because they bought, like, two hundred dollars of product, but I'm starving. Lunch was forever ago." She looked past him to Mitchell. "Mitchell, what would it take to get you to cater these meetings?" She held up her plate of cheese cubes. "This is not food." She glanced back over her shoulder at who was nearby—nobody—and then said conspiratorially, "I'd blow pretty much anyone for something from the restaurant right now."

Mitchell was staring at Hannah with his mouth slightly open. Damn, Ben understood that expression. He couldn't help picturing Hannah on her knees sucking him off, those pink lips wrapped around his cock, and Mitchell would have to be dead in the pants not to be picturing the exact same thing. What a thing to say right before the meeting started.

Mitchell recovered quickly and grinned. "I don't know, Hannah. Mixing prostitution and catering is probably not a good business move for us."

Hannah laughed, and Ben took the opportunity to look her up and down. On this unseasonably warm September day, she'd dressed in a pencil skirt and a sleeveless blouse that showed off all her curves. And fuck, she had curves. Wide hips, hint of a belly, generous breasts... She was the kind of woman he loved to wrap his arms around—and that other parts loved for different reasons.

Hannah popped one of the cheese cubes in her mouth and sighed. "It'll do." She gave Ben a once-over, tilting her head back to look him in the eyes. Most people backed up when he approached, just out of the reflex that he was so much taller than them, but Hannah stayed where she was. She was tall for a woman, but she was still many inches shorter than him. "Gotta say, I'm surprised to see you here."

He fixed her with a flirtatious, smoldering stare. "Mitchell said you'd be here, so I had to show up."

She rolled her eyes and snorted. "Nice. That line ever get you anywhere?"

"Now and then." He smiled more broadly, genuinely this time. He hadn't spoken to Hannah very much, only a few brief conversations in passing. How had he never realized how tempting she was?

"You should've brought a sandwich." She held up the cheese plate. "That would have gotten you a lot further than pickup lines."

"What if I take you out to dinner after this meeting?"

Hannah glanced just past Ben's shoulder, where Mitchell was still hovering. Interesting. Mitchell had never mentioned anything between them, but those two definitely saw each other on the regular. Maybe Ben just hadn't picked up on it before. When he looked over at Mitchell, though, the other man was pouring himself a glass of water and didn't seem to be listening.

"And why do you want to take me out?" Hannah raised an eyebrow, still skeptical. "You didn't eat, either?"

Ben skimmed his gaze down her body again, eyeing all those delicious curves. "Maybe I'm ready for dessert."

"Oh, brother." She shook her head and chuckled, the action bringing out two delicate dimples in her cheeks.

Before he could follow up, Barry Hammond, the director of the Chamber of Commerce, called them all together around the long conference table and began the meeting.

By the time conversation finally rolled around to the Mapleton Fall Festival, Ben had learned far more than he ever wanted to know about the workings of the businesses in this town. Mitchell was engaged the whole time, god bless him, taking notes on his iPad and occasionally asking questions. Ben was a top-notch brewer, and his PhD in organic chemistry certainly didn't hurt, but Mitchell had always been the driving force behind the business end of things. Ben had a grip on the marketing and promotion, but Mitchell had the financials under control, and Mitchell was the one attending these meetings religiously and maintaining good community relations. For all the shit he gave Ben about hating meaningless social interactions, Mitchell was a whiz at Chamber of Commerce stuff. Thank god they were partners.

He didn't have time to dwell on that, though, because Barry was moving on to talking about the festival, which was less than a month away now. He loved Fall Festival. They shut down Main Street to all motorized traffic, rerouting cars around the side streets to turn downtown into a pedestrian-only zone. Mostly, people parked in the fairgrounds field and walked in. In addition to extended hours in all the shops and restaurants, vendors set up booths and performance spaces all along Main Street. It was one of the best weekends of the year. Their pub always got a booth on Restaurant Row, selling quick bites and sometimes beer on draft, and they always had a good time.

Carla, who ran the stationery and paper-crafts store, handed out the festival schedule photocopied on autumn letterhead. Ben scanned the list of vendors, picking their name out on the Featured Restaurants list and then running through the other booths. Most were familiar from past years; people tended to stick with what worked for them. Some were crafts and skills booths: Carla's Stationery taught calligraphy workshops, and the Tangled Web yarn store did a crochet seminar. The White River spa taught basic massage techniques and then offered discounted massages afterward. Some shops just ran booths for specific sales. Challenge booths were always popular, with people competing in silly little game show–style activities to win prizes and tickets they could turn in for discounts at participating shops, and sure enough, there were a handful of those listed on the schedule. Maybe one year, they should do that. Could be more fun than just selling food. He scanned the list again. Interesting: Hannah's sex shop wasn't listed as a vendor. Although what could she even sell at a family event like the Fall Festival?

Barry was almost vibrating with excitement when he started talking again. "All right, folks. We have some really exciting news. I apologize for getting this information out to you so late, but we had a lot of loose ends to tie up. Carla, can you explain?"

"Thanks, Barry." Carla tapped a sheaf of papers into a neat stack. "As you all know, we've had concerns over the years about the limited opportunities the Fall Festival has for some of our businesses. Well, it's late, but it's happening. This year, for the first time, we're adding a new adult element to the festival with Mapleton After Dark. A number of you said you were looking for a way to draw in the adult crowd, so this is our solution. We're really excited." She beamed, pink cheeked. "We're going to take the town common on Saturday night from eight to midnight, and we'll have booths and activities geared for the grown-ups. No one under eighteen permitted. We can do twenty-one and over with wristbands, serve alcohol, maybe dancing—it'll be quite fun."

Hannah straightened visibly. She'd been leaning backward in her chair, and now she sat upright, rapt.

"But wait a minute," one of the other bar owners piped up. "The festival's just a few weeks away! How are we supposed to pull this together?"

"I know, Phil, and we're sorry for the short notice." Barry adjusted his glasses. "It's a very late-breaking addition. But to compensate for the short notice, we are discounting Mapleton After Dark booths 50 percent off the normal booth-rental fee."

Shit, half off? That wasn't bad. Murmurs broke out around the table. Many of the group—mostly the owners of businesses that needed an adult audience—looked pleased by this development. In addition to Hannah's sex shop, the owners of the other bars in town looked interested, as did the couple who ran the dance club/arcade that Ben had been known to frequent. He half listened to the rest of the info from Carla, dates for when booth proposals would be due, when they'd be approved or rejected, and a few other interim deadlines. Question-and-answer wrapped up the evening's session, after which the formality dissolved into the meeting-after-the-meeting.

With Mitchell deep in conversation with Carla, Ben made his way over to Hannah at the snack table.

"I'm going to get a complex about my eating if you keep

coming over here." She used the toothpick to spear a single cube of cheese from her plate, then ate it, closing her teeth around the small skewer of wood and sliding the cheese off. It was such a minute detail, but Ben was momentarily captivated by the flash of white teeth, the bite, something feral in its action. He lost his train of thought.

"I can leave you alone if you want," he managed after a moment's blank stare.

"No, that's okay." She skewered more cheese. "I just don't want you to think all I do is eat. I may be squishy, but I have other hobbies."

He gestured over to Mitchell, who was still talking to the festival organizers. "Mitchell is the workout fanatic. I haven't seen the inside of a gym since college. But anyway, Fall Festival." Ben leaned against the wall next to the snack table. "You're not on the vendor list yet. Are you gonna do a Mapleton After Dark booth?"

She shrugged one shoulder. "I'm considering it. I'm not sure how much interest I would draw, though. Adults-only event or not, I don't know that anyone wants to buy sex toys in the middle of the town common."

"It must be frustrating to run a shop with so much stigma attached."

Hannah pursed her lips, tipping her head to the side. "I don't think there's as much stigma as there used to be. When I opened the shop, I knew I wasn't selling shoes. I knew what I was getting into. People who are scandalized by this sort of thing aren't my target audience, anyway."

"Right."

"But I don't know that I've got enough of a draw to have my own booth. Plus, it's pricey, even at 50 percent off. I'm on a really tight budget." She folded her arms and tapped her lips with one finger, seeming to think aloud rather than to talk directly to him. "Maybe I need some sort of theme, or challenge, maybe, to draw people in, but I'm not sure what that is." Her expression changed to a polite smile. "I have a little bit of time to think about it." She glanced over his shoulder, and Ben turned to see Mitchell still in conversation, this time with Barry. "What about you two? Going to do a special booth?"

"I'm considering it. We always do the restaurant booth, but maybe we can do something more creative as well. Feature the beer in a more central way." He liked the possibilities that offered, and with their business performance still going strong, it wasn't a significant financial risk. "We'll see. I'll decide before the deadline, I suppose."

"I suppose."

"That dinner offer is still open, you know." He smiled down at her.

She angled her head and looked up at him through her lashes. "I don't know. How do I know you're not just a hallucination brought on by extreme hunger?"

He leaned down to her, speaking low enough that only she could hear him. "You could take a bite and find out."

Her cheeks flushed pink, and she laughed, a surprised chortle. "You're something else, you know that?" She lifted her chin to study him, contemplating. God, he wished he knew what was going on in that mind of hers. After a few moments of scrutiny, she looked right past his shoulder, and her expression relaxed. She took a step back, shaking her head. "Not tonight."

Had he failed some test? He hadn't realized he was taking one. "How about your number, then? Just in case?"

She handed him her phone. "I'll take yours instead. You want me, you can find me at the shop."

Better than nothing. Ben took her phone and entered his number.

Mitchell appeared near his shoulder, and Hannah nodded

to him. "Nice to see you, Mitchell. I'll catch you sometime this week?"

Mitchell nodded. "Probably."

The walk home with Mitchell was spent in generally companionable silence. Although the day had been oppressively hot, the temperature had dropped after sunset, and now the sidewalk radiated a pleasant warmth up at them in the cool evening breeze.

Mitchell might have been content not to talk at all, but after a few minutes of the silence, Ben broke it. "So, Mapleton After Dark. You want to try something different?"

"I was thinking about that." Mitchell nodded thoughtfully. "That could be cool. We've never done anything special before. It would be a nice year for it. Business is stable; we don't have any big equipment needs coming up. At half off normal booth rental, it seems like a low-risk investment."

The prospects, the ocean of possibility—this was the kind of business planning that got Ben's heart pumping. "We've already got the whole fall beer lineup. Maybe we should showcase the beers with their own booth. Or I was thinking maybe some kind of gimmick. A game or a contest, something like that." As he spoke, more ideas kept coming. "We could offer a design challenge, maybe, or get people to name a flavor and win a case...or some kind of matching? Match the beer to the food?"

"Any of that would be good." Mitchell nodded, quickening his pace as he got into it. "I like the matching idea. Beer and food would work, but then we have to bring all the food to a second booth. Maybe some other kind of game. People love that shit."

"Hell, *I* love that shit." Ben watched their shadows shift on the sidewalk as they passed into and out of the direct light of a streetlamp. "We can keep brainstorming."

Mitchell's expression stayed thoughtful in all these

moments, the measured balance to Ben's enthusiasm and excitement. People who didn't understand Mitchell thought he was overly serious, but his deadpan sense of humor yielded to far more excitement and exuberance once someone had earned his trust. Being included in that small group of close friends filled Ben with quiet pride. Once he'd thought there might be more between them, but when the moment came, Ben had decided to pull away. He and Mitchell had a good thing going, with a solid friendship and a seamless business partnership. The thought of losing their restaurant to a potentially tumultuous relationship was never worth the risk, not to mention the risk of losing their friendship. He cared about Mitchell too much to do something that would ruin what they had. After all, his ex-wife had told him in no uncertain terms that he was shit at commitment.

That line of thought was enough to turn him sour, so he purposefully put it aside.

"The festival's fun," Ben added. "It's a good community builder."

"Best part of the year," Mitchell agreed. He smiled at Ben, an expression so warm and open that it made Ben self-conscious.

"What?" he asked. Mitchell's shift from business mode to friend mode unsettled him with its suddenness.

"It's just nice to be planning with you."

The emotion twisted something in Ben, some kind of sweetness that felt distinctly uncomfortable. He'd pushed those feelings away for so long that he wouldn't know how to let them out, even if he could. "Yeah, well, don't get all sappy on me."

Mitchell put his hands in his pockets, his smile fading back to a comfortably neutral expression. "Wouldn't dream of it."

Chapter Three

When Hannah opened her front door that night, the warm air washed inside with her, but the calmness of her home did nothing to alleviate her own unsettled emotions. She felt shaken, like all her nerves were firing at once and she could barely hold herself within her skin. A normal Chamber of Commerce meeting shouldn't leave her feeling like this. A normal Chamber of Commerce meeting, though, wouldn't involve Mr. Tall, Dark, and Mischievous making flirty eyes at her all evening and talking to her in that smoky voice. She'd never really talked to Ben before. They had exchanged a few casual greetings in passing, not one-on-one conversations with too much eye contact.

She had no reason to be so shaken up. This conversation was, by all rights, as casual as any conversations she had had with acquaintances at these meetings, albeit more flirtatious. Rather than the content, it was Ben who made the conversation intense. Ben and his smart, effortless sexuality, casually asking her out to dinner and undressing her with his eyes. In the time since the meeting ended, she should have recovered. Even so, she felt just as unsettled as when Ben had first asked her out. This was ridiculous. If she was into the guy, she should have taken him up on his offer, and if she wasn't, then she shouldn't still be thinking about him.

She left the lights off and turned on the sound system, filling the house with instrumental music to drown out the emptiness. Then she slid open the doors to the back deck and let the balmy night air wash inside. With the front windows open, the cross breeze brushed past her like fingertips over her skin. Her house would cool throughout the night; hopefully her blood would as well. If she could help it, she hated turning on the air-conditioning, and turning it on during the last half of September in Massachusetts just felt wrong, even if she was a bit overheated. Still hungry from skipping dinner, she picked through leftovers in the fridge, making herself a sandwich. She ate it standing in the kitchen, the linoleum cool against her bare feet, and washed it down with some ice water. Damn, the night was still way too hot. She walked upstairs into her bedroom and pushed open both windows to cool that room as well.

In the darkness of her room, it took her a few minutes to identify the feeling running through her body. Arousal. She sighed. Just fucking great. She had spent an evening flirting casually with Ben and came home practically panting for sex. He wouldn't know how close she had been to taking him up on his offer for dinner. If she had, she'd probably be bringing him back here right now. He could be pressing her down into that bed with his giant frame, those large hands cupping her breasts, his beard tickling her neck and making her moan.

Instead, before she could say yes, she'd spotted Mitchell out of the corner of her eye. Mitchell, with his perpetually thoughtful expression and almost religious obsession with food, with whom she flirted on a near weekly basis, had been watching her with Ben. There had been no mistaking the longing in his eyes, naked and raw, an expression she had never seen on his face. As soon as he'd caught her looking, his guard was back up, his expression neutral, and that was it. She knee-jerk turned Ben down without another thought.

She was thinking now, though. If Mitchell wanted her, he could damn well say something about it. She'd given him enough opportunities. She was in there every week, for fuck's sake, even though she couldn't afford more than one beer most of the time. She flirted with him each time. He flirted back, but he'd never made a move. He certainly had no claim over her.

Ben's casual charm was intoxicating. And...it was nice to have a man look at her and make her feel wanted, after so many failed dates. The way he murmured to her, leaning in so it felt like they were the only two in the room, he'd exuded a magnetism that felt far too intimate for a Chamber of Commerce meeting. If he was like that in a professional setting, what would he be like on a date? Or here, alone with her in her house?

She turned away from the windows and stripped off her clothes. She owned a sex shop, for fuck's sake. If she was going to do this, she was going to do it *properly.*

Having long outgrown the nightstand next to her bed, Hannah kept her toys in a large wooden armoire in the bedroom. Although it took up more room than her bureau, she couldn't imagine giving up any of these toys to save space. She'd cultivated her collection based on her interests and wants, and each item in there served a specific purpose. Now, she stood in front of it the way other people might stand in front of a fully stocked refrigerator trying to decide what they were in the mood to eat. In a way, it was pretty similar...she just wasn't choosing something for her mouth.

She wanted to be overwhelmed. She wanted to lose herself in this, to imagine, to pretend that her fantasies could be real. Her thickest dildo would be almost too much, but the *good* kind of almost too much.

Rubbing the head of the dildo between her slick folds, she pressed it just inside. God, Ben would be like this. Broad, tall, solid, he would feel so thick against her. Yes, she wanted that burn and stretch, she wanted the pressure that was nearly pain, that delicious mixture of sensations that made her moan out loud. She wouldn't touch her clit, not yet, and focused instead on how her body yielded as the dildo split her open. It went on forever. Fuck, she felt so full, each inch sending ripples of pleasure outward through her body.

Finally, stuffed full, pussy clenching around the hard length, she let her fingers drift up to brush her nipples. They were hard, stiff peaks, tight with arousal, and running her fingers over them made her clit tingle like she was touching it. If only it was Ben. He could be here, his cock filling her so much better than this dildo, his hot body pressing her into the mattress. Instead of her fingers grazing her nipples, he could have his mouth on her, his beard scratching her sensitive skin, hot breath lighting every nerve on fire.

She had to touch her clit. She couldn't wait any longer, her body crying out for more. That first press of fingers on her tight, swollen bud made her arch up off the bed and moan out loud, *fuck*, electricity racing through her thighs and up her spine. God, she needed this, now, all of it, fingers speeding up over her clit. She fumbled for the base of the dildo with her other hand, and her slow buildup dissolved in frantic need. Short, hard strokes, like Ben couldn't hold back anymore, both of them driven on by instinct.

She was soaked, and the pads of her fingers slipped across her swollen clit like a tongue. Oh, a tongue, Mitchell's tongue, his talented mouth working her over, and her fantasy shifted to him between her legs. Determined, focused, he would draw his tongue across her sensitive bud and taste her like a fine dessert. She sucked in a breath, gasping for air. The fantasies blurred, as if somehow she could have Mitchell's mouth and Ben's cock, or maybe the other way around, Ben's beard scratching her thighs, Mitchell holding her tight and splitting her open, the images and feelings rolling over her like so many waves. She didn't even know she was coming until everything dissolved in a flash of color and light.

Her orgasm overtook her like a current, body moving instinctively into the razor-sharp pleasure. Ben, Mitchell, bodies moving against her, over her, inside her, and then her mind went blank.

When she relaxed, she sagged back down on her bed, eyelids opening again, hands falling away from her body. She stared up at the ceiling of her bedroom in the darkness, feeling drained in the aftermath. Fantasy was easy. She could get off, clean up, go about her life. Fantasy didn't come with any risks.

And it didn't come with any rewards, either.

So what was she doing lying here fucking herself instead of going after something better? Maybe it was ridiculous, or maybe it was too much time spent talking with Lori, but there was no reason she couldn't try for at least some of what she wanted.

These thoughts circled her mind as she cleaned up and got dressed. Ben wanted her. He'd asked her out, and she had said no, out of some strange impulse or loyalty to Mitchell. And yet she'd never asked Mitchell out. She'd made all kinds of excuses to Lori, sure, saying he was a commitment kind of guy, but she didn't know his opinions on the matter at all. She had just chickened out.

Fuck chickening out. She needed to do something, or she was going to fuck herself to death alone.

When she returned to the living room, the paperwork from the Mapleton Fall Festival was still lying on the kitchen table where she'd left it, so she brought it over to the couch and started leafing through it. The page of booth prices stared up at her. Damn, that was another issue. Even discounted, Mapleton After Dark was expensive. She couldn't swing this on her own, as much as she wanted to. Her bills were nearly insurmountable, and she didn't need to call up her accounts to know it. With the increase in rent, the sales were barely covering expenses, and she was still in debt for the extra money she'd borrowed for a marketing push. Nothing like a heavy dose of reality to squash any leftover horniness.

Hannah closed her eyes. Most small businesses failed. She'd known that going into this situation. She'd been determined to prove everyone wrong: her parents, with their well-meaning condescension, her boyfriend at the time, who thought she was overreaching her capabilities, and most of all, herself. She'd been mediocre for so much of her life, never achieving any greatness of note in school or in work. But then she was a business owner, something to be proud of. The thought of losing that paralyzed her.

She'd almost made it the full five years, too, the window in which most businesses folded. Somehow she'd thought this would be easier now, five years in. She hadn't counted on still barely scraping by.

Maybe they had all been right about her.

Although if she had a boost in income, that would pay off her marketing debt and send her into the holidays in the black. One big push might be all she needed. The best bet for this quick profit was definitely Fall Festival.

Renting a booth alone, though, was going to be a problem. Maybe she could finagle some kind of discount? But no, that wasn't fair to everyone else. She knew the Chamber of Commerce wasn't turning a profit on this event. The logistical costs of the Mapleton Fall Festival were high. The "free to the public" acts weren't really free; someone needed to pay for the entertainment, the infrastructure, setup and cleanup crew, etc. Those costs were covered by booth rental fees, supplemented heavily by official event sponsors like the supermarket, radio station, and usually city government. And it made sense, too. For most businesses, the festival was a huge boost in sales. It wasn't her fault that those people tended not to be buying sex toys along with their gourd wreaths.

Alternately, she could split a booth with someone. And that brought her back to Ben and Mitchell. The pub did a great business. By all accounts, they wouldn't need any financial boost to afford to participate in the event. Would they even want to partner with her?

But not needing help didn't mean they wouldn't welcome it. Maybe they'd want to do something different than just sell food and beer in Restaurant Row. She could save them half the cost of a Mapleton After Dark booth. They didn't need to know she was in dire financial straits. She wasn't about to disclose that to anyone, least of all these two successful, hot guys.

And if she got to spend some time alone with them in the process, that might have some secondary benefits for all involved.

Ben had given her his number, so she sent him a text.

It's Hannah. Guess you have my number now. Want to talk about the festival? You guys got time this week?

His response came a few minutes later.

Tomorrow? Drinks?

If it weren't for the fact that she'd mentioned both of them, this would have felt like a date. Getting together with two hot guys for drinks? The erotic story practically wrote itself.

A few more exchanges and they set up the location and time. Hannah tossed her phone onto the couch next to her and kicked up her feet onto the coffee table, the paperwork off to one side. Already, she had apprehensions. She couldn't deny her own layered motives. If they partnered for the festival, she couldn't just walk out if things got uncomfortable. Plus, Mitchell and Ben were roommates, and that seemed like an extra layer of complication. Fall Festival might be good for her business, but damn, it wouldn't be without risk.

· · ·

The nice thing about the Night Owl was its lighting. Ben spent a lot of time thinking about ambience, mostly in the way that beers could evoke their own sense of ambience, and the Night Owl created a pleasant coziness that went with chocolate stouts and oatmeal porters. As a rule, he liked to try new beer whenever it was available, but he was in the mood for something harder. He ordered a whiskey on the rocks from a sexy bartender with a pink pixie cut and took to people watching. He liked getting to places early, especially places with good people-watching possibilities, so he had about fifteen minutes to eye the place before he estimated Hannah would show up.

Hannah apparently had a similar idea to him, because less than five minutes after his drink arrived, she walked in. God, what a knockout. She was wearing a tank top with little ruffles around the neckline, a pair of knee-length shorts, and sandals. He got caught up looking at those calves as she walked to the bar and placed a drink order with the cute bartender. Then, before sitting, she turned to scan the room, her gaze finally landing on him.

"You know, I almost didn't even look around. I almost just sat at the bar." She slid into the booth next to him. He'd taken the corner booth, the wraparound, plenty of room for four or five people even though Hannah slid right up alongside him. Although she wasn't pressed against him, her arm rested next to his on the table, an expanse of soft skin, and she smelled wonderful.

He was never one to hold back his thoughts. "Can I say that you smell good, or is that weird?"

She grinned. "It's a little weird, but you can say it." She tossed her hair over her shoulder. "Is it my hair?"

This was a perfect opportunity to lean in, and she definitely shivered as his nose brushed lightly against her ear.

"That's part of it, yeah." He drew back before it got awkward, but the space between them had suddenly become about ten degrees hotter. "But if I keep smelling your hair, there's no way we're going to talk about business tonight."

She returned his grin with the same tenor, mischievous with a little uptick at the corner of her lips. "Pretty sure of yourself, hmm?" Resting her chin on her hand, she looked at him, her eyes that indefinable shifting color between gray and green, framed by those black librarian glasses.

Whatever she might be thinking, *his* thoughts were completely impure. "I have my ways."

Her free hand rested on the dark wood of the table. Those long fingers would look amazing wrapped around his cock. Better change the subject before he popped a hard-on right here in the bar. Fortunately, a waitress brought Hannah's drink over to them, which created a shift in the tone. "What are you drinking?"

"Scotch and soda." She sipped from it, then sucked in a breath through her teeth. "Heavy on the scotch."

"I'm a whiskey man myself." He held his up. "In all its forms."

"Cheers to that." She clinked her glass with his. "So what happened to Mitchell? I thought you both would be here."

Ahh, the Mitchell question. He wasn't sure himself, what with Mitchell being kind of cagey last night about the whole thing. His reasons for missing the meeting seemed thin: work to do in the restaurant, mainly, along with some kind of bullshit about not wanting to be in the way. Ben had pressed, but Mitchell had refused to elaborate. "He's got a bunch of stuff to do in the kitchen. Besides, I usually handle the marketing side of things for the business."

"Oh." She seemed mollified by that, if perhaps a bit... disappointed? He couldn't tell. "He work a lot of nights?"

"Mostly mornings, actually. Some nights when it's busy, especially on weekends. He doesn't cook as much as he manages. He's working in the office as much as in the kitchen." Their respective roles had evolved substantially in the almost seven years since opening the restaurant, and while Mitchell liked to cook and made time for it as often as he could, Ben had eventually convinced him to turn over most of the dinner cooking to his sous chef. Kitchen management took far more time.

"You guys must both be really busy." She rested her chin on her hand, brow furrowed in thought.

Ben shrugged. "You know how it is, running a business. Hard to keep your head above water."

Hannah snorted. "Don't I know it." She took another sip of scotch and shook her head. "Whoo. That burns."

"Just like I like it." Ben tipped back some of his whiskey, the liquid searing his throat in the way he had come to love. "So, tell me about this interest in Mapleton After Dark."

The mention of the festival brought her out of flirtatious mode and into business mode, which somehow made her look even hotter. He could see why Mitchell was so smitten with her, even if that foolish man refused to do anything about it. She pushed her glasses up the bridge of her nose. "I think Mapleton After Dark sounds good, and I think it would be a nice boost for business, but I don't think I can justify that kind of business expense on my own, even with the discount. I don't think I'd sell enough product to make up the investment, and I don't have a selling point beyond my products." She took a breath and let it out, her hands balling into fists on the table like she was steeling herself. "I thought maybe we could do a partnership. Beer and sex toys. You know, 'What beer goes with this vibrator?' and, 'Hey, if you like hops, try the rabbit,' stuff like that. Silly things, but some kind of marketing that normalizes the sex toys." Tucking a strand of hair behind her ear, she took another sip from her drink and set the glass down on its cardboard coaster. "It would save us each the cost of paying for a full booth, and we could each market our products. Like a temporary partnership."

"And we would split the cost fifty-fifty?" He stroked his beard. This plan definitely had an appeal.

"Right. And our individual sales would be our own. Now, it all depends on you guys being willing to partner up with a sex shop." She shrugged, but the shrug looked stiff, as if she were holding extra tension in her shoulders. "Not all businesses want to do that. I don't know if it would drive away your customers if they saw that you were in bed with me. Financially, I mean," she added quickly. "It's an expression."

He smiled. When flustered, she was extra cute. "So why our business? Why me and Mitchell?"

Hannah ran her finger around the rim of her glass. "I know you both, or at least I know Mitchell a little bit, and I know your business. I trust you. I thought you were better than approaching some random person at the Chamber of Commerce meetings. Plus, I think alcohol aligns with sex toys probably better than anything else does, for better or worse."

"Fair enough."

"I was going to write up something formal, but that felt weird, so I just figured I'd talk to you." She paused, then asked, a bit hesitantly, "What do you think?"

He couldn't see the harm in it. "I think it sounds like a good plan. I have to run it by Mitchell, but he was already talking with me about doing a booth for Mapleton After Dark, so this is a natural extension of that."

"Do you think he would have any aversions to partnering with me? I don't know if he's uptight or something like that." Hannah bit her lip. "I make a lot of crude jokes with him, but it's not like he ever makes them back."

Ben had to laugh. If only Hannah knew the half of it. "He would *not* have a problem with sex toys, trust me." Taking a sip of his whiskey, he thought to some of the more lewd encounters he'd enjoyed with Mitchell, including some truly crude dirty talk. "Although he doesn't own any. Maybe you could change that."

Hannah's mouth opened slightly, and after another pause, she took a drink. "So you two are close, then," she said when she had recovered. "I wasn't sure. I know you're friends, but there are lots of levels of friendship."

"Yeah." He thought about whether or not to say anything further, but if he was hoping to take things further with Hannah—and he was—then she should probably know. Plus, it would be worth it to see her expression. "Mitchell and I are the kind of friends who fuck."

Hannah's eyes widened, then narrowed, her expression turning puzzled as she probably tried to reconcile her worldview to the information she had just received. "I didn't know you were dating." She laughed, a nervous laugh. "I've been flirting pretty hard tonight."

"I like your flirting." Ben smiled. "And Mitchell and I aren't dating. It's nothing serious. Just two guys letting off steam."

A bit of color flushed her cheeks. She was pretty glib most of the time, so with her momentarily stunned into silence, he pushed the subject. "You're blushing. Does that turn you on? Are you picturing it right now?"

Hannah started laughing, and then downed a large gulp of her scotch and soda, shaking her head as she swallowed. "I can't believe you just asked me that."

"What? I know some girls are into that. Just wondering if you're one of them." He set his hand on hers where it still rested next to her glass, his fingertips tracing a circle on her skin.

She looked down at their hands, her wordlessness persisting for a few more seconds before she found her voice again. "I'm pretty equal opportunity with my porn, even if I do happen to only be attracted to men." Her ensuing smile was a little bit naughty, a little bit guilty, and quite a bit intrigued. "I imagine that's quite a sight to see."

"It's not like we invite an audience." He loved this: the tension, the way she leaned into him like a flower toward the sun. Anticipating what might come next kept him alert, his senses tuned in to her every response. "But maybe for a special occasion. Mitchell and I, we don't let gender stand in the way of a good fucking. It's part of the pleasure of being bi."

"I imagine that would be an advantage." Hannah turned her hand palm up beneath his, her fingernails scratching lightly across his tender skin. "What are your policies on mixing business and pleasure?"

"Every chance I get." Ben dropped his voice lower. "I've been fucking my business partner for a few years, after all." For sex, it was easy. Sex didn't have to mean anything. Romance was a different animal entirely, one he was happy to avoid. But they weren't talking about romance. "How about you? Do you like mixing business and pleasure?"

"My business *is* pleasure." She licked her upper lip, perhaps chasing a stray drop of scotch, but her eyes were only on him. "Is this why you agreed to meet with me tonight? Hoping to get me into bed?"

"It was a perk, yes." He slid a bit closer in the booth, closing the space between them. "It's a shame Mitchell didn't join us."

"Oh?" Hannah's breath caught. He noticed it, the slight hitch on her inhale, the way her eyes widened. "Do you two share women?"

"Never." He looked down at her mouth, those full lips that he was definitely going to kiss into swollen softness. "I could imagine there's a first time for everything."

She leaned in, and he met her halfway, his mouth pressing against hers in a first kiss that was far too hot for a bar, even a dimly lit bar like the Night Owl. She didn't hold back, slanting her lips against his and parting them to tangle their tongues together. She tasted sweet, but laced with the burn of whiskey, a combination that flooded his senses and drove him into immediate, pulse-pounding desperation. Fuck. This kiss was supposed to be a tease, a little touch that hinted at more, but her lush mouth opening beneath his had him coming apart. He was reaching up to take a fistful of her hair when she pulled back. "He's not here. It's just us. Either of you going to have a problem with that?"

"No problem here." Ben's breath came quick alongside his heartbeat. "Mitchell knew how this might turn out."

"You assuming I'm a foregone conclusion?" Hannah shook her head, still smiling. "I don't know how I feel about that. Maybe I should say no and make you wait."

"And why would you do that? Especially when you know how much fun this could be." Ben slid a hand to her leg, resting it halfway up her thigh, which yielded softly beneath his grip. He wanted to keep going, drag his hand all the way up to cup her pussy, make her press into his palm, and it took a lot of restraint to hold himself in check in this very public space. He leaned in for another kiss and she let him, kissing back, tantalizing him with the promise of more. "You'd be punishing both of us for no good reason." He moved his lips to whisper against the pink shell of her ear. "And not the kind of punishment that either of us might like."

Hannah sat back, her eyes sparkling. "You know, my store is literally across the street. Maybe we should settle our tab."

"I've never been inside your store. Are you offering to show me around?"

"In a manner of speaking." She poked the tip of her tongue playfully out from between her lips. "It's a lot closer than my house and probably yours."

"You're up to no good, and I love it." He leaned in one more time, kissing her sweet mouth, impatient for more. "You'd better finish that drink."

She tossed back her drink in one gulp, and he did the same with the last of his whiskey. His body was singing with the adrenaline coursing through his bloodstream, adrenaline that doubled when Hannah's long fingers squeezed the hard outline of his erection through his pants. Fuck. He froze, hand squeezing shut reflexively and knocking over the empty whiskey glass as his mouth fell open.

She smiled and raised her eyebrows. "What's the matter, butterfingers?"

"Just can't hold my liquor, that's all." He sucked in another breath as she ran her palm up his length. "You should be careful what you're doing down there."

"I know exactly what I'm doing down here." She gripped him firmly, locking eyes with him. Yeah, he was going to enjoy the challenge she offered. "Come on. Let's pay up and go."

Chapter Four

Hannah kept hold of Ben's hand as they crossed the street and headed up onto the sidewalk in front of her building. She fumbled the keys out of her pocket, fingers trembling more than she'd expected.

"Back here, huh?" Ben peered past her through the glass door. "No store frontage?"

"I thought about it." She unlocked the door and pulled him into the hallway that led to her shop. "But I can't really do Main Street window displays anyway, and the rent is cheaper back here." She led him down the hallway, passing the paper-crafts store between her shop and the street, before arriving in front of the actual door to Yes, Please.

"Still must be expensive as hell. Shared entrance or not, your door is right on Main Street." Ben looked behind her toward the street, frowning, eyebrows drawn together.

He didn't know the half of it. This location had seemed perfect when she was first looking, but back then she'd had higher hopes about the revenue she'd be bringing in every month. God, did he have to bring that up right now?

As if reading her wishes, before she could reach her key to the lock, Ben turned her and pressed her up against her own door, boxing her in with his large body. He made her feel *tiny*, like having him this close was enough to overwhelm her senses. He took a handful of her hair in his hand, not pulling, just holding her in place, and kissed her deep and thoroughly. Fucking hell, the man could kiss. This was the kind of searching, probing kiss that didn't belong in a bar or anywhere in public, quite frankly, especially when he reached his other hand up to cup her breast and squeeze it. A shock ran through her body, and he swallowed her gasp. Perfect. He had trapped her here against the wall and she didn't want to get away; she wanted him to strip her down and have his way with her. Vulnerability plus arousal left her drunk and dizzy, knees weak, clinging to his arms so she didn't collapse down to the floor.

This had to stop, or she was going to let him fuck her right here in the hallway. She put a hand on his chest and sucked in a breath. "I've got to let us in."

"Don't let me keep you." He turned her back around to face the door, letting her hair go but cupping her breast again. She could barely work the key in the lock with the mind-fogging intensity of his body flush with hers. His erection pressed against her lower back, promising that overwhelming pleasure she'd thought of when touching herself. But she had to open this fucking door first, if she could only focus. Ben wrapped his other arm around her waist, holding her more tightly against him, thumb starting to brush the hard, sensitive peak of her nipple.

"You're killing me." She laughed breathlessly, pausing to rest her forehead against the door, key dangling in the lock.

Ben chuckled. "Here. Let me help." He turned the key at the same time he rolled her nipple between his fingers, and Jesus, her knees really did buckle at that. He could play her body like an instrument, and they were both still fully clothed. Excitement and nervousness rolled over each other in waves inside her.

The room was bathed in red light from the emergency exit signs, and Hannah went around flicking on the lamps. Fluorescent lighting would have been too harsh, so she used natural light whenever possible, brightness spilling from every angle to illuminate the room with warmth instead of starkness. The moment of distance from Ben gave her a chance to catch her breath.

"Wow, look at all this." Ben turned in a circle, taking everything in. "I want to try everything."

Hannah laughed and took his hand again. "Well, you can't. I've got most of the samples at my house. This is all for sale, and none of it's cheap." She took a condom out of one of the bowls and held it up. "Except these. These are cheap."

Ben took it from her hand and tucked it into his pocket, then crowded into her personal space and wrapped his arms around her. "Have I told you how much I want to fuck you?"

"You haven't, no." And there was that breathlessness again. How was she supposed to think straight with his body slotting against hers? She ran a hand down his broad chest. "You barely know me."

"I know you enough to want to fuck you."

Well, no one could say he wasn't direct. It was kind of nice, actually. So many guys played games, and she didn't have time for games. But if all he saw her as was a piece of ass, this business partnership was going to be a challenge.

"Do you want to get to know me?"

"Yeah, I do." He slid his hands down to cup her ass. "Don't you think I'll get to know you in the next few weeks?"

"I suppose you will." Weeks of this, of him. The thought made her smile.

"Do you want to get to know *me*?" Ben teased her lips

with his once more, a gentle, light kiss.

"Mmm-hmm." She kissed back, nibbling at his lip. "This is a good start."

Ben's kisses made her mind go fuzzy, a haze that made thinking difficult and reduced her to the tactile sensations in her body. His beard against her face electrified her nerve endings, and those large hands against her back kept her pressed flush against him. Somehow he was both overwhelming and delicate, large and playful. She couldn't stop smiling even as he made her body throb. Fuck, this was going to be fun. But she couldn't lose her head yet. There was something more.

"Business first." She pulled back and rested her hand on the front of his shirt. "I just got tested last month and came back negative for the whole gamut." She tickled her way across his chest, fingertips working up toward his neck and making him duck his head and pull away, grinning. "How about you, ticklish man?"

He grabbed her wrist and pulled her hand away. "Yeah, end of summer. Me and Mitchell both. Everybody's negative."

"Testing together. Nice." She nodded approvingly at his comment, then sucked in a breath as he started to nibble the arm he'd caught tight in his hand. "Oh," she breathed.

"Who's ticklish now?" he teased. Then he bit gently into the skin, and her sigh turned into a much louder moan. "Mmm, I like the sound of that." He used her wrist to pull her closer again, moving his mouth from the tender skin of her inner arm to the sensitive curve of her neck. "I need you out of these clothes."

Fuck, yes. Hannah was a few minutes away from lying down right here on the floor, but she had her head together enough to know that was a terrible idea. She stepped back. "Come on. Not here."

"Holy shit." Ben started to laugh the moment she turned

on the light of the storage room. "Tell me you don't have a sex swing in the back room of your shop."

"All right. I don't have a sex swing in the back room of my shop." Hannah walked over to what definitely *was* a sex swing and tugged on the webbing. "Then this is some kind of mysterious alien artifact, I think."

"This is wild. I've never seen one of these in person. Only in porn." Ben shook his head and looked it all over, picking up the various straps and cushioned supports and buckles and then letting them hang. "Why do you have this here instead of in the shop? Are you shooting porn back here?"

"I do not shoot porn." Hannah sat down on the hanging seat part of the swing. "First, it's a fun place to sit. Second, it takes up too much floor space in the main room, but if a customer wants to see how it looks and works, I can take them back here for them to check it out." She grinned. "And now it's got a third purpose, which is that I am going to have you fuck me in it."

Ben licked his lips, showing her exactly what he thought of that. He walked a complete circle around the swing. "This is pretty crazy."

"I'm pretty crazy." She looked up at him, daring him to meet her on this, to play like she wanted to play. "You in?"

"Fuck yes, I'm in." He stepped up to where she sat and pulled the swing, bringing her legs to either side of his hips. Bending, he kissed her again, rougher, before letting her back down. From there, Hannah's mind went foggy again under the influence of his kisses. He stripped off her clothes with single-minded focus, large hands deft at buttons and zippers, baring her skin to the cool air. When her bra fell to the floor, he paused, and yeah, she could definitely get used to being looked at with that kind of lust.

Sometimes, being exposed like this in front of a new person was uncomfortable, but Ben's gaze was nothing but awe. "I wish…" he started, then paused. "I wish I could lay you out and really take my time with you."

Not like that, not tonight. Some nights were for slow, leisurely sex, but Hannah already burned from the inside out, and she was not going to wait. "I don't want you to take your time." She tugged his shirt up and off, standing on tiptoes. "I want you to fuck me."

Ben cupped her breasts in both hands, and all her words disappeared again. His warm palms pressed against the cool skin. More. God, she wanted more than this soft touch; she pushed forward. The pads of his fingers brushed lightly on her nipples, too lightly, a tease that made her moan in frustration. Her pussy was throbbing and he hadn't even really *touched* her yet. But then he rolled her nipples between his fingers like he'd done earlier, no clothing in the way this time, and she shivered all the way down to her toes.

She needed him naked, now. Tugging at his clothes, she got him to let go of her enough to get undressed, and finally, she could get a look at him.

Holy shit. His cock was ridiculous, large and thick and gorgeous, swollen and leaking at the tip. She could close her fist around it, but barely. Her tight grip made him groan, his eyes falling closed. She could watch him like this forever, his openmouthed pleasure at her gentlest touch.

Ben moved quickly, dragging her against him to kiss her hard and rough and with all the need she was feeling as well. They wanted this. She wanted this. The sex, the closeness, the breathless desperation… She wanted all of it, couldn't get it fast enough.

"Easy," he murmured against her mouth, his hand closing over hers. She'd been stroking him harder, faster, in her excitement, and she stilled beneath his hand. "You're gonna get me too worked up." He smiled and kissed her again.

Without any further preamble, he squatted and picked

her up, a sudden quick lift with his arms wrapped around her thighs. She gasped, hands going to his shoulders for balance.

"Fuck!" She looked into his eyes, now at their level.

"What, nobody ever picked you up before?"

"Not in a really long time. And never like this." She smiled, the exhilaration of arousal and playfulness combining into a really heady aphrodisiac. Ben lowered her onto the swing, where she clung to the straps for a moment of unsteadiness until she found her balance. Her feet were only about a foot off the floor, but it felt way higher, like she might slip out at any moment.

"You're not going to fall," he said as if reading her mind. "Relax. It looks like you can lean back on this strap right here."

"Right." She let out a shaky laugh. "This feels different than hanging in it for just lounging around." She kept a death grip on the straps as she leaned back, and yeah, the back strap cushioned her and kept her mostly upright. Her body teemed with conflicting sensations. Dizziness from being weightless, excitement, a touch of fear that made her all the more aroused.

Ben took a moment to see how everything worked, then threaded her legs through the separate leg straps, sliding them up so that each of her thighs was supported. In this position, she was exposed, her thighs spread wide, her legs bent at the knee and feet dangling. Her heart was going to beat out of her chest. Fuck, this was too much; she was in over her head here, and she wanted more.

The first stroke of his fingers over her cleft shocked her body like electricity. He brushed over her, light touches up and down the folds of her pussy, not lingering anywhere she wanted him for too long.

"You're so wet." His voice sounded rough. "God, you're soaked."

A blunt pressure stretched her open so perfectly, those same fingers working into her, sliding through her slickness.

She couldn't do much more than moan in response, her body limp under his caresses. In the swing, she couldn't reciprocate, and lying here under his touches was going to drive her mad.

"More, please." She tried to shift closer and couldn't.

Ben finally moved up to her clit, right where she wanted his touch, and began rubbing in slow circles with his thumb. His fingers deep inside her pressed against her G-spot. *Yes, holy mother of god.* Fuck, his touch made her struggle to speak or think. The cold air of the storage room contrasted with his hot fingers and with her own wet folds, a combination that set her trembling.

"Please," she begged. To hell with how desperate she sounded. "Please fuck me."

"You're kind of demanding, you know." Ben grinned.

Watching him slick the condom over his erection was enough to make her pussy twitch again. He was huge. He was going to push inside her, impaling her, exactly how she wanted. He stroked himself, hand moving over his latex-wrapped shaft. He was beautiful.

Ben lined up between her legs, the thick head of his cock pressing against her entrance. Grabbing her hips, he began to guide himself inside.

"Oh, fuck." Hannah felt that penetration all throughout her body, and her curse dissolved into a moan.

Ben had his eyes closed, and the strain of not fucking all the way into her was written on his face. He moved achingly slowly, taking his time, easing into her, filling her up. He seemed to go on forever. Just when she thought there couldn't be any more of him, he kept going, and she took him even deeper. The all-consuming helplessness was intoxicating, the pleasant fullness and rippling spasms running all through her pussy. She let the slow, deep penetration overtake all of her senses. When he finally bottomed out, balls-deep inside her, she clenched a few times to test the sensation. She'd never been full like this. Ben stretched her to her body's limits, and each clench made her shiver. Hanging like this, she couldn't move against him, couldn't thrust, had to just take it.

Ben breathed out steadily, slowly, and opened his eyes.

"You're burning hot." His cock twitched inside her, pressing against some spot that made her gasp again. "Jesus. You're killing me."

"Fuck me, *please*." She tried to shift her hips, wiggling again so he moved against her. "I can't even *move*."

"Mmm. So impatient." He smiled, then took her by the hips and began to move more steadily.

That made her lose her words. She wanted to talk more, tell him what he was doing was good, so good, but she couldn't do anything but breathe and moan. Each thrust lit her up like the first, impossibly good, impossibly deep. How could she think like this, her body strung out at its limits?

Ben reached out to take her nipples in between his fingers, twisting them. Each thrust pulled against his grip, and suddenly, she was on the edge. Where had that even come from? Flailing wildly, she caught hold of the webbing straps, some measure of stability, something to keep her anchored to this moment.

Her orgasm didn't wash over her as much as slam into her full force. The world went white, then black, her pussy clenching around his cock, body trembling, all her muscles seizing up as nearly unbearable pleasure exploded outward from her core. Ben was still moving within her, dragging out her orgasm with each deep stroke, and she gasped and cried out. Another few strokes and he was coming as well, holding himself deep inside her, his climax so intense, his cock pulsed against her inner walls.

"Holy shit." Ben pulled out, gasping and shaking his head, already taking care of the condom with shaking hands.

Hannah took a few moments to catch her breath as well. The emotions of orgasm still rolled through her body, bliss and vulnerability, a desire for closeness that she could push aside.

"I have got to get me one of these swings," Ben said, returning to her side.

The jokes came easy, her mind floating free as her body. "Yeah? You want to hang it in your place for all the good fucking?" She tried to wriggle herself free but then gave up and waited for him to help. "Think Mitchell would like it?"

He began lifting her legs out of the straps, letting her free one step at a time. "I'm not used to talking about sex with one person after having sex with another, you know." He smiled.

"You don't think it's hot?"

"Maybe a little." His smile was light, lascivious, and fun, and she instantly relaxed tension she hadn't realized she'd been holding. Rather than bring her to her feet, he bodily lifted her out of the swing and into his arms, then set her down on the floor. She wobbled, and he caught her, holding her until she was ready to stand. She started to pull on her clothes.

"Oh, not going to sit naked on all the furniture in here?" Ben grinned and started to get dressed as well.

"Definitely not." Hannah laughed.

"It conditions the leather, you know."

She pressed a hand to her head. "You're something else. I like laughing with you. I don't always feel like laughing after sex. Which is a shame, because fucking is fun."

"That's for damn sure." Ben sighed.

"Do you and Mitchell laugh a lot?"

Ben pulled his shirt over his head. "During sex, or otherwise?"

"Well, I was thinking of sex, but anytime." Picturing them together made her more curious, not less.

Ben looked at her for a few seconds. "You really want to ask about me and Mitchell, huh?"

"I'm curious."

"All right." He sat down on one of the chairs, and she sat down in her desk chair. "Sometimes Mitchell takes it a little too seriously, but usually I can get him to loosen up."

"So you two..." She wasn't sure how to ask the question about Ben and Mitchell's relationship. "I mean, you're not dating, but clearly you're not exclusive, or you wouldn't be here, I hope."

Ben shook his head. "Oh. No, Mitchell and I both date other people." He paused. "Well, not lately for me. And not in a long time for him. But that's it. Just sex. And really good friendship." He folded his arms, and he made a fine sight sitting there. If she hadn't literally just finished a fantastic orgasm, she'd consider going for round two.

"I see." She could appreciate the arrangement. "I didn't mean to pry."

"Nah." Ben shrugged. "I don't think it's a secret." He paused as if realizing something. "I don't *think* it's a secret. I'm realizing we never really talked about whether we talked about it or not."

"Well, have you ever told anyone else?"

"No." Ben tapped his lips with a finger. "And I don't think he has, either. Shit, I've gotta tell him I told you."

"I'm sure it'll come up." She hadn't expected so much of their postsex time to be spent talking about Mitchell, but a curiosity remained, and it was definitely rooted in the naughty, dirty fantasies she'd been spinning about him. "So you said he's bi, too?"

"Yeah." Ben nodded. "I don't know if he has a preference, but he goes both ways."

"And you? Do you have a preference?"

"I prefer that they're as excited as I am." Ben grinned. "Otherwise, I don't really care. What about you? You said earlier you're just into guys?"

"I am sadly heterosexual." Hannah smiled. "I disappointed a roommate back in college with that, but I have to admit, I have no sexual or romantic feelings for other women." After pausing, she added, "But I can appreciate that they are beautiful."

"Obviously."

"You and Mitchell." Hannah put her arms on the armrests of the chair, spinning the chair back and forth a few inches as she thought about how to broach this subject. "You guys get jealous?"

"How do you mean?"

If she brought this up directly, she might ruin any future plans with Ben, but it was important to clear the air so she knew. "What if I wanted to ask him out? Would you be cool with that?"

Ben pursed his lips. "Sure. We're not dating. And even if we were, I don't own you. I don't control who you see." He looked honest, too; there was no guile in his expression. "And I already talked to Mitchell about where I had hoped tonight might go. We're cool."

"Okay. That's...okay. He didn't strike me as the casual-sex kind of guy." And maybe that wasn't all the way true, maybe it was just an excuse, but she didn't have to admit it out loud.

Ben chuckled. "Mitchell's a lot of things he doesn't seem to be at first. Give him a chance." He raised his eyebrows. "In fact, I think you'll be pleasantly surprised."

Chapter Five

Mitchell unbuttoned his chef's jacket and stripped it off, the fresh blast of cool air hitting him like a balm after so long in the hot kitchen. Everything was set for tonight, dinner service was well underway, and he could finally head out after being here for—he checked the clock on the wall—ten hours. Not bad, as his days went. He would normally stay later, but his sous chef had pretty much kicked him out of the kitchen. She might only be just a hair over five feet tall, but she had the no-nonsense demeanor it took to boss Mitchell around when necessary. Most of it was good-natured, like how she insisted he have some free time and leave the kitchen at a decent hour now and then.

All right, fine, he'd go. He hadn't hit the gym yet today, so he could go there, then pull some food together for his own dinner, maybe something for Ben, too, if he was home.

Passing through the dining room, Mitchell stopped abruptly at the sight of a familiar face hanging out near the front of the restaurant. Hannah had one arm slung along the back of the booth, her face turned expectantly toward him.

Well, damn, he hadn't expected to see her the day after she'd gone out with Ben. He hadn't expected to see her at all, at least not until maybe they talked about Fall Festival together. When she smiled and beckoned, he couldn't help but slide into the booth across from her.

Hannah leaned closer and breathed in. "You smell delicious."

"Thanks?" He was never sure how to take that compliment; he tried his hardest not to smell like the Fryolator most of the time. "What brings you in tonight?"

"I was looking for you."

"Oh?" Well, that was a surprise.

"I asked about you, and the hostess said she thought you were heading out soon." Hannah nodded to the front of the house, where Opal was organizing the stack of menus.

"And here I am." Too bad he wasn't dressed more presentably, instead sitting here in just his white undershirt and chef slacks, jacket tossed on the bench beside him. "So what's up?"

"I met with Ben last night to talk about some ideas for the Fall Festival."

He'd heard all about that. "Yeah, he told me."

Hannah rested her chin on her hand. "I was disappointed you couldn't join us."

Knowing what had happened last night, at least from the gist he'd inferred from Ben, this was definitely a flirtation, especially delivered as it was with Hannah looking up through her lashes. Was she rubbing it in, or was she possibly inferring more? "Seems like you two did enough 'talking' for the both of us."

Hannah didn't look away, smiling instead, her tongue caught between her teeth. "Yeah? You get all the details?"

"A few." Ben wasn't the type to brag about sex like it was a conquest, but he'd come home absolutely floating last night.

Hannah didn't look bothered at all, not with that Cheshire cat smile.

"Hmm." Hannah looked to the sides, making a show of ensuring they were alone. "Disappointed you didn't get *all* the details?"

All right, this was definitely flirtation. If she was still going to flirt while sleeping with Ben, then maybe that wasn't so serious. Maybe he hadn't given up his only shot. Smirking, he leaned in. "Maybe you should give me all the details so you can make sure he got the story right."

Hannah chuckled and nodded. "Maybe I'll have to do that sometime."

And that was it, just a smile and nothing further, and curiosity pressed at him along with a little annoyance at how obtuse she was being. "But really. Why were you waiting for me?"

Hannah's expression returned to neutral, drifting away from the sauciness she had been presenting. "I really did want to talk to you about the Fall Festival."

"Ben went over your proposal with me. I think it sounds fine." He leaned back again in the booth. "You could have emailed, too."

Hannah's plump lips turned down in the barest hint of a frown. "You know, if I didn't know better, I'd say you were trying to get rid of me."

"I'm not trying to get rid of you." He wasn't, but it was hard to sit here and ignore the fact that last night he'd jerked off while imagining watching Ben fuck her senseless. "I'm just...confused." Confused about where he stood with her, about why she was flirting, about the nature of whatever was developing between her and Ben. "But we can talk about the festival if you want to."

Hannah bit her lower lip. "Okay. I do want to talk about the festival. But also, I want to go out with you. See where things lead." She dragged out those last few words, making eye contact as she did so. Oh. That was clear enough. He'd wanted Hannah for so long, but he had never taken action, never even been willing to take that kind of risk. And then there were his loyalties to Ben, because didn't she literally just sleep with him last night?

"What about you and Ben?"

Hannah slung one arm along the back of the booth, angling her head to the side. "Ben didn't become my boyfriend last night, you know. Any more than he's become yours."

"Right." The idea of Ben as his boyfriend was not an idea he entertained much anymore, except sometimes when he was a little drunk. Afterward, he always blamed the alcohol. He wanted to say yes to Hannah. There was no real reason to say no, other than his own fear about where that path might lead. But she wasn't asking him for a relationship. She was asking him for a night. "Yeah. I'd like that."

"You free tonight?"

Damn, if only he could. "Not tonight. I'm headed to the gym, need to make dinner, run through some orders for next week. But, um..." He thought over his schedule, the times his sous chef was scheduled, the hours he had committed to doing dinner service instead of morning prep. "I could do tomorrow, if you want."

Hannah smiled. "I could make that work. I close at eight. You want to come by my house after that?"

Her house? Fuck yes. "Sure." He slid out of the booth. "You staying for dinner? Or do you want to walk out with me?"

"I'll follow you out."

Hannah tailed Mitchell out to the lobby, where he paused. "I've just gotta grab some paperwork." He gestured to an unmarked door in the foyer.

"The secret lair?" Hannah bobbed up onto the balls of her feet. "Can I see?"

Was she serious? "It's a storage area. It's not that exciting."

"I love behind-the-scenes things."

"Okay, if you want." He opened the door and let her inside, flipping on the light. He wove around boxes to get to the desk in the far corner where he kept the weekly and monthly order forms, then started leafing through for the ones he'd need to check.

"Wow, you weren't kidding about the storage area part." Hannah's voice came from the other side of a tower of boxes. "What's down this staircase? The brew tanks?"

He didn't need to look up. "Yup. But if you want to see those, you should ask Ben. That's his domain."

She picked her way back over to where he was standing, maneuvering around the piles of clutter, and came to stand with her hands on her hips in front of him. "How come you never used this space?"

"What? We do use this space."

"Yeah, but for storage. This is a good-size area." She glanced around. "You could expand your foyer, maybe. Or do extended seating."

This space hadn't been anything other than storage in a long time. Even thinking of it differently felt weird, like he was back in time when they first bought the place. "We bought a few different parcels of this building side by side in order to convert it into a restaurant. Our original business model included a retail storefront, but we ended up not needing it. We sell all the merch right out of the foyer, and this space was just left over." He shrugged. "We don't need the restaurant to be any bigger than it is."

"So you converted everything else and not this?"

"There were some weird construction issues with knocking out this wall." He gestured to the wall where they'd come in. Figuring out those plans had been such a pain in the ass. "Plumbing and wiring or something. It was going to raise our reno budget. We decided to put it on hold until we had more capital and eventually decided it wasn't worthwhile." He started to leaf through his papers again.

"You own the whole building?" Hannah looked around. "What's upstairs?"

"Event room." Mitchell waved his arm vaguely toward the ceiling. "And I already told you we've got the brewery setup downstairs." Finding the last papers he needed, he tucked them into a file folder and slipped it under his arm. When he turned to leave, though, Hannah was blocking his only clear exit. She took a large step closer, and he sat down on the desk in surprise, making her chuckle.

"Did I scare you?" She stepped closer, right up against him, eye to eye. Her expression dared him to make a move. That defiant look on her face triggered a spark inside him. Oh, Hannah. She definitely thought he was shy, didn't she? She had no idea what he could *really* be like.

Hannah's eyes widened as she saw *something* in his expression that she clearly hadn't seen before. She took a hasty step back, but Mitchell was faster, reaching out to catch her wrist in his hand. When he pulled her back up to him, he watched her response: her quickening breath, the dilated pupils, the soft openness of her mouth—these were signs of fear…but Hannah definitely wasn't afraid. He had seen this look on a few people, the ones who liked his dominance and yielded to it gladly. Mitchell didn't even have to stand up, instead staying where he was, sitting on the edge of the desk. He tugged her closer, leading her to the space in between his legs. When he released her arm, she could have backed away, but instead she remained right where he'd brought her. Moving deliberately, he cupped the side of her face and ran his thumb across the swell of her lower lip. Hannah let out an almost imperceptible sigh, her eyelashes fluttering. He wanted to go further. He wanted to take her just like this, pin her down on this desk and have his way with her. Those noises she would make, hands gripping the edges of the desk, breath coming in gasps as he thrust into her wet heat…his cock throbbed in his pants.

"Interesting," he murmured and made himself pull his hand away.

Hannah came back to her senses with a start. "What? What's interesting?"

Mitchell shook his head, because they both knew and he wasn't going to say it. "Your house tomorrow night?" Watching her respond to his dominance, tomorrow night had suddenly become an even more enticing prospect.

She nodded and took a step backward, her motions unsteady. "Nine o'clock. I'll send you my address."

"Sounds good." He got back to his feet, gathering up his jacket and file folder. "I'll walk you out."

. . .

"What the fuck did you tell Hannah about me last night?" Mitchell was barely in the door of the house that night before he was already lighting into Ben. A full Crossfit workout had left his body sore but still as electrically charged as standing in the storage room with Hannah, none of the tension dissipated in the intervening time. No, his adrenaline had him just as revved up as he had been in that hormonally saturated moment.

Ben looked up from the brewing magazine he was reading. "What?" He frowned. "Nothing weird. I mentioned we were fucking, but I already told you that last night. Why? What did she say to you?"

"She wants me over her house tomorrow night."

Ben grinned. "Oh yeah? Nice."

"I don't get it." Mitchell looked down at his phone, where

a text message was now displaying her address.

Ben rolled his eyes. "She wants to fuck you, Mitchell."

Clearly. "Yeah, I got that. But..." He couldn't explain exactly what he was thinking. In the time since his workout, his brain had begun to catalog all the ways in which she shouldn't want him. "She literally just saw you last night."

Ben stared at him without commenting for a minute, incredulous. "So?"

"So why didn't she just call you again? You two already have a thing going."

"We have a thing going? What is this, high school?" Ben tossed his magazine onto the coffee table and folded a leg beneath him. "Listen. She's probably wanted to fuck you for a long time. She told me last night that she didn't think you were the type of guy for casual sex. That's probably why she never asked."

"Oh." He was a pretty serious guy, so that wasn't an unreasonable conclusion. "And you told her I am?"

Ben gestured between the two of them. "Well, what do you call this?"

Mitchell had avoided defining that for a long time; when he really delved into those thoughts, they led nowhere safe. "You're my best friend, though. It's different."

"If you don't want to fuck her, tell her." Ben shrugged. "No harm in that."

Mitchell laughed. The way she'd looked at him at the end of the night, her eyes filled with that open, haunting vulnerability, there was no way he was turning her down, even if it probably did make more sense for her to stick with Ben. "No, I definitely want to."

"So why the hesitation?" Ben tilted his head to the side. "Is it because you're kind of a freak?" He smiled, no harm intended.

Mitchell shook his head and laughed, walking into the

kitchen. "Fuck you."

"I'm pretty sure Hannah's not gonna be put off by your freakiness. Quite the opposite, as a matter of fact." Ben spoke louder to be heard as Mitchell headed for the fridge. "I've got leftover pizza in there."

"Hell yeah." Mitchell carried the entire pizza box into the living room along with a can of soda.

Ben stretched out his arms along the back of the sofa. "Don't get too attached, though, right? I don't want to fuck up the Fall Festival partnership."

Sure, because obviously that would be Ben's concern. Can't mess with business. Can't let emotions get in the way. Heaven forbid anyone get *attached*.

"It wouldn't be the worst thing in the world, you know." Mitchell slid a piece of pizza onto his plate.

"What wouldn't be the worst thing in the world?"

"Getting attached." At Ben's raised eyebrow, Mitchell kept talking. "I'm just saying, it's possible to get close to someone without everything going wrong." Ben was still looking at him with incredulity, so he shifted his gaze to the pizza and picked off a slice of pepperoni.

After a pause, Ben made a disparaging noise. "Well, not in my experience. Not when there's so much at stake."

It was the closest they had come in years to talking about what came before. Neither of them brought up those days out of some tacit agreement, but Mitchell remembered what Ben was like after his marriage ended, when he seemed so broken it was impossible to believe he could ever put himself back together again. But he did, slowly, and somewhere along the way, he added walls to keep it from ever happening again. At least he didn't seem to find friendship a threat to their business success.

Mitchell cleared his throat in the awkward silence and grabbed the remote. "Come on. Red Sox are on tonight."

Chapter Six

Mitchell always had a presence about him, but it hit Hannah way more intensely when he was standing in the doorway of her home. He wasn't a large man, but he seemed to take up more space than Ben did, and Ben was quite a bit taller. Ben's charisma and charm filled the space, but with Mitchell, it was something more quiet and intense. That intensity drew her and simultaneously kept her frozen in place in the doorway.

After a moment, he gave her a wry smile. "You gonna let me in? Or are we having this conversation on the doorstep?"

Hannah stepped aside, laughing but also flustered. "I was thinking about asking you some riddles before I let you in."

"I don't have much patience for riddles. You'd be better off with Ben. He's the genius in our partnership." He looked around. "This is a nice house."

"You want the dime tour?"

"Sure. Show me around." Mitchell strolled in, hands clasped behind his back, casually looking around like he had all the time in the world. She walked him around the first floor, half-heartedly explaining some things about the house. Really, though, it was hard to keep herself calm in his presence. He was like a whole different person right now, his energy all different. Did she even know him at all? She seldom saw him outside of work mode. He was either at the restaurant, moving briskly from one task to the next, or he was at the Chamber of Commerce meetings, taking notes and representing his business. Yeah, he was always intense, but this was different intensity. She could *feel* him near her. He had barely touched her last night, and her body had burned like a thousand matches caught fire under her skin. She'd been so cavalier about inviting him to her house, expecting that under that reserved exterior was someone shy who just needed some coaxing. As he brushed past her to look at a painting on the wall, moving like a lithe animal, it seemed she might have been very, very wrong. He hadn't been shy. He had been waiting. And damn, that was sexy as hell.

She grasped for a topic of conversation. "You want to talk about Fall Festival?"

Mitchell put his hands in his pockets and turned. "Ben went over all of it already. You can go over it again if you want, but I think it sounds great. We're ready to move forward."

She should have known. "So, you don't need to talk more about it?"

Mitchell raised both eyebrows. "Hannah, neither of us is here so you can go over Fall Festival information with me." He tipped his head to the side. "Right?"

Hannah licked her lips. "Well, I'm here because I live here."

Mitchell chuckled. He always gave her those tight-lipped smiles, but his laugh was low and rough, a laugh she could feel. "And you invited me." He looked toward the staircase, then back at her. "Do you want to take me upstairs, or not?"

The breeze blowing in from outside had cooled Hannah's bedroom to an early fall briskness, but the moment Mitchell stepped in the room with her, the temperature jumped several degrees. He didn't waste any time, stepping into her personal space so she backed instinctively against the wall, pinning her without touching her at all. Fuck, she was wet, and he hadn't laid a hand on her. It shouldn't be possible to want this much all at once. Mitchell braced himself with a hand on the wall next to her head, studying her like he was seeing her for the first time.

"I don't do this a lot, you know."

Hannah felt a rush of different emotions. "Ben said you two have been fucking around for a couple of years now."

Mitchell smiled. "Yeah, that's right. But this." With his free hand, he touched her lightly on the breastbone, one finger resting on her sternum. "Casual fucking. I don't do it a lot."

His touch, that one point of contact, burned like a live wire even through her clothing. Hannah's voice sounded breathless in her ears. "I don't imagine you do very much that's casual."

His eyes sparkled. "Now you're getting it."

"I don't have to do casual." Hannah wanted this, wherever it was going, and the heat under her skin threatened to consume her before they even got started. "But I am going to explode if you don't touch me soon."

Mitchell smiled. No, not smiled. *Smirked.* He smirked like he knew exactly what he was doing. Somehow, she had never realized Mitchell Fredericks was a Dominant, and damn, what an oversight to make.

"Touch you?" He moved his hand up from her chest to the back of her head, sliding his fingers through her long hair and then tightening his hand into a fist. He pulled her hair perfectly, just hard enough to send tiny needles of pain through her scalp and tingles of pleasure into her clit. With that grip, he held her in place and lowered his mouth to her ear. "I can touch you if you'd like."

Jesus. She wanted his mouth on hers, but instead, he began nibbling his way from her ear down her jawline. He held her motionless as his lips evoked sparks and shivers from her oversensitized nervous system. She let out a whimper, and his lips curled up in a smile against her skin.

"I like that sound," he whispered hot on her jaw.

He moved down, tipping her head to the side to give him better access to her neck. When he reached the sensitive dip of flesh where her neck met her shoulder, he slowly sank his teeth into that pressure point until she let out a moan that she had never made beyond the context of actual sex. Mitchell didn't let her squirm; she shifted, but she couldn't go far. She was trapped, and just thinking about being trapped beneath him heightened all her senses. Maybe, right here, she would collapse.

"Hannah." He brushed his lips against her collarbone and then lifted his head. She had to struggle to focus on him. "You want this?"

She nodded, feeling his hand still in her hair, loosely cupping the back of her head.

"Can you use words?" He smiled, teasing, and she relaxed a bit. This was Mitchell, and she knew him; he wasn't just this dominant stranger taking her apart with barely any effort at all.

"Yes, you ass, I want this."

"Good." He let go of her hair, settling his free hand down on her hip in a neutral position. "Safety talk?"

"Mmm-hmm." Hannah smiled. "I talked to Ben about this. He told me you guys get tested regularly."

"Always negative, always protected." He waggled his eyebrows. "You?"

"Same." She grabbed his shirt. "Now, will you please keep going?"

"You getting bossy?" He cupped her breasts, thumbs brushing her nipples through her bra, light and teasing and not nearly enough. "Hmm?"

"Yes. I'm very bossy." She slid her hands over his shoulders and down his back. Muscles. Yeah, she could stand in support of those. "And what I really want is for you to kiss me." She tipped her head. "How's that for using my words?"

Mitchell gave her a half smile, his eyes darkening with desire. She pulled him up against her, his hard body pressing into hers, and he wrapped his arms around her to finally—*finally*—kiss her on the mouth.

Mitchell kissed like he seemed to do everything: methodically, thoroughly, purposefully. There were no teasing nips or licks, just deep, soul-baring exploration, no holding back on the intimacy that he dropped into headfirst. Hannah didn't usually feel like she was being consumed by a kiss, but just in this space, right now, she could dissolve into him and never have existed. This was not just intense. This made her nerve endings go frazzled, short-circuiting her brain, and she didn't even register that he'd moved her away from the wall until she felt her knees hit the side of the bed and she tumbled backward.

"Holy shit." She propped herself up on her elbows, feet dangling off the edge of the bed. "You really don't do this halfway, do you?"

"I don't, no." Mitchell smiled wickedly. "Now, take off your clothes for me."

He said it so casually, but his tone didn't invite refusal, and that order curled her toes on its own. He watched her as she undressed, and her hands shook like crazy under his focused gaze. Hannah pulled off the rest of her clothes and tossed them aside, and now she was grinning even though the very air felt charged with sexual tension. He looked at her like he wanted to devour her, and man, she could get used to this.

Hannah stretched out on her side, facing him, and he took his time looking her up and down.

"You are...gorgeous."

She flushed. "What about you?" He was still completely clothed. "You going to get naked anytime soon?"

"We'll get there."

Mitchell climbed gracefully onto the bed with that litheness she'd noticed downstairs. He moved like an animal, measured and precise, maybe like a big cat. He climbed onto the bed next to her and, with a hand on her shoulder, rolled her onto her back on the bed. Then, without further ado, he inched his way down her body and pushed her legs apart.

Fuck, just like this? No preamble, no other touching, and he was staring right at her folds, his strong hands holding her thighs spread. Embarrassment and arousal warred inside her: being so exposed wasn't supposed to turn her on like it did. She was dripping. Hannah slid an extra pillow below her head, propping herself up, looking down the length of her body at the highly erotic sight of him lying down between her legs and studying her like one might study a rare flower. She had to breathe. She was going to pass out if she kept holding her breath, but breathing seemed way too difficult.

Mitchell traced his fingers up and through her wet folds with a steady, slow swipe, running two fingers through her cleft and up over her clit. The arousal hit her like a jolt, hips arching up off the bed out of reflex. *Fuck.*

He chuckled. "Are you a little sensitive?"

Hannah nodded, gripping the comforter, smiling even as she felt overwhelmed and, honestly, a little nervous. This was all happening in the wrong order; she didn't know what to expect from him. The unpredictability shook her more than she had thought it would.

"I love looking at you like this, close up." Mitchell spread her folds open, using his fingers to part her lips and expose the heart of her sex. "It's beautiful. You're beautiful."

He sounded reverent, and god, if that didn't push all kinds of weird buttons inside her. Hannah couldn't respond. Her throat had closed up, tension and emotion and vulnerability and just plain raw arousal silencing her.

Mitchell put his mouth directly over her clit and sucked the entire thing into his mouth.

Hannah cried out and twitched, her thighs reflexively trying to close and squeeze him away, but she was held in place by his hands. Oh, that was intense. Intense, amazing, overwhelming, everything all in one, and she suddenly couldn't parse exactly what he was doing with his mouth because it was *yes, this, now, good.*

She was making noises, mindless whimpering noises. Fuck, how did he get to be so good at this? Slowing her breathing, she tried to calm herself down, to keep from ratcheting up and over the edge too quickly. Deep breaths. Deep, slow breaths. With her attention focused again, she could feel the long, steady laps of his tongue over her bud, alternating with suction, a changing variety keeping her on the edge of an orgasm but not quite bringing her there.

When he stopped, she couldn't help pushing her hips forward, toward his mouth. He lifted his head, mischief in those eyes. "You want more?"

"Yes."

"Ask nicely."

"*Please.*" She had no intention of playing games here, not with a potentially incredible orgasm just a bit beyond her grasp, and she wriggled in his grip. "Please make me come."

"Do you really want that?"

Hannah looked down, incredulous. Was he serious? "Why the fuck would I *not* want that?"

He swiped his tongue once over her clit, and she jerked in

his grip reflexively.

"Because," he answered, "sometimes it's fun to be teased."

"Okay, yeah. Sometimes. Not right now." She tried to push herself forward into his mouth again. "Please?"

He held eye contact, his mouth so close she could feel his breath whispering across her skin, making her wait an interminable length of time. Finally, he nodded.

"If you insist," he murmured.

It wasn't often that Hannah's brain became so hyperfocused during sex, but it wasn't often that she got eaten out with such precision, either. The climax built all the way from her ankles, rolling up through her body, thin currents of electricity that tingled and sparked and warmed her until yes, there it was, right there, the edge that she so desperately sought, the pleasure building right beyond the peak.

Her climax overtook her like a force of nature, seizing up her muscles in a paroxysm of overwhelming pleasure. She came hard, his mouth on her the entire time, sucking and licking her through, drawing out the waves longer than should have been possible for her, her hips jerking as she arched up against his mouth. She gripped the comforter, threw her head back, and lost herself in the searing-hot intensity of orgasm.

Coming down, she flopped her limbs off to the side, boneless in the aftermath.

"Fuck. Me."

She couldn't move right away. In her limp relaxation, Mitchell got up, left her line of sight for a couple of moments, and then stretched out on the bed next to her with a smug grin on his face.

Mitchell smiled. "I like doing that."

"Yeah, you think?" In the giddy aftershocks, Hannah had to laugh. "You might have killed me. I'm completely unable to move. Exhausted." She let her head loll to the side and closed her mouth, tongue out in a parody of death.

Mitchell made an exaggerated noise of despair. "Oh no! Death by orgasm! I killed her!"

Hannah opened her eyes again and smiled. "You have. I am dead."

"That is a shame. I am most definitely not dead." Mitchell cupped his erection through his jeans, and Hannah felt a flutter of interest again. Damn, that was sexy.

"Well, I think my death is temporary. A little death, as it were."

Mitchell grinned. "Are you making a French joke? *La petite mort?* The little death?"

Color her surprised. "I am. Since when do you speak French?"

"I don't speak French, but I know that one." Mitchell scooted closer. "And I can cook French."

Hannah reached up to pull his head down to her. "And kiss French." She tasted her own muskiness on his lips.

Mitchell groaned quietly against her mouth. "I want to fuck you."

"I want to be fucked."

"This is a good arrangement." He grinned. Sitting up, he pulled off his shirt.

Damn, those muscles. She had to ogle. "Fuck, how often do you work out?"

"Six days a week." He didn't sound like he was bragging, but he was very matter-of-fact about it.

"Doing what?"

"I do Crossfit and yoga. Sometimes I run or swim."

Hannah let out a breath of laughter. Great. "I am *so* not that ambitious."

"You own your own business. You're clearly more than a little ambitious."

Hannah's smile felt stiff. Sure, her own business. The

business that was about to go under if she didn't turn things around. The business that she had been so determined to run on her own, to prove that she could be independent and successful. The damn albatross around her neck.

Mitchell must not have noticed the change in her smile, and who would have in these circumstances? Regardless, her mood changed quickly when she saw his gaze return to the armoire. He got to his feet and walked over, hands on his hips, shirtless but still half dressed. "A bureau, a closet, and this. So what are the odds this is full of clothes?"

Ha. "Not very good."

He smiled. "Can I look in here?"

"Please." A guy who was intrigued by her toys? Perfect.

Mitchell opened both doors and whistled. "Damn." The cabinet was filled, each shelf organized and stocked wall to wall with a whole array of her favorite items. Mitchell picked up a paddle hanging just inside the door. He slapped his palm with it. "You like this?"

Hannah flushed. She didn't let just anyone spank her. Her partners never took it seriously, never did it the way she liked it, and she didn't want to get her hopes up. "I do, yes."

Mitchell smacked the paddle against his hand again, and that satisfying thump made Hannah's pussy clench. "How much?"

She could play it off here, like she usually did, but something told her not to. "A lot." She swallowed. "Have you ever paddled someone before?"

"No." Mitchell smacked it against his hand again. "But I've given some really good spankings, I think. Now and then I get a partner who's into it."

Damn, that was a mental image for the ages. Mitchell, calm and serious, holding someone down and spanking their bare ass. Holding another woman down. Holding Ben down. Fuck, no matter who she pictured, it was hot as hell. Hannah swallowed. No way she was going to turn this down. She got onto her hands and knees.

"Okay. Hit me. Medium."

Mitchell paused. "Don't you want a safe word?"

Hannah sat back on her heels. "I'd rather just tell you what I like. If it's okay with you, we can stick to no meaning no. I don't generally use safe words unless I want to struggle and fight and say no and not have you stop." She smiled, biting her tongue as she did so. "But I don't want you to fight. I want you to hit me. Give me what you think is a medium hit." She got back onto her hands and knees and wiggled her ass at him.

Mitchell wound up and smacked the fleshy part of her bottom with the paddle. She let out a yelp, but it was out of surprise instead of pain. That light sting was gorgeous.

"Oh. Nice." She let her head hang. "Harder? That was... like, a five. Can you give me a seven?"

His next stroke was a bit harder, landing on the other cheek, and it made such a satisfying sound, the resonance running through her body, that she had to groan. "Fuck. That's good. Just like that?"

"Absolutely." His voice sounded husky with want.

The man could paddle. Like, really paddle. A few strokes and he was into it, confident and powerful, and Hannah was a mewling mess in no time at all. He wasn't hitting too hard, except once or twice, and with the strength and control he had over his muscles, he was able to hit her perfectly over and over. Her ass must be red, the color probably blooming under his strokes, her skin burning hot. Everything dissolved except the solid sound of the paddle on her ass and the stinging of her skin.

His sudden light touch on her warm flesh made her jump, the contact of his hand rather than the paddle pulling her out of her meditative state. She'd let her head and shoulders collapse down to the bed, and now she lifted them to look behind her. Mitchell's eyes looked dark and feral, and he still held the paddle in one hand. Damn, she was suddenly as horny as if she'd never come.

Hannah needed to get her hands and her mouth on him, right now. She crawled over to him and then sat up on her knees to unfasten his belt buckle, needing what was inside, needing to get at his body. He let her undress him, helping her push the pants and boxers down over his narrow hips so the rest of his clothes fell in a pile to the floor.

Mitchell had a really nice cock. It wasn't a monster cock like Ben's, sure, but she didn't want to have that all the time. Slightly over average length, if she could judge by sight, but thick, hard, perfectly proportionate to this average-height, muscular man. And she wanted it in her hands, in her mouth, in her pussy.

She wrapped both hands around him and began to stroke, and Mitchell let out his breath in a huff. "Not wasting time, huh?"

"Nope." She shifted to sit back on the bed but then yelped as her sore ass landed on the bed. She paused in her stroking. "Fuck! That stings."

"Good sting? Or bad sting?"

"Good sting." She adjusted to carefully sit down. "So good. I can't describe it." That searing burn brought her into her body and out of her head. She slid off the edge of the bed, kneeling on the floor in front of him. Without further preamble, she took him down into her mouth.

Sucking cock was seriously underrated. She loved the thick weight of him, the way he filled her mouth, the sweet, clean smell of his skin.

Mitchell's hand went reflexively to the side of her head, but he didn't pull, touching and then moving away. No, she didn't want careful. She had had a touch of his dominance and wanted more. Grabbing his wrist, she pressed his hand into her hair.

Thank god for quick learners. He closed his fist on her hair, gripping her tight enough to hurt her scalp, and then began to slowly fuck her face. Hannah relaxed her jaw, closed her eyes, and relished this helpless sensation. She couldn't overpower him. She couldn't get away. She was at his mercy, fucked in the mouth like a whore, and that fantasy had her dripping in no time.

Her clit slid between her fingers, soaked and needy, and she began to rub.

"You like sucking my cock?" he asked, his voice sounding strained. "You want me to fuck your mouth while you play with your pussy?"

Jesus, she hadn't expected dirty talk, and it was amazing.

"Don't come, though. Get yourself nice and close to the edge."

Hannah's pussy clenched around nothing, and she sucked harder on the cock in her mouth. This was exactly what she wanted. She let him fuck her in the mouth, hard and deep, almost too deep, almost enough to make her gag. Then he pulled back, all the way, slipping out of her mouth and leaving her reaching for him.

She stayed on her knees for a moment, dazed, enjoying looking up at him. "*Please* fuck me."

Mitchell smiled down at her, cupping her face with his broad hand. Shit, that pushed some serious submissive buttons in her, and she closed her eyes at the emotion threatening to overwhelm her. "Yeah, look at you. All right."

He walked over to the open armoire and set the paddle down where he found it, then grabbed something off one of the shelves. As Hannah got a condom from the nightstand, Mitchell stretched out on the bed. She climbed onto the bed with him and tore open the wrapper, eager to get it on his dick. He watched her as she carefully unfurled the latex, sheathing his wet cock and moving to straddle his hips. She could not get him inside her fast enough.

"Jesus." His curse sounded like a prayer as she sank all the way down onto him in one hard slide. He exhaled, the muscles of his abdomen clenching as he controlled himself. In this position, his entire physique stretched out beneath her, those exquisitely sculpted muscles twitching with the feeling of her pussy wrapped around his cock. She shifted her gaze to his eyes, and he was staring right back. After his paddling, his dominance, his single-minded approach to this visit, this raw vulnerability on his face shook her more than the physical sense of having him inside her. She'd nearly forgotten that beneath the dominance, the confident sexiness, the playful intensity, this was Mitchell. Here, though, with his hands on her hips and his eyes locked on hers, everything crashed back: months of flirtation, tiny details of conversation, all of that culminating in this moment of raw, honest nakedness.

Hannah looked away. She was not ready to deal with all of that right now. Right now, he was gorgeous, he was throbbing inside her, and she was going to ride him until he went to pieces beneath her. She shifted her hips and began to rock against him.

In this position, her clit rubbed against his cock with each stroke. It might not be enough, though. As if reading her mind, he reached over to the nightstand and held up a small vibrator, which must have been what he'd grabbed earlier. His smug expression made her smile. That vulnerability from earlier was gone, and she wasn't sure how she felt about that. But then he slid the vibrator into place between them and switched it on, and all thought vanished for a breathless second.

"Pretty proud of yourself, there?" She shifted her hips to press her clit harder against the vibe. Damn, that was nice.

He nodded. "You could say that."

She could come like this, no problem. With that thought at the back of her mind, she focused on him, noting his every reaction and response.

Watching a man in the throes of passion was one of her favorite parts of bringing a partner to bed. Mitchell's guard slowly came down again. His eyes were glazed, lips slightly parted, and he opened and closed his mouth a fraction of an inch with every breath. He held on to her hips as she moved, and even though he had been so dominant before, now she was in control. Control was a heady, beautiful feeling. God, she wanted to know him, really *know* him. What lit him up? Running her hands over his chest, she found his nipples, small and dusky rose colored, neither fully brown nor fully pink, and rubbed across them with her thumbs.

He huffed out a breath and smiled. "Good girl."

Well, fuck, that wasn't something she expected to turn her on like it did. She might have control right now, but just like that, he reminded her that he was *letting* her have it. And damn, that was sexy.

His cock twitched inside her each time she brushed those sensitive buds, even more so when she pinched. Her orgasm threatened at the edge of her senses, but she held it off, teasing them both. Lightly pinching his nipples, she rode his cock as his heavy breathing turned to soft groans. The vibration transferred through both of them, surely, since it was lined up directly with his cock as well as her clit. She ground down against it, starting to quiver.

Unguarded, vulnerable, she had another moment of clarity about how fucking beautiful this man was. Damn, getting emotional during sex was not her style at all, but this was Mitchell, with his perfect body and mysterious demeanor, whom she knew and yet didn't know at all, Mitchell who was twitching and gasping and starting to shake apart beneath her. She should focus just on the sex, but no, she couldn't stop thinking of him, this man she had come to care for, and those feelings tangled with her arousal and wove the two together.

Tightening all her muscles around his cock, she held her position flush against his hips, squeezing him as hard as she could, pressing against the vibrator and holding his dick all the way inside her.

"Fuck!" He slammed his head back against the pillow. "You're just... I'm gonna..." He began to thrust up into her, letting loose like he hadn't before. She held on to his chest and rode out the thrusts as he came closer and closer to the edge, loving his inarticulate words, his frenzied thrusts, the expression of complete surrender on his face. She was so close, too, and pinched his nipples hard one final time.

Mitchell was completely silent as he came. He arched up, tucking his head, his eyes squeezing shut as his face contorted in a rictus of pleasure-pain. Just like that, she yielded as well, her own climax a surprise in its intensity and suddenness. She lost her balance, tumbling forward onto his chest and clinging there as she clenched around him. The vibrator was merciless, powerful and unmoving and directly lined up between her folds, and she kept clenching over and over again even as her body lost all strength.

When Mitchell relaxed, his muscles going limp below her, Hannah carefully untangled their bodies and slid off him, fumbling the vibrator off as she did so. Mitchell reached over to her nightstand for tissues. Hannah lay there, overwhelmed and sated and still breathless. Fuck, this was supposed to be a lighthearted experiment. But there was no way she was letting this be a onetime thing. She already wanted to do this again.

After going to the bathroom to clean up, Hannah returned to her bed, where Mitchell now sat in his boxers, leaning against her headboard and looking contemplative.

Cuddling wasn't normally her style, but that pull was too strong to resist. She joined him on the bed, scooting up next to him and resting her head on his shoulder.

Silence stretched on for a minute before she had to break it. "Well, it wasn't casual."

Mitchell started to chuckle. "I said it wouldn't be casual." He wrapped an arm around her back, stroking her skin. "Your bum feel okay?"

Hannah grinned. "Did you just call it my bum?"

"Well it *is* your bum, isn't it?" His brow furrowed.

"It's such a cute word. I don't think I've called it my bum in years. Like, maybe middle school?"

"I like that word!"

"Don't get defensive." Laughing, Hannah set her head back on his shoulder again. "It's adorable. You're adorable."

"I don't know if 'adorable' is the kind of compliment somebody wants after sex." Mitchell sounded grumpy, which was even cuter, but she wasn't going to tell him that.

"My bum is okay, yes, thanks. You're good at paddling. I'm gonna need some of that again sometime."

"Yeah?"

She wrapped an arm across his waist and squeezed him. "If you're up for that."

He paused, and her stomach dropped. Had she gone too far? Was this a one-and-done thing? Normally she was the one who was ready to dismiss a guy after sex, but now she'd been interested in two, back to back. That wasn't what she'd been expecting… but that didn't matter, right? As long as they were both game, they could do this again, as many times as they wanted.

"I…would like that." He squeezed her hand, smiling. Compared to the mind-blowing sex they'd just shared, that look shouldn't feel as intimate as it did. She'd always wanted to be looked at like that. Something tightened in her throat, some emotion she hadn't felt in a long time and didn't really want to feel now, when she was still riding the euphoria of her orgasms.

"I really have to get going, though." He grimaced. "Work is early. And never-ending."

"Don't I know it."

She unwound herself from him and slid off the bed. No need to dwell on how nice it would be if he could stay. Those thoughts weren't going to help anyone. This was fun, and they could do it again, and that was all she needed.

• • •

Ben wasn't waiting up for Mitchell, even though he was up later than usual, dozing on and off while sprawled out on the sofa rather than going to bed. He was merely enjoying the weather: the late September heat had finally yielded to fall crispness, and he got the cross breezes better here in the living room than in his bedroom. That was the only reason he was lying here, half listening for Mitchell to come home. He wasn't at all nosy. Curious, sure, but…not nosy. Not at all.

Mitchell's key in the lock jolted Ben out of another light doze, and he sat up, blinking away his grogginess. Ben had seen Mitchell every day for years, and the guy definitely had a look when he'd just gotten laid—a look he was wearing tonight. Well, thank god. He sure needed it.

"You still up?" Mitchell tossed his keys into the key bowl and went straight to the fridge.

"Yeah, I was just brainstorming spring flavor profiles." Ben gestured to the notebook still open on the coffee table, which he legitimately *had* been working on before dozing off.

Mitchell handed Ben a beer from the fridge and sat down in the armchair with his own. "Hannah wants to get together in a few days to talk specifics for the Fall Festival. Figure out a game for the booth."

"Sure, sounds good. Did you spend a lot of time going over your plans together?"

Mitchell looked at him with a neutral expression. He had to know what Ben was asking, especially as Ben couldn't stop from grinning. Finally, Mitchell sighed and relaxed in the chair. "No. We didn't talk about plans at all."

"Nice." Ben exhaled.

"This isn't weird for you?"

"What?"

"Us both having fucked the same woman, like two days apart." Mitchell shifted, crossing one ankle over the other knee. "That doesn't weird you out? I've never done that before."

With everything Mitchell knew about Ben, almost twenty years of friendship, seven years of close partnership, Mitchell should know better. "Asking me something like that, it's like you don't even know me, dude."

Mitchell shrugged. "I don't know. We've never dated the same person."

Well, that was an understatement. He hadn't seen Mitchell date anyone at all in a long time, actually. First, they were both consumed with the pressure of opening the restaurant, but even when business settled into the hectic-but-manageable pace of their lives, Mitchell stopped giving excuses. He just didn't date anymore, and Ben didn't ask. This evening with Hannah was a nice, unexpected change.

As for him, though?

"I don't care if we date the same person. Romance isn't for me. You know that. I can't imagine coming home to the same person every day, day after day. Not anymore."

Mitchell tilted his head to the side. "Except for me?"

Ben opened his mouth, then paused, the beer raised halfway to his lips. Mitchell did have a point. He shrugged.

"Yeah, I guess. Except for you." Funny how Mitchell was the exception to so many things. After his marriage to Viv ended, he swore that he would never live with another partner, never settle down, never let those walls down with another person. Mitchell was Mitchell, though, friends since high school, drifting apart and then reconnecting just when he needed it, right when his whole life was falling apart. No matter how deep his feelings for Mitchell might be, he had to keep them firmly labeled as friendship. Friendship wouldn't put everything at risk, not when they'd worked so hard for their business and each other. "You're different, though."

"I'm not like other girls." Mitchell grinned, teasing.

"You *are* really easy." Ben tapped the lip of the beer bottle against his cheek. Banter was much easier than getting deep into emotional shit. "I can get you into bed without even trying."

Mitchell put a hand over his heart in mock affront. "Benjamin, are you calling me a *whore*?"

"The dirtiest slut I ever took to bed." Ben grinned. "Does it bother *you* that we fucked the same woman?"

Mitchell pursed his lips, looking off into the distance, absentmindedly rubbing the side of his beer bottle with this thumb. "I'm pretty sure it's hot."

Ben had to laugh. "Oh? You're pretty sure?"

"I'm pretty sure. I might have to watch you both to be totally positive." Mitchell gave him a wicked grin.

Fuck, that was a sexy thought. Ben hadn't really considered it, and Mitchell's teasing caught him off guard. He had to focus intently on the muscles necessary to drink from his beer bottle and then swallow without choking. Mitchell had that laser stare locked onto him, the one that felt like being examined under a microscope, and just the *thought* of getting that stare while he was fucking Hannah was enough to make his cock twitch and take interest.

But the bigger idea, that was also intriguing. Him, and Mitchell, and Hannah. Together. "You know, that could work."

"What could work?"

"The three of us. All seeing each other."

Mitchell rolled his eyes and looked up to the ceiling of their condo. "This is not *Letters to Penthouse*, Ben."

"Jesus, nobody reads *Penthouse*, Mitchell. You still getting your porn by mail?" He shifted on the couch, sitting up straighter. "But really. We could be a group thing. Like a love triangle, but nobody's heart gets broken."

Mitchell grabbed his beer again. "Nobody does that."

"Sure, people do that." Now that he was thinking about it, this was a really good setup. "You and me, we've got a good thing going. We get along, we make good business partners, we're great in bed. And we both like Hannah, right?" At Mitchell's tentative nod, he continued. "And neither of us wants a romantic relationship. So, let's just…bring her in." Not to mention, if they both were sleeping with Hannah, maybe everything would feel less serious between him and Mitchell. Maybe he could distract himself from wanting something different than the stable, safe situation they currently had.

Mitchell pursed his lips, picking at the label on his beer with his thumb. "What makes you think I don't want a romantic relationship?"

Was he serious? "You haven't dated anybody in years. You haven't been seeing anybody in years."

Mitchell blinked at him, looking hurt for some reason that it took Ben a heartbeat to understand.

Oh. Mitchell hadn't been seeing anybody in years… except for him.

That wasn't the same thing, though, right? They weren't boyfriends. They never talked about their feelings or confessed their love. That distinction was mutual, right? He could run through all their encounters in his mind if he wanted to, all the way back to when he'd first approached Mitchell before that restaurant inspection and they'd fucked his anxiety away. Sure, there had been some ambiguity with the nature of their relationship at first, but Ben had made his limits clear. And Mitchell, being Mitchell, had never pushed.

Of course Ben would have assumed Mitchell wanted the same things. If Mitchell didn't agree, why didn't he say something?

Ben cleared his throat. He wasn't prepared to deal with feelings like this now. "I think we should both see her again. Maybe together." He waggled his eyebrows up and down, but it felt forced. He was trying too hard to lighten the mood.

Mitchell smiled, though. "You're just all erection all the time, aren't you?"

Ben raised his beer. "Giving bisexuals everywhere a bad name. That's me."

Mitchell put his feet up on the coffee table. "You know, your sluttiness makes it really hard for people to trust us."

A hot spike of anger rose in Ben, a swell of emotion like a pot of water boiling over.

"Hey." His voice cracked, and he cleared his throat again. "I've never cheated on a partner. I've always been totally up front with everybody I've been with." He'd gotten louder, and he tried to quiet his tone even while his heart raced. "I don't lie, and I don't cheat."

Mitchell visibly softened. "Sorry. I'm sorry." He spoke more quietly. "I forgot that was a thing with you and Viv."

A thing? That was putting it mildly. He remembered Viv standing in the kitchen, her arms folded, looking up at him with hurt and indignation in her eyes. *What do you mean, you're bisexual? Now I have to worry about you fucking guys, too? Why didn't you figure this out before?* The implication was that she could have gotten out of it if she'd known beforehand. Standing there, looking into the eyes of a woman he'd sworn to spend his life with, knowing he was breaking her heart not because of anything he did, but because of who he was? That was an experience he wasn't keen to repeat.

"You know she had trust issues," he said, which was enough. He'd spilled it all out to Mitchell years ago, when Mitchell had first found him in the well of his postdivorce depression. He didn't need to rehash it again. It had all been for the best, certainly. Viv had ended things over the fact that he was bisexual. He couldn't be with someone who didn't accept him for who he was, no matter what kind of history they shared.

"You're not a cheater. None of us are." Mitchell clinked his bottle with Ben's like some kind of peace offering.

They drank in silence for a few minutes, with Mitchell making the contemplative faces he always made when he was chewing over a deep thought. For a man who was so reserved to so many people, every time he was with Ben, he didn't hide his emotions. It was really nice, actually. And Ben could be himself with Mitchell, too. Mitchell didn't ask for anything other than Ben was willing to give.

He felt the small press of guilt inside him. Mitchell didn't ask for anything.

After a minute, Mitchell finally spit out his question, looking a little sheepish. "You really think there's room for something between the three of us?"

Ben took a sip of his beer. "I don't see why not." He'd definitely heard of people having arrangements like this, even if he didn't know any of them personally. "Let's feel it out when we talk with her about the festival." He glanced over at Mitchell. "You want to give me some of the details about your night with her? I could use something to jerk off to."

Mitchell laughed, getting up off the couch. "You're on your own there. I don't kiss and tell." He crossed past Ben, headed to his room.

Ben called after him, "So don't tell about the kissing!

Will you fuck and tell instead?"

Mitchell was still laughing as he shut the door to his room behind him.

Ben lay back on the couch, staring up at the popcorn ceiling in the silence of midnight. He had a lot to do this week. There were special seasonal advertisements to sign off on, batches of fall beer to check for quality, temporary workers to bring in to decant the latest brews. Instead of planning all that, though, his mind gravitated back to thoughts of Hannah...and Mitchell...and Hannah and Mitchell together. It was probably just horniness; threesome fantasies were practically required for sexual beings, and he was within reach of making that fantasy a reality.

But other aspects of the idea were appealing, too. Mitchell could use an excuse to do something other than manage the restaurant and work out. The guy had literally no social life aside from hanging out with Ben. Seeing Hannah would be good for him. And Ben was certainly intrigued by her, the way she flirted shamelessly and approached sex as enthusiastically as he did, the confidence and poise she exuded. She was fun, and she challenged him. He was always up for a challenge.

Ben closed his eyes. Sometimes, in moments like this, with the apartment silent except for the hum of the refrigerator, he felt completely alone. Mitchell was just a room away, but sometimes he felt alone with Mitchell, too. The problem with shutting down any intimacy other than friendship was that it grayed out the nuances of emotion, simplifying them down into one nebulous haze. He'd been flippant for so long. Even if he wanted to open up, he wasn't sure how.

Fortunately, no one was asking anything else of him. All they were talking about was friendship and sex, and those were two arenas he could handle.

After getting reluctantly to his feet, Ben set his empty beer bottle in the recycling bucket and headed to bed.

Chapter Seven

Having company always made late-night shipment sorting go more smoothly, even if that company was Lori sitting at the desk typing endlessly while instrumental music echoed through the storage room. Hannah sliced open another box and sorted through the collection of lubes, bringing some up front to restock and setting the rest of them on the appropriate storage shelf. It was so damn frustrating to be moving product and still be in the red.

"Well, that's about all the thesis work I can handle for the night." Lori shoved her laptop away from her and spun on the desk chair, looking over to where Hannah was sorting through lubes. "How about you? Just about done?"

"Just one more box." Hannah returned to her task. This final box was filled with books that she'd ordered, the newest releases that aligned with her brand. Lori followed her onto the sales floor, where she started rearranging the bookshelves to make room for her newest titles.

"Is this your holiday rush shipment?"

"Should be." Hannah set a copy of another book about

female orgasms in a prominent display place. "I've also got some online orders to fill."

"How are you holding up, financially? Still above water?" Lori was always there to ask the direct questions.

Hannah winced. "Things are tight." In truth, every month was putting her farther behind.

Lori made a thoughtful noise. "You talk to that financial adviser yet?"

"A few weeks ago." Swallowing her pride had been the worst. "It doesn't look great. Basically, I need some strong festival sales or holiday sales. Online is trending upward, and my marketing campaign is going well, although it's costing me out the ass. If I can cover the debt from that marketing investment and then make it through the holidays, I should be in the clear."

"Good." Lori climbed up on the stool behind the counter. "I didn't want to see you go under." Lori was never one to mince words to make someone feel better, but she really was on Hannah's side through all this. "Oh, and I'm glad you're doing the festival. I know you weren't sure before."

Hannah nodded. "I'm sharing a booth with Ben and Mitchell." She headed back into the storage room immediately, not lingering to possibly give something away by a look or a smile, even though Lori was totally going to get this out of her eventually. After only a moment, the door to the back room swung open and Lori came in. She leaned against the shelving unit next to the door and crossed her arms.

"All right. Tell me all the shit you're trying not to tell me." Lori sat down at the desk, then looked over at the corner. "Like where your sex swing went."

"I took it home to wash it and haven't brought it back yet." Hannah carried the flattened boxes out the back door to the shared cardboard recycling bin next to the dumpster. When she came back in, Lori was giving her an irredeemably smug look.

"Which one did you fuck in the sex swing?"

So much for stealth. "Ben." Hannah reached up to remove her hair tie, letting her bun come loose. Her hair spilled down around her shoulders. "I fucked Mitchell in my bed."

Lori whistled. "So much for 'Oh, I can't ask Mitchell out, he's only looking for a serious relationship.'" She imitated Hannah with an exaggerated expression and air quotes, ridiculous enough to make them both laugh. "Tell me how this happened. You two have been making eyes at each other for a year."

Hannah recapped her first encounter with Ben at the Chamber of Commerce meeting, then their subsequent date at the Night Owl, rehashing what she had learned about them along the way.

Before she got any further, Lori held up her hand. "Hold up. What did you just say?"

"I said that Ben told me he and Mitchell fuck sometimes."

Lori shook her head. "Shit, I didn't even know Mitchell was gay. I mean, bi. He's bi, right?"

"Bi," Hannah confirmed.

"Bi." Lori nodded. "Do they each know you fucked the other one?"

"Yeah, of course they know. I'm not just gonna fuck two business partners, two *best friends*, back to back without telling either of them about the other." Hannah dusted her hands off on her jeans. "That about does it for inventory."

"You want to go get some tea?" Lori asked. "My treat."

"I feel bad when you treat me."

Lori rolled her eyes. "Don't. Consider it payment for the sordid details."

"And if I don't give you sordid details?"

Lori fixed her with a death stare. "Make some up. I am on a sex drought and writing a thesis about polyamory. It's the least you can do."

Hannah laughed. It was hard to argue with that.

Lori kept peppering her with questions as they walked down the block to the teahouse, which would be open late. After some general discussion about the quality of the sex (excellent) and whether she'd compared the two guys (there was more than one kind of awesome), Lori moved onto the heavier questions.

"So what's next? Was this a one-and-done thing? Notches on your headboard?" She sat down across from Hannah at a small table in the front window of the warm, cozy teahouse.

Hannah stared out into the darkness of the empty street. She'd been asking herself this same question. "I don't know. I want to see them again. Both of them. But that seems like a terrible idea. I've been trying to convince myself that there's a way to make it work, but I might be better off just leaving both of them alone and keeping this strictly business."

"Why don't you just date them both?" Lori tipped her head to the side, looking at her like it was the most obvious question in the world.

"Well, yeah, but I can't do that forever." Eventually she'd have to either choose one or choose neither.

"Why not?"

Hannah blinked. She probably should have expected this, with Lori's dissertation topic, but having the idea of polyamory actually applied to her life felt way different than discussing the vague hypotheticals from Lori's research.

At her silence, Lori pressed on. "There's nothing deceitful about it. You don't have to choose one. You could date both of them. You could even date more than just the two of them. You could sleep with them and not have a romantic relationship. You could have a romantic relationship with both of them, or all three of you together." Lori ticked off the possibilities on her fingers.

Hannah pressed a hand to her forehead, suddenly overwhelmed. "I don't want a romantic relationship with anybody." Those kinds of relationships involved giving up too much and taking too much risk. Every guy she'd ever dated had wanted to be her one and only, to be the person she talked to about all her issues, to be more important than all her friendships. She couldn't live like that. She liked her independence rather than being beholden to anyone. She didn't like having no one to come home to, but that was a silly reason to get into a relationship. That was a reason to get a cat.

Plus, the thought of failing something else in her life was appalling. None of her relationships had ever worked out, and after a while, it was hard to pretend the problem wasn't her. She didn't need that kind of blow to her self-esteem, not when her business was already tanking.

"Okay, so that's not on the table." Lori was unfazed. "If you don't want romance, then just date them. Fuck them. Something. But don't force yourself to choose where there's no choice that has to be made."

The tea arrived, a delicious spread that included local milk and honey along with tiny ginger biscuits, and Hannah took the time to pour each of them a cup of the tea while trying to articulate the number of thoughts running through her head. Was it really as simple as Lori implied? She'd done casual dating before, but almost always in serial monogamy, where she'd see one guy for a couple of dates and then switch to a different guy when the first guy wasn't working out. She sometimes had a few first dates within a few weeks of each other, but most didn't lead to second dates. It felt wrong, somehow, to be having dates with multiple guys, even if there was no expectation of exclusivity.

"That doesn't feel like polyamory to me." Hannah sipped her tea. "That feels like...I don't know. Sleeping around."

Lori shrugged. "So what? It doesn't have to be polyamory. You don't have to be in love or have some deep emotional connection. You could just sleep around. I'm just saying, you're inventing a problem, and there's not a problem."

Maybe she was right. Hannah contemplated the possibilities in silence, steam curling up from her tiny teacup.

Lori gave her a sly smile. "Lord knows it would be good for you to get some decent dick into your life. Talk it over with both of them. See what happens."

Hannah shrugged, not wanting to make any commitments. It would be hard enough to shake Lori of this idea once she'd latched onto it. "Maybe. Enough about me. Tell me about how school is going for you."

• • •

The moment Hannah walked into their living room, Mitchell thought, shit, this was a mistake. They should have picked a neutral space. Her presence filled up the living room as soon as she stepped through the door. Ben was like that, too, but Mitchell had mostly grown used to it. Plus, Ben was six and a half feet tall, so he definitely had a presence. Hannah, though, was only his height, tall for a woman but not unusually so, and yet she suddenly seemed to have sucked all the air out of the room.

"So this is where the magic happens." Hannah put her hands on her hips and turned around in their living room, looking around at everything.

"The fucking usually happens in one of the bedrooms or the shower," Ben offered helpfully, coming out from his bedroom. "Unless you mean something else by 'the magic.'"

Hannah smiled. "I meant the restaurant planning, you doofus."

Doofus? Mitchell hadn't heard anyone called a doofus

since he was a kid, and it made him chuckle. He flopped down onto the couch.

"But," she added, "it's good to know that you have your fucking limited to just a few key places."

"This couch sometimes, too," Ben added, as he sat down on it next to Mitchell, and Mitchell rolled his eyes.

"I cannot believe you are going to talk like this." Mitchell gave Hannah a long-suffering expression. "Please don't let him talk like this."

Hannah smirked. "I think it's kind of hot." She sat in the armchair next to the couch. "But you're right, you're right. We have a lot of stuff to plan before the festival."

"I've submitted all the paperwork," Mitchell offered. "I gave the description like we talked about, and I put down the deposit."

"Right! Thanks for reminding me." Hannah snapped her fingers. "I brought my half of the deposit. Is it okay if I pay the rest the day before the festival, when it's due? I'm waiting for some stuff to clear." She bit her lip as she rummaged around in her satchel, first pulling out her checkbook, then a tablet computer.

Mitchell nodded. "Sure." He took the check from Hannah and went to tuck it into his wallet.

"Now, about the festival." Hannah began tapping through some screens on her tablet. "I started to brainstorm some ideas for events. I thought if we could come up with enough content, we could have a selection of events that run throughout the evening. So people could come to multiple ones. We could put up a schedule earlier in the day and then try to attract a steady crowd." Mitchell watched the tapping of her long fingers. He should probably find the notes he'd taken with Ben earlier that week.

"Here's what we have." Ben was already going through the notebook in which he wrote everything. It was just for show; Ben could remember whatever they'd talked about without having to put much effort into it. It was a talent Mitchell didn't share, and one he frequently admired, even though Ben seldom talked about it.

"I agree. Pairings is a good place to start, while people are first getting warmed up to the idea." Hannah had produced a pen from her bag somewhere and was tapping it lightly against her lips, which only brought Mitchell's attention to how full and plump they looked and how gorgeous they'd been stretched around his cock.

Oh, fuck, not good. He pushed the thought from his mind, trying instead to focus on the words Ben had written in the notebook, the words he could read from the side as Hannah examined them.

"I don't know much about beer, though." She looked up at Ben. "If I go over the sex-toy descriptions with you, will you try to figure out what matches?"

"Yeah, that's fine, or Mitchell, you could do that, too." Ben looked over at him. "If you want to pair appetizers, we could add those."

Mitchell frowned. "I've been thinking about apps and planning out the logistics of doing full food when we've been running a food station all day, and even just apps are going to be more than I want to handle. If it's all right with both of you, I'd like to keep it to beer."

"I'm fine with that," Ben said. "Hannah?"

"Sure, sure, we can keep it simple." She pointed at the notebook with one long finger. "What's this mean here? It just says 'Mitchell's Game.'"

"Oh." Mitchell looked over at the notebook, even though he hadn't written anything specific in there about the game. "I had this idea when I was itemizing the kitchen inventory the other night."

"That's Mitchell's idea of a good time," Ben cut in.

Mitchell put his hand on the side of Ben's head and shoved him away. "Nobody asked you."

Hannah grinned, watching the two of them, and the expression on her face gave Mitchell a flush of warmth.

Mitchell cleared his throat and tried to focus. "Anyway, I realized that a lot of the stuff we use is really obscure, and I thought we could play a game of 'sex toy or kitchen gadget.'"

Hannah's eyebrows raised, and then she started laughing. "Sex toy or kitchen gadget?"

Mitchell nodded. "It's perfect. It's silly, and it ties in the restaurant with the shop. Everybody can play at once. We've got some pub swag for prizes, and you can give out... I don't know, condoms or cheap toys or some kind of favors. Whatever doesn't cost you a lot."

"Right." Hannah nodded. "I like that."

"So we've got the pairings, and the game, and what else do we need?" Ben checked the notebook. "How long do we have the booth?"

"We're there from eight to midnight," Hannah said. "It's a four-hour event. And not everyone's going to want to spend the whole night at our tent. So we should have more short events rather than a few longer ones."

"We could repeat some." Mitchell could see that being a success. "Two rounds of each. I don't know that they'll take more than a half hour for each one, right? Maybe we can stagger them and start a new one on the hour."

Ben crossed his arms. "Sounds good."

Hannah was nodding, but she had a faraway look in her eyes, like she'd gone down some thought pathway and couldn't get back.

"My main goal for the night is visibility." Ben flipped through his notebook. "Bring new people into the restaurant. Also, boost brand recognition for the holiday beers. I don't care as much about sales that night. We'll sell, but it isn't my top priority."

Hannah didn't seem to be coming out of her reverie, so Mitchell prompted her. "What about you? What are your festival goals?"

She looked a bit pained. "Honestly?" Her face said she didn't want to actually give her honest answer. "Money's tight. I'm trying to dig myself out of a bit of a hole with a boost in sales."

Mitchell's brow furrowed. "How much of a hole? Are things going okay for you?"

"Fine. I'm fine." She shook her head, like she was trying to clear it, and didn't meet his eyes. "Anyway, I'm hoping to make enough sales at this event that I can make up some of the difference."

Her dismissal of the question wasn't a good sign. Mitchell opened his mouth to push more, but Ben interrupted him. "Okay, so maybe we should envision some kind of third event or promotion to really maximize your sales."

There had to be something they could do in that department. "Shit, it's too bad you can't just force people to come through and look at your stuff. Like how when you go to Ikea, you can't just visit one section? You have to walk your way through the entire store."

"That's a great idea!" Ben jumped in. "What if we set up a sex-toy labyrinth?"

"What?" Hannah had already started to laugh.

"A labyrinth. We see if the committee will let us create a path of some kind to the booth, like with hanging curtains or cubicle walls or something, I don't know." Ben adjusted his seat on the sofa, tucking a knee under himself. "You can have sex toys along the way, maybe have people collect fun facts and trivia about them. At the end, you take a quiz, or maybe you try to name them all? Something like that. And we give you beer, and you win a prize."

It wasn't a half-bad idea, actually. Mitchell could see it working. "You pick your highest-profit-margin items to display. Then those are the toys you have available for sale. Oh! You could list their qualities, and then at the end, people have to match up which toys are best for which purpose, then that also helps people figure out what they might like."

"That is seriously smart." Hannah nodded slowly in approval. "I love it. We would have to get the festival coordinator to give us more space, though. I can't..." She paused, then said the last part fast. "I can't afford to spend any more on the booth."

"No, that's cool." Ben held up a hand. "I'll talk to him. We hit it off pretty well at the meeting."

Ben hit it off well with everyone, everywhere he went. He pulled out his laptop and started typing away, all his attention turned to the screen. At Hannah's quizzical look, Mitchell explained, "He's going to send the email right now, I assume. He'll tune back in to us in a minute."

"He always like that? Just dives right into something, tunes the world out?"

"That's what makes him good at what he does. Hyperfocus."

"I can still hear you, you know." Ben didn't look up from his screen.

Mitchell grinned. "Completely oblivious to the world." He started to poke Ben. "Like a mannequin."

Still without looking up, Ben reached a hand over and swatted at Mitchell, slapping him away and making Mitchell laugh. Hannah watched them with her own smile. "You two are cute."

"Ew. Don't." Mitchell shook his head. "Don't call us cute."

"Why not? You are cute." She got up and set her tablet down on the coffee table, then squeezed herself into the nonexistent space between them on the sofa. Mitchell pushed over, complaining loudly of the invasion while Hannah only laughed.

She fit herself neatly in between the two of them, with Mitchell pressed against one side and Ben typing away on the other. When Ben finished his email, he folded the laptop and set it aside. "You just moving in here?"

Hannah put a hand on each of their legs and squeezed. "I like this. It's cozy."

"It's hard to talk, though." Mitchell stretched his arm out along the back of the sofa, angling his body slightly toward Hannah.

She looked over at Ben, then turned toward Mitchell. "We don't need to talk, do we?"

Even having hoped for the evening to end up here, it still felt surreal looking into Hannah's gray-green eyes while Ben watched them both. She licked her lips, a quick flicker of tongue. Then, leaning over toward him, she cupped his jaw and brought his lips to hers.

Hannah kissed delicately, teasingly, none of the deep searching of their last kisses so recently in her house. She was testing him, testing out this idea of kissing Mitchell with Ben right next to them, and fuck, it was hot. He slipped a hand into her hair and pulled her closer, tilting his head to deepen the kiss. Knowing they were being watched, feeling the gaze on him, he opened his eyes. Ben's expression was rapt. His lips were parted, eyes focused on Mitchell's. Fuck, this was intense, with Hannah's tongue against his and Ben watching the two of them. Mitchell closed his eyes again to focus on the kiss, but Ben's gaze still felt palpable even without seeing it.

Hannah sat back, giving Mitchell a smug look. She kept eye contact for a moment, then turned to face Ben. Without looking back at Mitchell, she leaned into Ben and kissed him, slow, steady, and Ben closed his eyes as Mitchell watched them. His cock stiffened in his jeans, this private pornography unfurling right in front of him. Damn, he was going to jerk off to thoughts of this for a long time.

Hannah climbed onto Ben's lap, straddling his hips, then gave Mitchell a smoldering stare.

"Do you like watching?" she asked Mitchell, running her hands over Ben's shoulders.

"Fuck yes."

Hannah licked her lips, then turned to Ben. "What about you?"

Ben smiled. "Isn't it obvious?"

"But I like to hear you say it." She rocked her hips against him.

"Yes, I like watching."

Mitchell had fantasized so recently about telling Ben how to fuck Hannah. Reality sizzled like fantasy never could, and if he wanted something, he had to go for it. "Kiss him again," he ordered.

Hannah's eyes widened, and she looked between Ben and Mitchell, smiling and then ducking her head away. Oh, interesting. This situation made her shy, and that was both adorable and smoking hot.

Mitchell smirked. "You like it when I tell you what to do?"

Hannah turned pink, color rising in her cheeks, but she made eye contact again. "Yeah."

Mitchell stretched an arm along the back of the couch. "Then do what I say."

Hannah hesitated only a moment before leaning back into Ben to kiss him once more.

Ben returned her kiss, his hands sliding up Hannah's back, holding her against him. Mitchell couldn't believe how much he *wanted* this, surprised by the depth of his desire, the intensity of his longing. Leaning in, he slid a hand into

Hannah's hair. She broke the kiss with a gasp at the sudden touch, looking over at Mitchell with wide eyes. Like he'd done in her bedroom, Mitchell carefully closed his hand into a fist, pulling just enough so she would know he was here. With her held in place, he asked, "Do you want more?"

She tried to nod, then weakly whispered, "Yes." Her voice had already grown husky.

Mitchell looked to Ben, who nodded. He knew Ben, knew where this would head, and he was ready. He released Hannah's hair.

Ben touched her cheek. "Come to bed with us."

Chapter Eight

Hannah had gone into this meeting with a clear sense about what she wanted, and with the hopes of getting these men into bed with her, but that didn't mean that she wasn't nervous. Her heart was thrumming full speed, ratcheting against her ribs, hindering her breathing. That had to be the reason she was so light-headed, right?

Or maybe it was because of Mitchell standing right behind her as she followed Ben into his bedroom. Mitchell was close enough that he could keep a hand on her back, guiding her firmly forward. It wasn't like she couldn't get away. She didn't even want to get away. But his gentle pushing felt like the perfect kind of control she liked in bed.

Ben's room was a surprise. She had anticipated a blue or gray bedding set, like what a bachelor typically used, maybe some action figures, probably some shit about beer and some family photos. Instead, this was a comfort paradise: a king-size bed with a large, fluffy white comforter dominated the space, but the nightstands—there were two—had candles on them and one of those aromatherapy liquid jars with the wooden sticks. He had decorated his walls with art; she recognized prints from Klimt and Van Gogh. The flat-panel television and gaming consoles fit her stereotypical expectations, as did the bookcase filled with—from what she could tell at a quick glance—mostly science fiction, but the rest was a complete surprise.

"Not what you expected?" Ben asked.

Mitchell sighed. "I tell him all the time, nobody's going to believe you like women at all when you have this room."

"I love defying stereotypes."

Hannah pointed to what was illuminating the gauzy drapes. "You know these are twinkle lights, right?"

"I don't understand why my desires for comfort are an indication of my sexuality at all." Ben put a hand over his heart in mock haughtiness. "It isn't my fault that Mitchell wants to live like a monk."

"Oh?" She turned to Mitchell. "So no twinkle lights and king-size bed for you?"

"He sleeps on a futon," Ben offered.

"I do not." Mitchell rolled his eyes. "I have an actual bed. I just don't go for all the…" He waved his hand, looking for the word. "…trimmings."

Ben scooped her easily into his arms. Shit, she was not going to get used to that. Hannah felt small in Ben's arms, and she never felt small. He grinned at Mitchell. "Speaking of the trimmings."

His tone ignited her from the inside, as did the way Mitchell looked from Hannah to Ben like he couldn't decide who to eat first. Fuck. This just might kill her tonight, and that would be a hell of a way to go.

Ben tossed her—actually tossed her—onto the bed, and she landed in the middle, dazed and laughing. Then Ben turned to Mitchell. "Where do you want to start?"

Mitchell's answering smile was wicked, the kind of smile

that made her toes curl. "Hannah's wearing too many clothes. Don't you think?"

"Oh, definitely. Definitely." Ben approached her, climbing onto the bed, but paused before he touched her. "You'll say if we start to do anything you don't want, right?"

"Yes, *obviously*. Get on with it."

Ben chuckled, starting on the buttons of her blouse while Mitchell climbed onto the bed with them. "Somebody's impatient."

Mitchell held her chin, fixing her with that smoldering, mischievous stare. "Better not get too greedy. Anything could happen yet."

They went for her clothes, and Jesus, this was like being in the middle of a whirlwind. Hannah was naked before she knew it, and before she had a chance to get nervous about it in any way, Ben started kissing her with a thoroughness that wiped all thoughts from her mind. She lay back, and he followed, stretching out alongside her and continuing to kiss her as one of his large hands encircled her breast. He swallowed her gasp. How was it possible to be this overwhelmed when they'd barely begun? He moved his hand, but before she could catch her breath, a mouth sucked hard at her nipple.

Fuck, that couldn't be Ben, because she was still kissing him. Hannah broke the kiss to breathe. Mitchell's hot lips pulled at her flesh, teeth pressing into the skin. Ben caught the other nipple in his mouth. Holy shit, her pussy flooded, the stimulation connected directly to her clit. Hot, wet lips and sharp teeth, twin sensations of pleasure and pain, and there was not enough air in this room.

"Ohh," she breathed, not sure what to do with her hands, lifting them a few times and then letting them drop to the bed, limp. She couldn't help lifting her hips into the air, reflexively.

Mitchell smiled at her, then at Ben. "She likes that."

Teeth dug sharply into her nipple again, the bite like a jolt through her sensitive skin. Ben lifted his head. "She does, yeah."

Being talked about like she wasn't here was somehow even hotter than what was literally happening.

"Have you tasted her pussy yet?" Mitchell asked Ben. "It's fantastic." Hannah clenched around nothing.

"Well, I'll have to get in on that." He winked at Hannah. This focused attention on her was more than overwhelming; exhilaration and fear mingled in her blood. His playfulness, though, eased that tension somewhat.

Mitchell moved to sit up against the headboard, then shifted Hannah in between his legs so she was leaning back against his chest. In this position, he could reach down and pull her legs apart, spreading her open. Here was this exposure again, the kind that triggered all her mixed, aroused feelings about being vulnerable. She couldn't cover herself and had to take what they wanted to give her, and a whimper escaped her.

"Perfect." Mitchell murmured his words right into her ear. "That's how I like to see you."

Ben casually slid between Hannah's thighs, looking up at the two of them. Still keeping that eye contact, he leaned in and licked her clit.

"Fuck!" The flash of pleasure made her jerk in Mitchell's arms, and he held her more tightly.

Long, firm licks over her clit had her twitching in seconds, and she was going to fall apart. This was *too* much, and with Mitchell holding her thighs spread, Ben could take his time with her. His beard tickled her thighs, but she couldn't squirm away even as she writhed. She gripped at Mitchell's wrists where he held her open, but she wasn't strong enough, and fuck, she didn't want to be. Being forced to sit here and take it was everything she hadn't known she wanted.

A sudden pressure at her pussy made her look down, opening eyes that she hadn't realized were closed. Ben's fingers, two of them almost as wide as a cock, slid inside her with no resistance, and suddenly she was full. God, she couldn't get enough air. Hannah sucked in breaths, a familiar pressure pulsing inside her as he hit her G-spot. With Ben's mouth on her clit, fingers inside her, her climax was bearing down on her like a tidal wave.

"You want him to make you come?" Mitchell asked her. "Is that what you want?"

Hannah couldn't form words. When she tried to speak, only a low moan came out. She was already starting to tense up around his fingers, trembling with arousal, but it wasn't quite enough. She wasn't there yet.

"Ask for it." He brushed her earlobe with his mouth again, hot and tingling. "Ask to come."

God, what were words? She moaned and swore. "Fuck. Oh. May...may I please come?" That high-pitched voice couldn't be her own, like the words were coming from the end of a long tunnel. Now she was hovering on the precipice of orgasm. Who was she asking? Ben? Mitchell? She needed that rapture, but she wanted permission, wanted him to *make* her come.

Mitchell kissed her neck. "Not yet."

Hannah whimpered and squirmed. She hadn't expected him to tell her no, and now her body seemed doomed to betray her, teetering so close as she tried to fight the climax she desperately wanted.

"Good girl."

His praise made her whimper, a reminder that she was at their mercy.

"Please," she begged. "Please, I can't wait."

Mitchell held her open, nibbling on her earlobe, while she panted and shook and squirmed against Ben's relentless assault on her tender flesh. Fuck, she wasn't going to be able to hold out, and she wanted Mitchell's permission so badly, wanted to *please* him so much it should frighten her.

He finally whispered the words she was desperate to hear. "Yes. Come."

Hannah exploded, euphoria crashing through her, pussy clenching tight around Ben's fingers as he sucked and licked her throbbing clit. And he didn't stop, carrying her through the pleasure, the sheer toe-curling intensity of orgasm. Mitchell held her, his presence a dim constant against her back through the searing climax, reminding her that they were both here, both taking her apart in different ways, both witness to this glorious, overwhelming ecstasy.

Hannah slumped down in Mitchell's arms at last, panting, and he released his grip on her legs. The skin tingled where he had been holding her so tight. Those sounds were probably Ben moving around, but she could barely lift her head, limp and catching her breath.

Fuck, that was amazing. Feeling had returned to her extremities, so she sat up and brushed her tangled hair back. "Holy shit."

"Good?" Ben sat back down on the bed, looking like he'd just cleaned up.

"Awesome." She laughed, postorgasmic looseness and relaxation weighing down her limbs.

"I had a sense you might like that, yeah." Mitchell reached out to touch her hair, more intimate than she'd expected. Turning, she leaned in to kiss him. Although his return kiss was tender and reserved, his hard dick pressed insistently against her thigh.

Sitting back, she looked between the two of them. They were beautiful, both of them. How much was she allowed to ask for here? This had been all about her so far, but curiosity about them together had been niggling at the back of her mind since Ben first told her the nature of their relationship.

"Can I watch you two?"

"Watch us what?" Mitchell smiled, teasing. The ass. He knew what she was asking. "What do you want to watch? Want to see us run the restaurant?"

Ben chuckled. "Clean the condo?"

"I don't think she wants to see any of that, Ben." Mitchell shook his head in mock disappointment. "I'm pretty sure she wants to see something *sexual*."

"I'm scandalized." Ben's broad smile made his eyes twinkle, his expression belying his words. "So scandalized."

Mitchell was already scooting around in the center of the bed toward Ben, who made room for him. Ben put his hand over his heart. "I think we're being objectified, Mitchell."

"Must be." Mitchell stretched out alongside Ben, and without hesitating, leaned in and kissed him. Ben tipped his head, angling to deepen the kiss, one hand gripping Mitchell's arm. Fuck, this was sexier than she had imagined. One of them gasped breathlessly—it was hard to tell who, and it didn't matter. They kissed like they had been hungry for it.

A sudden uncomfortable feeling settled in her stomach, like she was intruding in something much deeper and more intense than she had foreseen.

Mitchell's hand squeezed Ben's cock through his jeans, and Ben groaned and pushed into Mitchell's grip. Hannah stared, rapt, as finally Mitchell moved his hand away and Ben broke the kiss. Their faces remained close together, eyes opening, the moment between them heavy with unspoken intensity. Hot damn. A deep, primal longing surged in her body, and her urge to fuck them both overwhelmed any momentary past uncertainty about being a voyeur.

Ben and Mitchell both looked at her at the same time and then moved apart, like they'd realized at the same time they weren't alone. Mitchell cleared his throat, visibly getting his bearings.

"I want to watch Ben fuck you."

Hannah had no time to respond to Mitchell's statement before Ben kissed her hard, tumbling her backward, and she huffed out a breath of both surprise and laughter. God, he was massive, almost imposing as he kissed her. His lips tasted like her and like Mitchell, a weirdly intoxicating combination. She wanted more of this, wanted everything harder, faster, now, and reached down to try to touch Ben's body. Her hands gripped cloth.

Hannah twisted her head away to get a breath. "Listen." Looking up into Ben's eyes, she tried to make a serious expression. "You have got to take your fucking clothes off."

Ben started to laugh and rolled away to sit up. She rounded on Mitchell. "You too! I am the only one naked. I'm half of a porno here."

Mitchell tipped his head to the side. "I would say you look like a whole porno all by yourself, but I don't think that's a compliment."

Hannah brushed her long hair back over her shoulder. "No. No, it's not." She stopped to think about it. "Maybe it is a little bit." But then they started undressing, and all her attention focused on the swaths of skin unveiled by every piece of clothing the men stripped away.

Ben finished undressing first, so large he loomed over both of them even when he sat back down on the bed. Hannah took his cock in hand, stroking his length, savoring the velvety smoothness. He seemed to swell even more with her touch.

Mitchell shifted nearby, and she checked him out as well. There was so much to look at here. Mitchell was watching her touch Ben with hungry intensity.

"He's huge, isn't he?" Mitchell licked his lips.

She continued stroking him, fluid slicking the head of his

cock. He twitched in her hand with each stroke. "I can barely wrap my hand around him."

Ben's eyelids fluttered, his mouth open, breathing hard with her touch.

Mitchell smiled. "It's overwhelming, right?" He casually reached down to his own dick and began to stroke it with a light, graceful ease.

She pictured Mitchell and Ben together again, running through the variety of options she'd fantasized about. "Does he fuck you?" She looked at Mitchell.

Mitchell hesitated. "No. Not yet. I, uh..." He laughed. "Not sure I could handle that."

Ben spoke quietly, breath hitching. "You know...I'd take good care of you."

Hannah shivered. The words weren't for her, but the tenderness and seduction in that tone hit her straight to her core nonetheless.

"I like him to fuck me." Ben smiled at Hannah. "When we do it that way. He feels so good inside me."

Hannah rubbed her thumb across the slit of his cock. Her mind went to an image of Ben bent over the bed, his cock hanging heavy and dripping as Mitchell pumped in and out of his ass. God, she wanted to see that sometime, if she ever had the chance to do this again.

Ben put his hand over hers on his cock. "Easy. I don't want to come yet."

Hannah took the condom Mitchell tossed onto the bed. This process was so sexy, carefully sheathing a man's cock in latex, watching the condom stretch around his girth, anticipating what was to come.

"Get on your hands and knees. Face me."

She hadn't expected it to be Mitchell who directed her, but she probably should have. Mitchell sat back against the headboard, his cock in his hand, watching them. The dominance in his voice was almost sexier than what they were doing. Oh, in this position, kneeling and facing him, his cock was so close, she couldn't help leaning down to take it in her mouth.

Mitchell sucked in a breath and moaned. Fuck, that was so hot. She loved everything about this, his salty taste, the way he filled her mouth, the warmth of his body. He stroked a hand through her hair, then a gentle tug. Suddenly, she felt fingers at her pussy again, Ben behind her, opening her up more than before. Oh god, the stretch. Three fingers, probably, thick and full, and she whimpered around Mitchell's cock. Ben's thumb brushed back and forth over her clit, and she pushed her hips back, fucking onto his hand.

Mitchell tugged on her hair then, and she lifted her head, lips slick, looking into his eyes.

"I want to watch your face." He smiled and brushed her hair back. "Don't stop looking at me."

The bed shifted as Ben moved behind her. This position was always so deep, so full, and with a cock like Ben's, she was going to feel every inch. His thighs brushed hers, and then a blunt, solid force pressed against her pussy.

Staring at Mitchell while Ben slid into her was the most intimate, intense experience so far, and that was saying something. He held her gaze, probably watching the way her eyes widened and mouth fell open when the giant cock head— *holy fuck*—finally slipped inside. Every inch that he pushed forward split her open. The position, the threesome, all of this pushed her buttons, but nothing compared to Mitchell's unwavering, intense, soul-searching gray eyes. He was watching every expression, every twitch as Ben sank deeper and deeper into her slickness. She couldn't hide. She couldn't look away. When she tried, head falling forward because all her bones were going weak, Mitchell reached out and held her chin with a firm grip. Even though her expression glazed over, she didn't close her eyes as Ben finally bottomed out, his hips flush against her. Then, only then, Mitchell released her chin and smiled.

"Very nice." He sounded as shaky as she felt. Maybe this was as intense for him as it was for her. Now, though, he looked up over her to where Ben was kneeling. "Fuck her nice and slowly."

Hannah let her head hang again as Ben began to pull back. The drag was amazing, the friction perfect. She'd wondered before if anything could top the sex she'd been having, but damn, this was light-years ahead of anything she could have imagined. Mitchell was watching her get fucked while Ben stroked gently, steadily in and out of her with that mammoth cock. The whole experience seemed surreal, and only the stretched-out, fucked-full feeling kept her grounded in reality. This was not just fantasy.

"How does she feel?" Mitchell asked.

"Ah, fuck." Ben's voice sounded strained, like he wanted to be thrusting much harder and couldn't. "She's so tight. Like a vise."

"You should see her face. She's gorgeous."

Hannah turned her head away, blushing. She couldn't really respond, though. The exposure, the comments on her body and her appearance, they were objectifying...and so smoking hot because of it. Somehow, they'd figured out her kink, and it was fantastic.

Mitchell's warm hands closed around her hanging breasts, his firm grip sparking her nerves like he'd touched her clit directly. Ahh, damn, he knew she liked it rough, and he began to twist and tweak her nipples. Each of Ben's thrusts pushed her forward, pulling her breasts against Mitchell's grip, exaggerating the pain that also turned her on. She clenched around Ben's dick in response, making him moan.

Ben kept up that frustratingly slow pace. God, why

wouldn't he speed up? She groaned. "Faster. Please."

"Not yet." Mitchell pinched her nipples again, and she yelped at that shock of pain. Mitchell's expression was all dominance, the kind that made her shiver all through her body, his smile wicked. "I like watching you frustrated. I want you to ache for it."

She shivered at the command in his voice. "I do. God, I want more."

"Mmm." His noise was noncommittal. Also, his cock was right there, and she leaned down again to suck him as Ben pushed forward. She was suddenly, gloriously stuffed full at both ends. Mitchell's hands tightened reflexively on her breasts as he gasped. She bobbed up and down, needing this, needing him, mindless in her own desire.

"What a good girl." Mitchell crooned his praise. He twined his fingers in her hair and began to guide her, up and down, pressing her mouth down onto his cock. She relaxed her throat and let him take the lead. Soon, though, he lifted her head off, and she mouthed after him, missing that contact. She wasn't expecting him to lean forward and kiss her on her spit-slicked lips, Ben's cock still steadily shifting in and out of her.

He stayed close to her, cupping her chin in his hand. "You want to get fucked faster? You want Ben to make you come?"

Yes, please. She nodded.

"Fuck her faster, now. I want to see these gorgeous tits swing."

His crass words ignited something deep inside her, and Ben's next hard stroke felt doubly intense. Those slow strokes had driven her mad, but this was insane, intensity ratcheting up faster than she could catch her breath. She could barely keep her balance with his thrusts. Mitchell's hands kept working her breasts, and he was looking into her eyes, and before she knew it, she was right on the edge of her climax without anyone touching her clit at all.

"She looks ready to come," Mitchell told Ben. "You're doing a nice job."

Ben groaned. The comment seemed condescending, like a power play, but Ben didn't mind if his sexy groan was any indication. His hands tightened on her hips.

"You want to come, beautiful?" Mitchell asked her, and she nodded, like that was the understatement of the year. Sweet talk and brutal fucking, and she was going to lose her goddamned mind. She opened her mouth, trying to get more air, the heat in the room oppressive, sweat glistening all over her body. She couldn't stop twitching.

"You don't want me to make you wait again?"

She whimpered once more. If he did that again, she might die. She shook her head, struggling to find words.

"So sweet. So needy." Mitchell took her chin in his hand again. "Come on his cock for me."

Hannah felt her body shudder, vision going blurry, and her orgasm crashed into her. Mitchell stayed with her, his eyes locked with hers. No one had ever watched her like this as she came. Always, her partner was there trying to hold off his own orgasm, or else sometimes with his face buried between her legs, never able to just watch and savor her expressions. She collapsed as her arms gave way, body shaking and shaking like it might never stop. Mitchell gently stroked her hair. Ben was still thrusting hard, his cock driving her orgasm onward, spinning out the pleasure.

Mitchell moved away, getting off the bed, his words to Ben resonant with that same dominance.

"You want to come, too?" Mitchell's voice sounded like pure sex, whiskey dark. "That tight pussy feel good around your cock?"

"Fuck." Ben's deep voice was nearly a whimper. "What are you... *Fuck*, Mitchell." The thrusting suddenly stopped,

Ben's cock buried all the way inside her as he froze.

She could just barely hear Mitchell now, and maybe she wasn't supposed to. "I'd love to fuck your ass while you fuck her. But you'll have to make do with my fingers." A slick sound, maybe lube, and she did not want to miss this. Ben's face was contorted in pleasure, mouth open, eyes closed, Mitchell kneeling beside him with a hand out of sight. "Go on." Mitchell spoke low again. "Pull out of her. Push onto my fingers."

Ben's thrusts became jerky and erratic, and yeah, Mitchell had Ben fucking between his fingers and Hannah's pussy. This wasn't for her; she was his cock sleeve, something to fuck, and damn, that hit a whole new collection of kinks. Ben's uneven thrusts filled her, deep and sharp, and oh, she could come again. Shifting her weight slightly, she began to rub slick fingers across her clit.

Mitchell noticed, and he replaced her hand with his free one. His fingers were rougher, merciless in their intensity. He was rubbing her clit while fingering Ben in the ass, and hell, she had never done anything like this. Her brain was going to short-circuit.

"Oh god, I'm gonna... I'm gonna..." Ben's thrusts became harder, his hands tightening on her hips once more.

"Wait for it." Mitchell began rubbing her clit harder. "Wait for it. She's gonna come again. Wait for her to squeeze you so tight."

A breath, that sense of inevitability again, that inexorable climb, and then she was lost in bliss. Ben's cock twitched and pulsed inside her as he found his own climax with a loud, desperate, agonized cry.

They collapsed afterward into a sweaty pile of limbs, and Hannah caught her breath while Ben just groaned with a hand over his head. Mitchell vanished off to the bathroom, returning a few minutes later to stretch out on his side next to them.

He wasn't going to do anything else? "What about you?" She propped herself up on one shaky arm.

"I don't need anything." Mitchell smiled. "Just watching this was enough."

He couldn't end the evening like this, half hard and still wanting when she had had *three* fantastic orgasms. Leaning in halfway, she waited for him to push her aside, but instead he let her kiss him. His dick came back to full hardness with just a few strokes of her hand. His kiss faltered, his lips opening slightly as he did so, and she kept kissing him amid her own smiles.

"Mmm?" she asked.

He made a contented noise in return.

The bed shifted as Ben stretched out along Mitchell's back, meeting Hannah's eyes with a smile. She couldn't see exactly what he was doing, but then Mitchell jumped noticeably in front of her, his cock twitching in her hand.

"Oh " Mitchell smiled. "Turnabout?" He shifted to look back over his shoulder at Ben.

"Shut up. You know you like it." Ben grinned.

Hannah kept stroking, fascinated by how every time Ben pushed a finger into Mitchell, Mitchell's cock twitched. Mitchell didn't resist, his whole body limp except his erection. Damn, being sandwiched between them held a clear appeal. Without the urgency of her climax, playing with Mitchell felt relaxed, fun, and light. When he locked his gaze with hers, though, all his pleasure naked and open in those gray eyes, she fell right in. She couldn't look away from what was beautifully unfolding in front of her.

Mitchell came in a rush, tensing up and spilling over her hand, groaning low and rough. He was beautiful, lost in pleasure, and something twisted in Hannah's heart that could only be a longing for more of this. Finally, he sagged down onto the bed, and Hannah flopped out beside them. She hadn't known what to expect. This was the stuff of fantasies, and fantasies didn't always cross over well into reality. Though exhausted, her body thrummed with energy, every nerve ending tingling. This wasn't just sex. This was an experience. Tonight was like she had woken up from a long sleep and was seeing the world around her anew. She stared up at the ceiling. Something profound had changed. This couldn't be a one-off experience. She didn't want tonight to be the end.

And that was terrifying.

Chapter Nine

When Hannah returned from the bathroom, Mitchell was alone on the bed in his boxers. "Ben went to the other bathroom. You all right?"

"So good." If she lay down, it would be tempting never to leave. Maybe clothes would help, so she got dressed. Mitchell patted the spot on the bed next to him, though, and it would probably be rude to just *leave*, so she gave in to temptation and curled into his side. He ran a gentle hand through her hair, and she shut her eyes and leaned into the touch. It would be so easy to stay like this, taking comfort from his closeness, talk long into the night.

"I'm not used to the cuddling." Mitchell chuckled, but his laugh sounded awkward and a little sad.

"Ben's not a big cuddler?" That was surprising. The man was built like a giant teddy bear.

Mitchell scoffed. "Definitely not." He hesitated. "Or, not with me. But I think not at all."

What a shame.

"Well, *I* would cuddle you." She wrapped her arm across

him and gave him a squeeze. What harm was cuddling, after all? Cuddling was physical affection, shared warmth, coziness. It didn't have to be emotional.

Mitchell sighed. His fingertips brushed up and down her back, lightly stroking her through her shirt.

The door opened suddenly. "You guys want a snack? I was thinking…" Ben stopped abruptly in the door, staring at the two of them curled together on his bed. The moment stretched out into awkward silence.

"A snack." Mitchell made a thoughtful noise, still wrapped up with Hannah. "What do you think, Hannah?"

Staying here was nice—maybe too nice. Maybe dangerous. "I could eat." She disconnected herself from him with some reluctance. Snacks were probably safer than cuddling.

It was good to be dressed again, lounging in the living room. This felt normal. What had happened in the bedroom was starting to feel like a dream, something that someone other than her had done. She put her feet on the coffee table, leaning back in her chair, while Ben sprawled out on the sofa. Mitchell hummed to himself in the kitchen, making coffee and grilled cheese for all of them even though she never drank coffee this late.

"He makes a good cup of coffee." Ben nodded over to Mitchell, giving Hannah a conspiratorial glance.

"He's good at a lot of things." Hannah grinned, testing out the waters. Could they joke about this?

Ben grinned back, his shoulders relaxing. "Yeah, he is."

"You two talking about me?" Mitchell popped his head out of the kitchen.

"Only good things," Ben responded, flashing Mitchell a cheesy grin. "All lies."

"Humph." Mitchell made a face and went back into the kitchen.

This sweet domesticity between them was like watching

a married couple. Hannah hadn't expected this kind of intimacy. They were more distant in public. They were letting their guard down here, in their home, and she was getting to witness it. How could Mitchell say there was nothing between him and Ben? It was obvious to anyone with two eyes.

Grilled cheese really was the perfect comfort food, though, and its perfection was enough to distract her from whatever musings she'd been starting about Ben and Mitchell. "Shit, I don't know how you do this." Hannah held the perfectly toasted sandwich reverently in two hands, because it felt blasphemous to hold it any other way.

Mitchell raised his eyebrows. "It is literally just a grilled cheese."

"Nothing you make is 'just a' anything, Mitchell." Ben was making some seriously pornographic noises over his food. Mitchell give Ben a look so appreciative, so soft, it just made her want to shake both of them until they admitted their feelings.

Instead of saying something to Mitchell, though, Ben turned to Hannah. "So. Question for you."

"Okay?" She paused in eating.

"How do you feel about seeing both of us?"

Whoa, that was a flash of sudden déjà vu to her conversation with Lori. "At the same time?"

"At the same time."

She looked down at her sandwich again and took a bite, using the chewing time to put her words together.

"Well, I definitely don't want to choose." How crazy that she hadn't been the one to bring this idea up. "My friend Lori studies polyamory. It's her PhD thesis. She was just telling me how lots of people make this work." She hesitated. "I've got to admit, though, it seems complicated."

"Yeah, but I'm not talking about a romantic relationship." Ben stirred his coffee. "I'm talking about friendship, but with sex. Like what Mitchell and I have."

Oh. The grilled cheese stuck in Hannah's throat, and she swallowed it with some difficulty. Mitchell was silent, holding his cup of coffee. She wasn't sure what she had been expecting, but this felt...like something else. Yet wasn't she the one who always said she didn't want romance, and she wanted her independence? Was she really feeling sad because she wasn't getting involved with *two* romantic relationships at the same time?

"I like being friends with you. Both of you. And the sex is great." She had no good reason to say no. "So, sure. We can give that a try. Mitchell? What do you think?"

Mitchell tipped his head to the side, still looking contemplatively into the middle distance. Finally, his gaze focused on her again. "I think it's interesting, and I'm game if you two are."

"Great." Ben raised his cup in salute. "Now, what the fuck do we still need to do before the festival?"

• • •

After Hannah left that night, the house fell into an uneasy silence. Mitchell stayed up on the couch, messing around on his laptop, which he never did. It seemed weird to Ben to just go to bed without talking, even though he couldn't really decide what they would need to talk about, so he started straightening up the kitchen just to have something to do. He hadn't realized before how attuned he was to Mitchell's moods, but since Mitchell was clearly feeling unsettled, he couldn't help mirroring it.

"This guacamole still good?" Ben held up a container from the fridge, and Mitchell glanced over from his computer screen for a moment.

"No. Throw it out." He went back to typing.

Ben emptied the substance into the sink and rinsed out the glass bowl. That wasn't going to be a good conversation starter, was it? He washed his hands.

"So Hannah said she wants some help packing up before the festival. You want to give her a hand with that?"

Mitchell's brows drew together, his expression curious and puzzled. "You know a lot more about sex toys than me. I thought you'd want to do it."

Ben walked back out of the kitchen. "Come on. I don't know shit about toys. You're the kinky one."

Mitchell smiled, the first time Ben had seen him do so since Hannah left. It was a welcome sight; he hadn't realized how much he'd been waiting for that smile until he saw it.

"Sex toys aren't kinky. I don't own any toys. I happen to know for a fact that you own at least one dildo and a masturbation sleeve."

"Oh, god, don't call it a masturbation sleeve."

"What do you want to call it?"

"I don't know." Ben shrugged. "I don't talk about it."

"And yet you own them."

Ben rolled his eyes. "Do you want to go or not?"

Mitchell shrugged. "Yeah, I guess." He looked back at his laptop screen but didn't put his hands on the keyboard again. He kept doing that thing he did when he wanted to say something, where his bottom lip twitched as he started to open his mouth and then stopped.

Ben wasn't going to let him just sit there and twitch. It killed him to see Mitchell uneasy like this. And that was totally normal and didn't mean anything deeper than the fact that nobody wanted their friends to be upset, and he was sticking with that story, dammit, no matter how much it felt like a thin guise. He flopped down into the chair. "What's up with you?"

Mitchell pursed his lips. "I guess I'm not sure about this

three-people-dating thing."

Ben frowned. "Tell me more." He leaned forward, resting his forearms on his knees.

Mitchell set his laptop down on the coffee table. "It feels like the bottom's going to drop out on it eventually. Eventually, Hannah's going to figure out she prefers one of us, and then the other one is...whatever. Left out. Alone."

Oh. Ben didn't see this side of Mitchell much, since in general he was a pretty confident, straightforward kind of guy. It was easy to forget that Mitchell had his own insecurities.

"Hey." Ben moved to the sofa next to Mitchell. "Please say that you're shitting me."

Mitchell stonewalled him with a completely blank expression.

Ben hesitated only a moment, then moved his hand to rest over Mitchell's. Mitchell looked down at their hands, his blank expression turning to a slight frown of puzzlement.

"No, look at me."

Mitchell did so, his face wary.

"Neither of us is gonna end up alone, okay? No matter what happens with Hannah. We've still got each other." And damn, that sounded gay as hell, but Mitchell was hurting and he could justify this to himself in the morning.

"I'm not worried about that." Mitchell averted his eyes, so he was probably lying, because he didn't do it often and he sucked at it. "I feel like there's no way she's not going to have to choose between us. And I don't want to end up in a competition with you for Hannah."

There was an unspoken part of that, the idea that if he had to be in competition with Ben, Mitchell was sure he would lose. He squeezed Mitchell's hand. "Listen. Why does it have to be competition? Why are you thinking she has to choose at all? Why do any of us have to choose?"

"Forget it." Mitchell sighed. "I shouldn't have brought

this up." He tried to pull his hand away, but Ben held it there. So much for pretending he didn't care.

If he really didn't care, he wouldn't push, but dammit, he wanted Mitchell to be a part of this, whatever it was. He wanted this weird triangle, even if it was a risk to the stability they had now. Somehow, adding Hannah to the mix felt like it left him more room to be intimate with Mitchell, like some of the pressure was off. "Just...give it a chance. Fall Festival is coming up, right? Let's just give it some time until then. Let's see what happens."

Eyes to the side, jaw tight, Mitchell nodded. Fuck, they'd had such a great night tonight. Why did Mitchell have to be so down about it? Ben let go of his hand and moved closer, throwing an arm around Mitchell's shoulders. The hell with distance. Right now, he didn't want distance. He wanted a few more seconds of closeness. Mitchell hesitated, then leaned slightly into the contact, turning so the brotherly arm around the shoulders became a full embrace. They stayed like that, the silence stretching between them, and Ben should pull away, but fuck, this felt really nice. He closed his eyes, trying to ignore that little voice reminding him, *You could have this.*

He wasn't ready, and he let go. "Come on." Ben grabbed the remote off the armrest with his free hand, clearing his throat. "Let's see what's on."

. . .

Ben awoke with a start, momentarily disoriented. The TV was still on, some show playing that he didn't remember turning on. He had somehow stretched out along the couch, long limbs hanging off the side, and Mitchell was flopped against him, sound asleep, head pillowed on Ben's shoulder. Shit. This was *definitely* a cuddle. It was a sleep cuddle, and so neither of them could be blamed for initiating it, but somewhere along the line, he and Mitchell had dozed off together on the couch and ended up back in an embrace.

Just like before, this was…nice. Mitchell was warm, and in his sleep he looked vulnerable and sweet, face relaxed, worry-free.

They couldn't stay like this, though. He was already sore all over, and they both had to work the next day. He nudged Mitchell, who murmured and threw an arm across him, cuddling closer. Aw, shit. That was fucking adorable.

"Hey. Mitchell. Hey." He nudged him again. "Come on, Mitch."

"Don't call me Mitch," Mitchell slurred, making Ben smile.

"Yeah. Get up, you lazy ass. Go to bed."

Mitchell untangled himself, sitting up and blinking awake with a groggy, sour expression. "I was warm."

"Yeah, I know, but I don't fit on this fucking sofa, and we certainly don't fit on it together."

They would fit in his bed, though.

But that was too far. Things weren't like that between them.

Were they?

Before Ben had to face the extent of that question, Mitchell got to his feet and rubbed his eyes, saying good-night as he staggered off to bed.

Climbing into bed, Ben could smell the scent of sex everywhere. Fuck. So much for restful dreams.

Chapter Ten

Hannah looked around her quiet living room, the deep, unsettled restlessness of discontent skittering like an itch beneath her skin. Normally her solitude was nice. She enjoyed not having anyone to answer to, complete freedom to watch terrible television or listen to pop songs, or to either go to bed at eight or stay up until four in the morning if the mood struck her. Ever since the threesome a few days ago, though, she'd been restless. Hanging out with Lori had soothed her a bit, but tonight Lori was working late, and she wanted... what? Company?

Whatever this sensation was, loneliness or boredom, it sucked. Ben and Mitchell had been on her mind nonstop, and not just remembering the sex. She missed their company. They'd created a group chat, which she called up on her phone. So far, it had just been exchanging information about the Fall Festival, ideas or funny kitchen implements that might be sex toys, a couple of stories that someone had seen online and thought the others might enjoy.

She typed out a message.

Bored. You guys want company?

She hesitated a minute before sending, because maybe this was needy or something? But hell, she was allowed to ask for what she wanted, right?

After a moment, Ben responded.

Sure. We're just hanging out. Nothing exciting.

Clear message that there would not be sex, which…was fine. She didn't want to fuck. She wanted to visit. Relief eased through her like a balm as she got ready to leave.

A little while later, Mitchell opened their apartment door for her, smiling warmly, and on impulse, she stepped in to give him a hug. It felt like the right thing to do. He hugged back, wrapping those strong arms around her. The smell of his cologne took her right back to the other night, a flood of memories, but also an overwhelming sense of safety. She flopped down on the couch in the empty space next to Ben, who set aside his magazine to give her a smile.

"Where's my hug? None of that for me?"

Hannah leaned across him to give him a one-arm squeeze, awkward for their position, and Ben made a noise of disapproval.

"This is a shitty hug."

"I can't give a good hug when you're sitting down."

"Nope, come here." He turned and wrapped both arms around her, squishing her deliberately against him and tipping her to the side.

Laughing, she tried to pull away. "You're crushing me!"

Ben let her go, both of them grinning. God, this was nice. She shouldn't have missed this so much: it was still so new, so undefined, but also reassuringly comfortable. She kicked her feet up onto the coffee table, and Ben did the same, picking up his magazine, which appeared to be in…German?

"You read German?" Hannah raised an eyebrow at the magazine.

"Mmm-hmm." Ben didn't look up.

"Ben is a genius. He has a PhD in organic chemistry." Mitchell sounded like a proud mother, and the thought that he *wasn't* into Ben was laughable. "He did a year of his graduate work in Germany."

"Why Germany?"

"The beer." Ben raised his eyebrows like it was obvious. "I was already into it back then. I thought I could learn more in Germany, so I studied there."

"And did you?"

"I learned a few things." He gave her a small smile. He was secretive like that, never sharing too much, even though she tried to crack into his armor.

"So what's that magazine about?"

"It's a brewing magazine." Ben showed her the front of it, which had a German-looking person holding a golden beverage aloft. "I subscribe."

"You big nerd." Mitchell smiled into his own book.

"What about you?" Hannah nodded toward Mitchell. "What are you reading?"

Mitchell held up his book, which had a lightsaber-wielding woman on the front. "*Star Wars.*"

Ben cleared his throat. "My dear roommate likes to call me a nerd from over the top of his *Star Wars* book."

Mitchell cleared his throat louder, outdoing Ben. "I borrowed this book from your bookshelf."

Ben didn't look up. "I can neither confirm nor deny that fact."

Hannah laughed, their banter welcoming instead of exclusive.

"You bring something to do?" Mitchell asked.

Hannah held up a bag. "Crochet, motherfuckers."

"Look at you." Ben nodded approvingly. "I didn't know you were so domestic."

"I'm domestic as fuck." Hannah kicked her feet up onto the coffee table.

"You want a beer?" Mitchell got to his feet.

"Sure. What do you have?"

Ben and Mitchell looked at each other and laughed. "We have the whole set," Mitchell explained. "What do you like?"

"Oh." Hannah thought. "I don't know. I like a little of everything."

Ben set his magazine down on his lap. "More hoppy or less hoppy?"

"Either?"

Ben sighed, but he didn't look really irritated. "You like fruity, or more straight-up beer flavored?"

"I guess more regular beer flavored?" It came out like a question.

Mitchell put his hands on his hips. "Name some beers you like."

Jesus, what beers had she ordered lately? She started naming the ones she could recall off the top of her head.

Ben started to laugh. "You named two IPAs, a wheat, a stout, and two lagers."

"I like a lot of things!" Hannah laughed with them. "Jesus, I don't know. Whatever you give me, I'll probably like it."

"You're killing me." Ben hung his head and shook it, still grinning. "Mitchell, grab her an Autumn Leaf Red."

"I don't remember if I've had that before." She watched Mitchell disappear into the kitchen.

Ben crossed his arms. "How do you not know what beers we have? You are literally at our brewery all the time mooning over Mitchell."

"Hey!" Mitchell's voice came from the kitchen, at the

same time that Hannah yelled, "Hey!" at Ben as well.

Ben grinned broadly. "Yeah, okay. Whatever."

"I have not been mooning over Mitchell." She paused. After sleeping with them, was there any point in the deception? "Maybe a little."

"Ha!" Ben called toward the kitchen, where he was met with only silence from Mitchell.

"But," Hannah added, "I don't really pay attention to the beer. I just order whatever's first on the specials board." At Ben's mock horror, she spread her arms. "I'm sorry! I didn't know I was committing some kind of cardinal sin."

Mitchell emerged from the kitchen pouring a hand-labeled bottle into a tall glass. "It's a red ale. We call it Autumn Leaf Red, and then we brew a similar one for Christmas that's a little bit maltier, and that one is Santa's Big Red Bag."

Hannah laughed. "Couldn't go with Santa's Red Sack?"

"Tried it." Ben scratched his beard. "But the marketing team lost their shit about my suggestions for the label."

The beer, rich and malty, made Hannah pause midsip. "This is really nice," she said after swallowing. "It smells like something. Some kind of fruit? I don't know. It reminds me of fall. And…fireplaces."

"Cherries." Ben nodded knowingly as Mitchell flopped back down into his chair. "That's one of our favorites. I'm glad you like it."

Hannah looked between the two of them. "So this is a quiet evening at home for you? Beer and reading? You're like some kind of Hallmark ad or something."

"Ben plays a lot of Xbox," Mitchell offered.

"Not a *lot* of Xbox. A reasonable amount of Xbox." Ben took his own beer off the table, which was still in the bottle that had been labeled "pale" with a Sharpie on a piece of masking tape. "And Mitchell spends most of his free time at the gym."

"Not *most* of my free time," Mitchell retorted. "Seriously, there's no need to exaggerate because I called out your video games."

"You did not call me out. I am not at all ashamed of my video-game prowess." Ben straightened in his spot on the couch. "But you do work out every day. Literally every day."

"I like it." Mitchell shrugged. "It shuts up my mind sometimes."

"So no, we don't have quiet evenings at home like this a lot. But they're nice when they happen." Ben paused, then gave Hannah a lascivious grin. "Also, sometimes we just fuck."

Mitchell fumbled the book he had just picked up, making Hannah laugh out loud. Mitchell was so confident and dominant, it was incongruous to see him get flustered by Ben's bluntness. "I'd like to see that."

Ben winked at Mitchell, who was rolling his eyes. "Yeah, so you mentioned."

"I liked what I saw the other night."

It was the first time anyone had overtly brought up the threesome, and the reference hung between them for a moment before Mitchell responded, his tone tentative. "Well, there's more where that came from."

It wasn't an immediate come-on, and the playful banter felt comfortable and silly rather than a legitimate offer. They each turned back to their respective reading material, leaving Hannah glancing between the two for a couple of minutes, and then she pulled out her crochet and tucked her feet underneath her on the couch. This wasn't a bad way to spend the evening.

• • •

The next night, as Hannah was just getting home from closing up the shop, she got a message from Ben. *Mitchell's closing tonight. Want to come over and watch a movie?*

There was no harm in saying yes, right? So she went over to the condo, Ben ordered a pizza, and they flopped together on the couch with one of the latest superhero movies that had just come onto Netflix. Not a lot of conversation between them; they shared pizza and a bag of chips, drank a beer each, and watched until the final after-credits scene rolled and the screen returned to the Netflix main menu. Neither of them moved to put on something else.

With Ben's arm around her and a fuzzy blanket over her lap, warm sleepiness filled Hannah like a comforting weight. "This is nice."

"Hmm?" Ben stirred next to her. "Yeah. I like this."

The silence felt comforting, rather than oppressive. Hannah shifted to curl more deliberately into Ben, wrapping her arm across his chest and settling her head on his shoulder. "How long have you and Mitchell lived together?"

"Seven years, more or less." Ben smiled, his expression reflective. "He's a great roommate. Took me in at a pretty low point in my life."

She made a thoughtful noise, wanting to ask more but not wanting Ben to feel uncomfortable. "He seems like a good friend."

"He is. Most reliable guy I've ever known." He got a faraway look in his eyes. "You know he almost dropped out of high school?"

"Really?" Hannah couldn't imagine Mitchell being anything other than successful at anything he tried.

"Yeah. School was shit for him. He's got dyscalculia. Mixes up numbers and stuff." Ben swirled his fingers around. "Smart guy, though. Brilliant chef. He took home ec and aced everything. Decided to stick it out and then go to culinary school." Ben chuckled. "His dad was pissed. Wanted Mitchell to go into the military like he did."

She could Mitchell in a military environment. "He probably would've done fine there."

"Some of it? Oh, totally." Ben nodded. "Discipline, schedule, organization, that's Mitchell's jam. But he hates guns." Ben's lips curled in a soft smile, his affection for Mitchell written all over his face.

"And are his parents still upset?"

"About the military thing? Nah." Ben shook his head. "He was a star at the CIA." At her blank stare, he explained further. "Culinary Institute of America. Top marks, internship at a Michelin-star restaurant in New York City—trust me, his parents were thrilled." He paused, lips parted midthought. "They were not as thrilled when he brought home a boyfriend for Thanksgiving one year, though."

"Shit, I bet." Military family with a not-straight son? That couldn't have been pretty.

"They got over it, though," Ben added quickly. "They're not bigots. Good people. Just a little old-fashioned."

"They live around here?"

"Up in Vermont." Ben pointed up, like Vermont was physically hanging over their heads. "His dad teaches up at Norwich University, the military academy up there."

"And Mitchell left his career to open the pub with you?"

Ben tipped his head to the side. "Yeah. Crazy, right? But I guess it worked out." He leaned back against the arm of the couch, giving Hannah a space to stretch out alongside him and rest her head on his chest. His heartbeat thumped quietly in her ears, and when he began to lightly stroke her hair, she closed her eyes.

"You really care about him."

Ben's hand paused, then continued the stroking. "I do." She could hear the smile in his voice, and then he cleared his throat. "What's your story? How'd you end up selling sex toys in Mapleton?"

That went back a few years. "Took the scenic route. I went to UMass Amherst, majored in communication, wasn't sure what I wanted to do with my life. You know, the common story."

"Yup, I'm familiar with it." Ben's hand rested lightly on her back.

"I got out of school, couldn't get a job, so I went back to school, got a master's degree in the same field. Like I thought it would help." She snorted at her own naïveté. "Not that there's anything wrong with communications, but I literally had no idea what I was going to do, and I just ended up with more debt. Worked at a few bookstores, did some temping, couldn't find anything I liked. But there was a sex shop I used to love up in Burlington, where I'm from, and I realized there wasn't one here in Mapleton. So this space came up for rent on Main Street, and before I knew it, I was at the bank taking out a loan to start the business." A twinge of pride warmed her as she remembered those days.

"Wow. No business classes, nothing?"

"Well, yeah, I took some in night school once I figured out I didn't know what I was doing." She curled closer into his side, trying to think about how much she still didn't always know what she was doing. "It's been rocky, but I'm glad I did it."

"How long have you had the shop?"

"About four years now."

"Those first five years are hard."

God, he had no idea. Or maybe he did, because he was a business owner as well. She didn't want to talk more about this, though, because then she'd think about the hole she had dug herself into. "What about you? What brought you here?"

Ben patted her shoulder. "That's a mess."

"I don't mind hearing about a mess."

The silence stretched out endlessly, only their breathing interrupting the stillness. It seemed she wasn't going to get that story. Finally, Ben broke the silence. "I was married once. It didn't end well."

The mess from that could have been anything. She really didn't know very much about him at all. "Kids?"

"No, thank god." Ben breathed out a sigh, his chest moving under her ear. "That would have been really complicated. But, we're divorced now, and we're both a lot happier. She's remarried. Lives out in Worcester."

Maybe she shouldn't pry, but she was curious. "What happened?"

Ben exhaled. "Viv and I were high school sweethearts. She was my first love. I loved her from pretty much the time I knew what love was. We got married young, right out of college. Right about the same time, I was finally coming to terms with my bisexuality. I thought, hey, this doesn't matter, because I'm married. I chose someone." He stopped talking for a minute, his hand tensing up where it rested on her back. "But I felt like I needed to at least tell her. Like, I didn't want anyone else, but hiding who I was started to feel shitty. So, I told her, and she...didn't take it well. Thought I was going to cheat on her. She never trusted me again, even though I was faithful to her the entire time. We tried therapy, and it just wasn't working. So we split up."

Hannah squeezed him a bit tighter. "That must've been awful."

He was silent for another moment. "You know I have a photographic memory?"

An odd subject change. "Yeah? Mitchell mentioned it."

"Well, that just means that I can still recall every fight we've ever had, right now, every word of it. Any bad memory, any terrible thing, and I can recall it like it just happened yesterday."

Hannah propped herself up on one arm, her hair falling over her shoulder onto his chest. Ben's expression was more honest than she'd ever seen it, no playful witticisms, no flirtatious jokes to take away from the moment, and her heart went out to him. In the near darkness, his openness beckoned her, and she went.

He kissed her back, sweetly, softly, the exact right kind of kiss for this intimacy. Lifting her head, she brushed her nose with his. "You know, that also means you can recall the good moments. Your best moments. Like they just happened yesterday."

Ben smiled. "That's true."

She crossed her arms under her chin, now lying on her stomach half on top of him. "Did you always know you wanted to be a brewer?"

"Nope. I was going to be a chemist. I spent a few years in the pharmaceutical industry, and brewing was just a hobby." He lifted his hand to tuck her hair back behind her ear. "When my marriage with Viv ended, I went through a pretty rough patch. Fell into a depression. Stopped showing up for work. Lost my job. I was at rock bottom when Mitchell called me out of the blue. Said he was tired of living in New York and wanted to come back to Massachusetts. We met up, talked about how to change our lives, and decided to start the pub."

Hannah smiled. "That sounds like Mitchell. Did he know what kind of rough shape you were in?"

"He had to have known. But he didn't call me on it. Just said, 'hey, let's be partners.' And he was strict about it, too. Made me draw up a fucking contract and everything." He pointed toward the wall.

Hannah turned her head to follow his gaze and saw a small frame, just big enough to hold a standard-size piece of paper. That was worth seeing more closely. She climbed out from his cuddle and walked over to the wall to see what he had been pointing at.

"You framed it?"

"We had to." Ben grinned. "It reminds us where we came from."

Hannah skimmed down the list. The contract was just one page, written in tiny font, probably eight-point, minimal margins, but it outlined the roles and responsibilities of both partners of the Mapleton Pub. "Jesus. This is thorough for one page."

"He had a lawyer draw it up. That's actually still the lawyer we use today."

At the bottom of the page, both their signatures marked the available lines: Ben's a chicken-scratch scrawl and Mitchell's a precise, even cursive. Seeing this contract, hearing Ben's story, a whole new wave of affection for both of them washed through her. "This is really something, you know."

"What, the contract?"

She waved her arms, because there wasn't a way to encompass all the different elements verbally. "You two. The pub. This. All of it."

Ben grinned. "I guess so."

Hannah returned to where he was still flopped on the couch, then leaned down to give him a kiss. He smiled as he kissed her back.

"You want to stay the night?" he asked.

Oh. Her knee-jerk response was yes, because of course she did. The pleasures of waking up in someone's arms, the casual intimacy of sleeping in another person's bed—these were the elements of a relationship that she loved and missed. She could have that tonight, and without even the pressure of something romantic. Comfort, physical closeness, the warmth of someone close by. She wanted it so badly, her heart ached beneath her breastbone.

And that was why she had to say no.

She couldn't let herself want something like this, not this soon, not this deep. She couldn't handle the kind of vulnerability that would arise if she kept going down this path. Hating herself for it, but knowing it was the only way to keep her heart intact, she shook her head. "Nah. I should go. But this has been fun. Mitchell still gonna come help me pack up the shop later this week?"

"He's planning on it." Ben reached out to her and squeezed her hand. "Drive safe."

Back in her car, Hannah gripped the steering wheel and hung her head. She could still go back inside and spend the night with Ben. It wasn't too late. She could walk back up to that door, kiss him, climb into his bed, share this night together. Share other nights together.

And then what?

Lori had said she could have both of them, but wasn't that wishful thinking, an impossible delusion? She didn't know anyone who was committed to more than one person. People didn't do that in real life, and they didn't even really do it in the movies, either. Eventually, someone was going to make her choose. If she didn't fall in love with either of them, it would be easy. If she fell in love with one of them, it would be messy.

If she fell in love with both of them, she was doomed.

This was a friendship with fucking, nothing more. Romance was terrifying. There was a different kind of vulnerability if she were to fall in love. Surely it would hurt far more to walk away. She wanted to be *able* to walk away.

Love was about giving up control, and she wasn't ready to do that. Giving up control in bed was one thing: hot, fun, playful. But giving up control of her life? Giving up the independence she'd worked so hard to achieve, only to attach herself to someone else? Or to *two* someone elses? Having to consider more than her own needs? It was frightening. It opened her up, exposed her vulnerability. She could fail, say something wrong, give them a reason to leave, and she could lose both of them in the process.

Romance right now was an easy way to end up with her heart broken two ways at once. And as long as she could, she was going to avoid it.

Chapter Eleven

Mitchell pulled up in front of Hannah's shop and parked amid a pile of fallen leaves blown up against the curb. After summer had lingered too late into September, October had roared in with cold and frost all at once, and the trees responded with a cascade of leaves. Mitchell wrapped his jacket tighter as he stepped out into the brisk wind. He should have gone into Hannah's shop before this. He had nothing against sex toys and had always wanted a few of his own, but he'd never made time to actually go and buy them. Also, his complicated feelings for Hannah had probably been making him avoid the place.

"Knock, knock." He rapped on the closed door with its frosted glass and "18+ only" sign. The shop had closed a half hour ago, according to the hours stenciled on the door.

"It's open!" she called from inside.

Yes, Please was welcoming, warm and cozy, and he spent a minute getting acclimated as he stepped inside. Hannah stepped out from the back room wiping her hands on her jeans, and she brightened at the sight of him. The big hug she gave him in greeting pressed her soft body against him. Damn, she smelled good, and he couldn't resist inhaling the sweet scent of her hair. Stepping back, she held him by the arms, excitement all over her face. "You've never been in here before, right?"

"Nope." He glanced around. This would be intimidating for someone less difficult to intimidate. "Overwhelming" was a better word for the plethora of products covering every spare surface. "You have a lot of stuff."

"No, you've got to actually walk around and look at things." She grabbed him by the hand and led him over to a rack of dildos, every size and color of the rainbow, including some in an actual rainbow pattern. "Dicks ahoy."

"This is quite a collection." He scanned the racks. "I thought there would be, like, a couple of types and a variety of sizes."

"Variety is the spice of life." She squeezed his hand, which she was still holding. "I like to have a range of options for sale. People are picky. Or they should be. Lots of people think all dicks are alike, but they're not."

"Like me and Ben?"

Hannah looked up at him and smiled mischievously, her tongue slightly between her teeth. "Yeah, like you and Ben. Two different dicks, both great in different ways."

"I see."

"You got any of these?" She motioned to the dildos.

"Nope, can't say that I do. Ben does, though."

"Oh, does he?" She raised an eyebrow. "You ever use it together?"

He shook his head. "Not yet." It was an intriguing prospect, one that he should really pursue one of these times.

"Ever thought about getting one of your own?"

"I've thought about it, yeah. Just never got around to actually doing it."

Hannah tugged him over to a series of bureaus covered in vibrators. "The tour continues. These are things that buzz." Everything was out of the box, just waiting to be handled and tested. Mitchell looked without touching until Hannah picked up a vibrator and turned it on. It was a long silicone thing with a knob on the end, resembling one of those old-fashioned stick microphones like Bob Barker used to use on *The Price Is Right*, only thick. It wasn't a very sexy comparison. Hannah booped Mitchell on the nose with it.

"Hey!" He let go of her hand and ducked away from the toy, grinning.

Laughing, Hannah turned off the vibrator. "Okay, here you go. Come check these out." She pulled him to another rack covered in plugs. "For your butt!"

"I know what butt plugs are." He perused them, examining the different rows. "Now this I'd be into."

"Mmm-hmm. Butt plugs are good times." She picked up a steel one from the middle shelf. "This is my favorite. It's got a little loop, so if I wanted I could tie a tail onto it."

Mitchell took the toy, surprised at how heavy it was. "You like wearing a tail?"

"Maybe." Hannah shrugged and replaced the toy on the shelf. "Could be fun. I like lots of things."

"Hence this section over here?" This time, Mitchell was the one who tugged her over to a section of kink supplies. A rack of paddles, floggers, and crops hung, with more implements than he would probably ever use, and then a bunch of cuffs and collars lined another separate rack. "Damn. You really sell this much kink stuff?"

"Not as much as I thought I would when I invested." She frowned. "It mostly just sits here."

"Have you thought about marketing especially to some of the kink communities? I imagine there are some in this area." Mitchell rubbed his chin. "Or maybe do some online distribution?"

"Yeah, I have an online shop that does pretty well." Hannah frowned. Obviously there was something going on with that idea, so he changed the subject.

"Now what's here? Does anybody really need this much lube?" Mitchell gestured at the rack of lube.

"There's all kinds! People have allergies and preferences and like lube for different purposes. It's a high-margin item and an easy add-on, so I carry a lot of it." She tapped one of the bottles. "Good shit."

"So." Mitchell put his hands on his hips. "What are we packing up for the festival?"

"That's what I've been trying to decide. I was hoping I could talk over some ideas with you and see what you think? You're good at marketing."

"That's mostly Ben's department, but I help."

"All right. Let's start."

He helped her select a bunch of different items, mostly letting her do the choosing and then giving feedback if she seemed really stuck between two options. She didn't seem to actually need much of his help, but it was nice to hang out with her. Maybe that's why she'd invited him. That was nice to imagine.

"Do you sell more in your store, or online?"

"In the store. I do pretty well online, but most of my business comes from in-person sales. And I work with a marketing firm, but it's expensive, and I'm not seeing the exact results I want." Hannah fiddled with one of the dildos she was holding. It was an odd sight, watching her flipping a wobbly bright-blue dick back and forth in her hand without much thought. She sighed, setting the dick back on the rack and then leaning against the counter, tilting her head to look up at the ceiling. "I hate doing anything half-assed. I want everything to be just right, or I'd rather not do it at all. I don't want to be barely scraping by. I want to be a success."

"Perfectionism?"

She snorted. "Not that hard to tell, is it?"

Perfectionism never worked out well. Young chefs from culinary school dealt with that, approaching every dish wanting to get the exact right sear every time and determined to master one dish before moving on to another. If they couldn't break the habit, they never made it through. "Maybe you're being too hard on yourself. Small businesses are challenging, and you sound like maybe you've got unreasonable expectations."

Hannah made a face, and fine. He wasn't going to push the matter anymore. If she didn't want help, he didn't need to give her any help. She could do all of this herself.

Instead of pushing past his phrases with some kind of twisted logic, though, she changed the subject entirely. "So I've got a question for you. You've been living with Ben for almost seven years now, right?

Mitchell nodded. "Somewhere around there."

"When did you start fucking?"

That was a quicker memory. "Two years ago." The thought came back to him almost immediately, of Ben leaning against his bedroom door frame while he was pacing manically back and forth, worried about their upcoming restaurant inspection by a well-known regional food critic. Ben had been so calm, so nonchalant as he offered to take Mitchell's mind off everything. That was the first time they'd ever confronted the tension between them head-on, and after that night, it had become a regular occurrence, something they returned to without question.

He'd been spacing out. Hannah wore a little grin on her face. "You go back a ways there? Having a few good memories?"

His face heated. No use denying it. "A few." He smiled.

"You want to know what I think?" She lined up the cases of sex toys behind the counter and turned to face Mitchell, her expression daring him to comment.

He could go there. "What? What do you think?"

"I think you're both in denial. I think you're both pretending this is a no-strings-attached sex thing, but you're totally into each other." She nodded, completely smug.

Yeah, it made sense that she'd think that. Hannah, who he was beginning to think saw everything in black-and-white, was trying to fit them into the boxes she understood. "I've heard that before." He got to his feet and folded up the chair he was sitting on, returning it behind the counter. "It's not really that big a deal."

"You love him?"

Mitchell's stomach twisted. God, he hated this question. He ignored it every time it came up in his head, because it was a question he didn't really want to confront. "I care about him a lot. I want him to be successful and happy. I like spending time with him." That felt generic, and in some ways it was. "I feel that way about all my friends. The people I do Crossfit with, my employees at the restaurant, lots of people."

Hannah's face said she was not convinced. "Yeah, yeah, general love of humanity. Really vague and altruistic, *Mitchell.*" The way she said his name was like an accusation, but not angry. "Really. Ben isn't different? He's not special? You feel the same about him as you do about all the people in your restaurant?" She tipped her head to the side. "*Really?*"

"Okay, not exactly." Too bad there wasn't a wall between them right now. He wanted some space. "But he's my best friend. I'm not in love with him. I don't want him to give up all his other relationships and be with only me forever."

"Does he have other relationships?" she asked.

Mitchell frowned. "Well, not right now." Not in a long while, actually. "But I don't want him to give up the possibility, either. I don't want him to limit himself."

Hannah nodded slowly. "I see. And you think he would have to do that if you two were in love with each other? He'd have to be your one and only?"

Ahh. "This is a polyamory thing, isn't it?"

"Maybe." She shrugged. "I just think you should think about this stuff. You're clearly not unemotional about him. You care about him. He also clearly cares about you."

"There's also the business." Mitchell knew that was part of it. "Mixing business and friendship is risky enough, but adding something more than that? If it goes wrong, it could go wrong all over." He swallowed.

"Maybe it wouldn't go wrong."

"Why do you care one way or the other?" Her investment in this didn't really make sense.

She looked into his eyes. "Because you're interesting. I like learning about you. I like spending time with you."

She reached out for him, and he walked closer, drawn in as though she were pulling him forward by a string. He always felt like this with her, compelled by her magnetism, and he didn't know whether the conversation was over or not, but he leaned in and started kissing her before they could decide. Perfect: no more questions, just her mouth under his and those soft breasts pressed against his chest. He tangled a hand in her hair and kissed her, her body shifting against him, pressed between him and the door. He didn't need to examine his feelings right now when he could just examine her.

Hannah held his face between both hands and drew back to look him in the eyes. She pursed her lips in a pout. "Are you kissing me so I'll stop asking you about your feelings?"

"Definitely."

She laughed. "I figured."

Something about this wasn't sitting right, though. "What

about you?"

"What about me?"

Mitchell walked away from her, hands in his pockets, contemplating. "You have some pretty strong advice for me and Ben. But here you are, perfectly content to play this middle-of-the-road game. You say Ben and I could be serious without giving up all other relationships, but then you tell me you want to keep things at a friendship level between the three of us. Why?"

Hannah blanched. Her smile faded, and she looked away. "That's more complicated."

"Try me." He leaned against the door.

Hannah bit her lip. She might not answer. This confessional thing was still new between them, and she might balk at the intimacy. Finally, she sighed. "If things don't work out between you and Ben, you've got a solid friendship at the root of it. You're business partners. That's not going to change, even though I know you think it might. You'll keep working together, you'll keep being friends." She wandered away from him a step, running her fingertip down the handle of a flogger. "But let's say I go for this, all the way, and it doesn't work out. You two have each other, and I don't have anyone. Just another big reminder of where I fell short."

"Don't say that." Mitchell walked up to her, wanting to comfort her, not wanting to overstep his bounds. He put a hand lightly on her shoulder, and she turned to face him, her expression serious, hazel eyes looking large and vulnerable in the light.

"It's terrifying," she said.

He brushed his thumb back and forth against her shoulder in a gentle caress. "Sure it is. It's terrifying for me, too. The only person who doesn't seem to be afraid is Ben, but that's because he doesn't care about ever falling in love again." Mitchell snorted.

"That's bullshit, isn't it?" She wrapped her arms around his waist.

Mitchell wasn't stupid. If they were both feeling afraid, Ben probably was, too. "Yeah. It's probably bullshit." He gave her a half smile. "You think maybe we should all be brave together? Actually...let ourselves *care*?"

Hannah clapped a hand to her heart. "The horror!" Her smile, though, was gentle. "Maybe we should talk about it more."

Even this honesty felt good, if risky. "Nothing until after the festival, though. All right?"

She nodded. "Definitely. Now. I'll see you tomorrow night at setup?"

"I'll be there."

• • •

"Oh shit! I didn't know you'd be already setting up! I'd have come by earlier."

Hannah's exclamation made Ben turn from where he was hanging the last curtained panel of their sex-toy labyrinth. "They let me in to start hanging panels early, since nobody's using this site."

Hannah set down the two large metal cases she was carrying. "I've got more of these in the car."

Over in the parking area for vendors, Ben let out a low whistle. "Fuck yeah, you do." In addition to five more cases, she had several large boxes and a collection of small fold-up tables.

"I brought a hand truck." She unfolded the device from the trunk.

"You bring enough stuff?"

She put her hands on her hips. "I wanted to make sure I had enough. I can't sell product I don't have, Benjamin."

Ben grinned. "Benjamin? You getting all mom voice on me? Because let me tell you, I grew up with two of them, and this is so not my kink."

Hannah smiled back. "You want to help me move this shit, or you just going to pick on me all day?"

"How about I do both?"

"How about I drag Mitchell over here and he can show off how much stronger he is than you?"

"Ouch, okay." Ben put his hand over his heart. "You wound me."

"I'm vicious. Where is he, anyway?" Hannah looked around as if Mitchell would suddenly show up in the parking lot.

"He's still working the food booth. He should be along after cleanup." Ben started to load up the hand truck.

Two trips later, all Hannah's stuff was finally unloaded at the booth, and soon toys covered every surface of their tables. "Now." Ben surveyed everything, hands on hips. "Tell me what you've got in mind."

Hannah grabbed a rolled-up piece of paper from one of the tables and unfurled it.

"You made a treasure map?" Ben stepped closer to read over her shoulder, and she rolled her eyes at him.

"It's a map."

It was a hell of a map, actually. She had drawn the entire labyrinth and labeled stations along the way, showing which toys went at which place. "I made informational cards for every spot, too. And then there'll be a quiz at the end."

Ben listened as she explained, nodding, but mostly just watching her work. She was really beautiful, both for her physical attractiveness and her sexy depth of knowledge. Smart and gorgeous made an enticing package.

"Are you even listening to me?"

"Yes." He tried not to sound defensive, but she responded

with a raised eyebrow. "And I'm also checking you out."

She rolled her eyes, but her small smile said she didn't really mind. "How'd the labyrinth turn out?"

"Good, I think." He explained the layout. He'd set things up so people would turn back and forth a few times before ending up here in the main booth. From where they would be sitting, they could see the entrance to the maze and keep an eye on people as they entered. Didn't want anyone making off with all the sex toys or something.

Setup took a little while, and he had just finished setting out the final information cards in the maze when Mitchell's voice echoed from out of sight, addressing Hannah. "Hey. Sorry I'm late. Cleanup took forever."

Ben peered over to where Mitchell and Hannah were standing together in the main booth. Hannah moved away from the table display she was setting up, heading into Mitchell's arms with a smile. Watching them together stirred some affection in Ben, that latent desire for the kind of intimacy he used to have, the kind he had told himself wasn't worth the risk. When he had invited her to spend the night the other night, he had hoped she would say yes.

Mitchell and Hannah both turned in unison to look at him over the top of the hanging curtains. Mitchell gave him a classic "what the fuck are you doing?" face. "We can see you, you know. You're a fucking giant."

Ben laughed, weaving his way out of the labyrinth. "I forget sometimes."

"Yeah, right." Mitchell hoisted a paper bag he'd set down near Hannah's table. "I brought dinner. Thought you guys would be hungry."

With the sun slipping away, the space was quickly growing cold, and Hannah pulled on a large brown sweater over the layers she was already wearing. It looked supremely touchable, especially over her soft curves. Right, he was staring again. He helped Mitchell spread out a blanket he'd brought and gave him some shit about it.

"What?" Mitchell sounded defensive. "I thought it would be nice. Like a picnic."

"It is nice." Hannah touched Mitchell's arm. "You." She made eye contact with Ben. "Stop picking on him."

"He can take it. Mitchell is not a precious angel."

"I am a precious angel." Mitchell straightened and tipped his chin up.

"Fuck off." Laughing, Ben started pulling containers of food out of the bag.

They sat together on a blanket at the end of a labyrinth of sex toys as the sky above them turned to twilight. Eventually, it got too dark to see and Mitchell turned on the hanging lights they had set up for the purpose. These strings of Edison bulbs and twinkle lights were atmospheric, but also bright enough to read by, dozens of them wending through the labyrinth and filling the main booth. In the warm amber light, Ben shared time between eating a plate of chicken and watching Hannah and Mitchell. This, the three of them together on a blanket under hanging lights, it felt...nice. Better than nice. Without much of a stretch, he could imagine this scenario again: at a beach, camping in the woods, or maybe just in their living room after dinner. The thought made something warm settle on him like a blanket.

"The fuck is up with you?" Hannah elbowed him, bringing him out of his reverie. "You're just staring at us all googly eyed."

Ben shook his head. "Sorry. Just thinking." Yeah, and he was thinking in dangerous directions. He didn't want to want these things. He had done love once, had learned that forever wasn't always forever and the fallout could be catastrophic. But he couldn't help the hope blossoming in his breast. Maybe, with the three of them, this could be different.

When eight o'clock rolled around, Ben gave a final sweep of the area. Everything was lit, chairs were set up nearby, and thanks to the patio heaters they'd borrowed, the space felt warm and cozy. Hannah still wore that big fuzzy oversize sweater, the one he kept wanting to touch, and it distracted him until guests started making their way to the start of the labyrinth.

The first few visitors to the booth wandered out a few minutes later, laughing and talking about what they had seen. A bearded guy in flannel held the hand of a woman in a giant woolen peacoat that dwarfed her small frame, and despite the cold, they were smiling and chatting. This was a good sign.

"We have the answers!" The man held his fist aloft. "Where is the quiz? We want to win everything."

"Everything?" Ben leaned on the counter and faked horror. "But what about everyone else?"

"Fuck them all!" the woman responded, and both of them laughed.

"The entry form is in the corner. Ten right answers gets you a raffle ticket." Ben pointed to where Hannah was set up at her minishop, the pop-up mobile sexporium she had pulled together close to one of the heaters. "All the product is courtesy of Yes, Please, and Hannah is the owner. She'll get you started."

"How's it going?" Mitchell sidled up to him, and Ben jumped.

"Shit, you snuck up on me." Ben nodded to where Hannah was working. "Seems all right." A couple more people were looking around, confused. "Raffle entries are over there, folks." He pointed. "We should have made more signs."

"I can make signs." Mitchell nodded like he'd been given a solemn task.

"I thought you were gonna help me sell beer?"

"You don't need me for that."

He was right; Ben didn't need him for that. "I'd like you to help anyway, though."

Mitchell smiled, open and warm. "You just can't bear to be away from me, can you?"

Ben made a gagging noise. "Don't read into this, you big sap."

Mitchell still grinned, and Ben squeezed his hand. There was that tenderness again, the one he didn't want to acknowledge, the one that told him maybe it would be okay to hold Mitchell's hand every once in a while.

"Jesus, look at her go." Mitchell was watching Hannah again as more people went over to talk to her and enter the raffle, several of them picking out items to purchase. "Never would've known there was that much of a market for sex toys in Mapleton."

"She's been keeping it up this long, so there must be." It couldn't be easy, though. When they'd started the restaurant, they'd faced so many pressures, and their business wasn't even controversial.

Mitchell leaned on the high counter they had set up, which for Ben was not a high counter at all. "How many shops have opened and closed downtown? It's tough out there."

"We got lucky, I guess." They had spent enough nights up late worrying about every penny of outgo. Those days were gone.

"Not lucky in business, but lucky to have good guidance." Mitchell's expression was serious, distant as he presumably thought back. "I guess she doesn't need our help."

"No, she doesn't. She's independent, Mitchell. Stop trying to save her when she doesn't even need saving."

Mitchell's expression flashed with annoyance, his lips tightening as he glanced over at Ben. He didn't argue, though. Good. He had to know this was one of his most common flaws. Always wanting to save people, even when people needed to figure things out on their own.

"Hey, why don't you go back through the maze and see how people are doing?" Ben nudged him toward the labyrinth entrance. "Make sure nobody's stealing display model sex toys. Or using them."

Mitchell blanched. "Oh god." He headed toward the entrance without another word, caught up in that horrible thought.

Ben hadn't set any sample beers out yet, just a table topper that announced beer tastings at nine, so he had no real reason to stay by the counter. He meandered over to Hannah, hoping to look as casual as a six-foot-five guy could look in a space like this. She was deep in conversation with someone about one of the sex toys. Damn, it was hot watching her wield it, holding it expertly in her hands as she explained things he couldn't really hear from where he was standing. He moved over, ready to listen, and a guy stepped between them. "Hey! Is there beer?"

"Not yet, man. Beer starts at nine. Check out some sex toys?" Ben pointed him off to the minishop, and the guy went. Thank god.

He moved closer to Hannah during a momentary lapse in customers. "You need some help?"

Hannah looked around at the table of toys. "No, I think I've got it under control." Her hair was falling into her eyes, and he reached over to brush it out of her face and over her ear, surprising himself.

Hannah smiled up at him. "Hey, stranger. Looking to buy yourself a sex toy?" Her dimples deepened in her cheeks, and he wanted to cup her face in his hands and kiss her. So he did, stepping in, bending to kiss her smile. Her eyes widened in surprise just before she closed them. The kiss was brief and sweet, and when he stepped back, her eyes were filled with tenderness. Too much tenderness, and he stepped back. This was public. They weren't public, not yet, not together.

"I, uh, sent Mitchell into the sex-toy maze. You think he'll come back out anytime soon, or will he be lost forever?" Ben peered into the maze, but he couldn't see Mitchell's short blond hair over the edges of the hanging curtains.

"He's gone forever. I'm going to have to send in a search party." Hannah turned to greet a young woman who had just come up to the table with a bottle of lube, and Ben watched the encounter with an ever-growing softness in his heart.

Well, fuck.

He went back to manning his counter until nine o'clock finally rolled around.

"All right, folks! Pull up your chairs, your blankets, your freezing-cold bits of ground." Ben raised his arms to beckon everyone closer. Mitchell scanned the perimeter of the tent area, walking around and watching for stragglers he could shoo inside. What was this, twenty people? Thirty? More if he counted the ones in the back. Shoot, this was a good turnout.

Ben rubbed his hands together. On one side, Hannah was set up with one of her tables and a selection of sex toys. On his other side, Mitchell stood behind the counter, leaning on one elbow and grinning at both of them. Here between them, Ben felt right at home. "This is the moment you've all been waiting for! I don't know if you've ever had this problem, folks, but I can't ever seem to figure out what beers go with my wide and varied collection of sex toys."

The room tittered, folks relaxing at Ben's joke, and he pressed on with more. "Plus, the opposite problem is true! When I really like a beer, and I want something fun to match it with, I just can't tell what's a good pairing. Can you match vibrators with wheat beers? Do they clash? I don't know." He turned to Hannah. "Fortunately, I've got Hannah here, of Yes Please, the toy store we all know and love right here on

Main Street. Hannah?"

"Thanks, Ben!" She flashed her winning smile and dimples at the audience. "I don't know if you've ever tried pairing beer and sex toys, but we have put together a tasting menu of sorts for you. Only, please taste the beer and *not* the sex toys."

The audience laughed, taking the sheets of paper Mitchell was passing around. He moved smoothly through the crowd, making a few quiet jokes that Ben couldn't hear, but people chuckled in response.

"So." He turned to Hannah. "You've got a hell of a something blue right there."

Hannah held up the small vibrator that fit in the palm of her hand, shaped sort of like a leaf, and began to describe it to the audience, explaining a bit about the type of vibrations, their intensity, and how people might use it. Then she turned back to Ben.

"So what beer goes with this one?"

Ben held up a bottle labeled with a river flowing through a mountain pass. "Well, we pride that company on their fine German engineering, so we had to go with a German-inspired beer. High quality, sharp and refreshing, just like you want from your sex toys as well." He motioned Mitchell to come up, and Mitchell did. "Now, folks, if you'd like to try the German beer and feel this vibe, go ahead and line up. We'll have two tables going at once."

Folks shifted, moving to the front of the room, and Ben started filling tiny cups as Mitchell took over giving out the samples. Mitchell slid into that role easily, confident in the product and in his one-on-one banter. As he and Hannah talked to people, he handed them tiny cups filled with their German beer until everyone had had some and held the vibe. Then Ben stepped up for the next pairing, and both Hannah and Mitchell moved smoothly back into their places.

They moved efficiently through the list of five pairings, sharing tasting samples of all the beers, making small talk, demonstrating how the vibrators turned on and cycled through their settings. The focus shifted swiftly to sales, with both vibrators and six-packs flying off the shelves as the evening wore on.

The next game, sex toy or kitchen gadget, was an equally big hit. Mitchell, with his deadpan delivery, was a hoot. When Mitchell held up a spiky Wartenberg wheel and asked Hannah if she thought it could double for sealing ravioli, Ben almost pissed himself. People laughed, they asked questions, they bought toys. By the time the evening came to a close, no one would doubt that the night had been a huge success.

They had just finished loading the last of the boxes into Hannah's trunk, and Ben opened his mouth to suggest going out to get a drink, when Mitchell let out a monumental sigh.

"I am exhausted." Mitchell slammed Hannah's car trunk closed and leaned against it. "What a night, right?"

Hannah slid up against him and elbowed him. "Come on. The night is young. It's only…" She checked her phone. "Twelve thirty. Bars don't close until two. Let's go get a drink." Awesome. Woman after his own heart.

Mitchell made a face. "I was up at six."

"You don't have to get up at six tomorrow, though." Ben could be the voice of reason here. Mitchell needed to get some social time with them. "One drink wouldn't hurt."

"Except it's not going to be one drink, it'll be two or three or four drinks, and then I'll be up all night." Mitchell folded his arms. "You two will have more fun without me, anyway."

"Bullshit." Ben gave him a light shove. "It's not the same without you. Right, Hannah?"

"He's right." Hannah took his arm. "You don't seem to believe us when we say we want you around. I'm developing a complex about it."

Mitchell made a great show of rolling his eyes. "Okay, fine, fine. One drink. Tell me where we're going."

"Want to come unload product with me first?" Hannah batted her eyes up at him. "Then the Night Owl?"

Mitchell sighed, but he was also starting to smile. "I think you only want me for my ability to lift heavy things."

"Maybe."

"Fine. Let's go."

• • •

With Hannah safely in her cab, Ben and Mitchell walked home, the streets silent now that it was after two in the morning. Their breath fogged in the cold night air, but with his steady buzz, he didn't feel as cold as he had earlier. They turned down their street, right on the edge of town.

"This is never gonna work." Mitchell spoke aloud into the silence, his hands thrust in the pockets of his coat. He glanced over at Ben. "Right?"

"What?" Mitchell could be talking about anything.

"All of it." Mitchell took a hand out of his pocket to wave his arm. "Us and Hannah. One of us is gonna fuck it up. Probably me."

"So don't fuck it up."

Mitchell sighed. "Maybe I'm not cut out for this shit. Feelings? Romance? I don't know."

"Hey, who's talking about feelings and romance?" Ben tried to laugh, nudging Mitchell with his elbow. Mitchell stumbled, and Ben reached out to steady him as they turned onto their front walkway. "Yikes. You're pretty far gone."

"A little bit." Mitchell grinned. "I don't drink much, you know."

"I know."

Mitchell squinted up at him. "Do you know how much I

love you?"

Ben froze, his heart stuttering in his chest. Mitchell was staring up at him like his statement was the most interesting puzzle, like maybe Ben could help him figure it out. All Ben could manage was "Oh," a totally inadequate answer. Maybe Mitchell would be too drunk to remember he said this.

"Come on. Let's get inside. It's cold out here." The cold had to be the reason for Ben's hands to shake so profoundly as he tried to fit the house key in the lock, finally managing on the third try.

Mitchell didn't ask anything else of him, walking past him into the living room. "Fuck the gym tomorrow," he said, disappearing into his room and shutting the door behind him.

Ben's soberness came suddenly, like someone had dunked him in an ice bath. Mitchell wouldn't remember this in the morning, surely. And even if he did, he probably wouldn't bring it up again. This was their rule: they didn't let feelings get involved. They were friends, they fucked, and they didn't make a big deal out of it. But Mitchell, dropping a fucking L-bomb on their front steps in the middle of the night? That was completely uncalled-for.

Whatever had happened these past few weeks with Hannah had clearly changed things, and breathless panic settled on him. Normally he could will those feelings away, but tonight they hung on. If he and Mitchell crossed this path, they weren't going back. Shit, Mitchell was his bedrock. And now he was trying to change their deal? That was unfair, and it was terrifying, and it was both of those things precisely because he wanted it so fucking badly.

He wanted all of it. He wanted Mitchell and Hannah, both of them, and he wanted love, and great sex, and stability, and two people to come home to. He wanted it so badly that he ached for it, and the depth of his own need took his breath away. If this was love, it was different than the love he had before, and he didn't know how to process it.

Unsettled, shaken, and feeling suddenly alone, Ben forced himself to go to bed. It would probably take him a long time to fall asleep.

. . .

Hannah was still pretty tipsy in the cab, but by the time she got into the house and took a shower, she had sobered up enough to look at her numbers. No way she could go to bed without *knowing*. The alcohol was wearing off, but the euphoria of a great evening stayed in her system. She had sold so much product. This had to be enough to cover her losses and tip her over into the black.

Finally in pajamas, she pulled out her computer and sat down at the kitchen table, tossing aside today's mail that she'd just brought in. She opened up the programs she used to track her sales, watching them populate with tonight's figures, her spreadsheet automatically filling in where necessary. While it did so, she grabbed a cup of water to try to stave off tomorrow's hangover. This felt good. Relaxing. Life was finally on the upswing. She flopped back into her kitchen chair again and scrolled down to her final results.

Well, fuck. That was a *damn* good night. And if she kept up her steady sales, she could pull herself out of this hole by the end of the year.

She punched the air, even though there wasn't anybody around to see her, grinning about business for what felt like the first time in a while. She was feeling so good, she could open all the mail now rather than procrastinating about it. Bills, always bills, and in the bottom of the stack, a thick letter from the owner of the building where she rented space.

She stared at it. This was going to be her lease renewal. With fumbling fingers and an increasing sense of dread, she tore it open and pulled out the contract.

Just a few lines in, her heart stuttered in her chest. The language was formal, professional, all this "due to increasing interest rates and economic circumstances beyond our control," blah, blah, blah—bottom line was they were raising her rent again.

All Hannah's positivity evaporated with whatever residual buzz she'd still had from the bar. Shit. Fucking shit. Goddamned motherfucking shit. She wasn't going to be able to break even at these new rates. Even with this boost in sales pulling her out of the hole, she was just going to turn a profit with the *old* rent, not to mention this new rent. Even though she knew what the results would be, she scrabbled for a scrap piece of paper and found a torn-open envelope, then started putting down the numbers by hand, adding them up like she might somehow do it better than the computer. The proof stared her right in the face. Jesus. If she signed this new lease, with the rent change taking effect on the first of the year, she was going to be out of business by March.

She was going to have to move, and she couldn't even do that. She looked at the rental listings all the time, and every place in town was out of her price range, except for one spot owned by the church, which had emphatically turned her down when she'd inquired about a leasing opportunity last year. Her pleasant feeling was gone, replaced by something sick and sour in her stomach. Christ. How was she going to make ends meet?

The hot press of tears in her eyes made her angry. What the fuck was she doing crying? Crying was absolute shit. She swiped the tears from her eyes. Okay. So she needed a next step. She had to have a next step. She always did this independently, and she could do that now. After a few mediocre attempts to deep breathe her way into calmness, she finally gave in and let the tears come. How could she be so stupid? Most businesses failed. She knew that when she applied for the loan to rent Yes, Please in the first place. She'd told herself that she was smart; she took business classes, read everything she could find, launched into this endeavor with both feet firmly on the ground. She was a person who got things done. Now, though, she was a mess. She was going to lose her business and do what? Get a job somewhere? What could she do? She had worked a string of shit jobs, and nothing suited her. She loved running her own business, but apparently she sucked at that, too. Maybe the only thing she was actually good at was fucking. God, how pathetic. Everyone who had doubted her, everyone who had told her not to get her hopes up, they seemed to gather in the empty space around her like ghosts. At the center of it all, her own self-doubt, her self-loathing, that tiny voice inside her reminding her that she'd never done anything worthwhile in her life.

Hannah put her head down and gave in to the self-pity for a few minutes of horrible, racking sobs, the kind that burned her face and left her feeling sore and swollen all over. They subsided eventually, leaving her with sniffles and a wrung-out feeling of exhaustion. Fuck this. She had to move forward in some way. Maybe she'd look at this again in the morning and somehow things would be better.

Yeah, right.

Chapter Twelve

Lori was all snark as Hannah let her into the house. "You know, I was starting to think you had left me for all these guys you're fucking."

"It hasn't been that long," Hannah said weakly as Lori blustered past. Lori hung up her coat and pulled off the tall black boots she liked to wear, immediately flopping down on the sofa once she was free of her fall layers. Hannah went into the kitchen and grabbed the plate of cheese and crackers she'd put together that evening after work.

"You giving me fancy party snacks now?" Lori took the tray and the can of seltzer Hannah gave her.

"It's cheese and crackers. Literally not fancy." Hannah sank into the chair across from Lori.

"Easy. I'm just joking around with you." Lori picked up a piece of cheese and a cracker and made a tiny open-faced sandwich, which she popped whole into her mouth and chewed. "What's with the long face? Fall Festival was a success, right?"

"I've got a lot on my mind." The dilemma of how much

to burden Lori with her business shit was always a delicate balancing act. She didn't want to weight their friendship with too many problems, so while Lori was a good sounding board, Hannah was also capable of getting these things worked out on her own eventually.

Usually.

When she wasn't dealing with business-ending shit.

Lori's expression indicated she wasn't fooled, but instead of pressing it, she changed the subject. Small miracles. "I wanted to ask you something." She shifted on her couch. "I've got a project happening for my thesis. I was hoping you could help me out."

Anything to not talk about her business. "What is it?"

"I'm doing a polyamory workshop. I've got a couple coming out who have experience coaching and mentoring polyam groups, and we're hoping to have a session locally." Lori gestured to Hannah. "I thought you could come. You and the guys."

"Oh." Hannah hadn't seen the guys since Saturday night, although they'd been talking steadily on the group chat in the few days since. She had used the excuse of being busy to avoid seeing them until she'd figured out what to do about this business thing, since she wouldn't be able to hide her sadness in person. The light, funny group chat had been a balm to her high levels of stress. This workshop, though, was something she probably shouldn't turn down.

"I can ask. What's it like?"

"It's going to be discussions about common issues in polyamory, ways to communicate better, pitfalls people don't usually think of."

That sounded serious. "We're not really *polyamorous*. We're not in any kind of romantic relationship. It's really just sex." She said it, but she knew it wasn't true. They cared about each other, and everyone knew it, even though they usually just talked around whatever was blossoming between them.

Lori raised an eyebrow, and damn, she looked like she wanted to argue, but after a moment of silent judgment, she just shrugged. "Still. I'm not sure how many people are going to show up. Most of the people who I've asked to attend are folks from my thesis research. They're people who have been doing polyam for years. I need some new people, too. Or people who are interested. Or might be interested. I really want to fill the room."

"Where are you having it?"

"The library offered me a room, but I was hoping for a space where we could have a little more privacy, so I'm still looking." Lori crossed her legs. "I thought about your shop, maybe bring you some extra business, but I don't think you have the space."

"I don't." Hannah thought back to her conversation with Mitchell a few weeks ago. "The pub has an event room upstairs. Maybe you could have it there."

Lori perked up. "Can you ask? I want to set it up next week. Midweek, probably, so I don't take up people's weekend. We're getting close to Halloween."

"Sure. I can ask." Even thinking about time passing raised Hannah's stress levels. Each week that passed was a week her business got closer to its end, and she'd been living with a sense of general sickness for days.

Lori eyed her. "Thank you. Now. What's really up with you?"

Hannah grimaced. She could tell Lori, and Lori would listen, and maybe give her some advice, but...damn, she was not ready to get input yet. She wanted to fix it *herself.* She had plans to talk to the building owner this week, ask about the possibility of a lower rent payment next year, negotiate the terms of the lease. "I'm not really ready to talk about it yet."

Lori's raised eyebrows said everything she needed to say,

but bless her, she didn't pry. "All right. I'm not pushing. You want to talk, you tell me."

"Thanks." There had to be some other topic of relevant conversation. "Why don't you tell me about you instead? What's happening at the paper?"

Lori let out a mighty sigh, the kind of sigh that indicated there was going to be A Significant Story coming, and that was a kind of relief. Lori's stories were always interesting: anyone studying any kind of psychology field for a PhD tended to have some thoughtful analysis of their own and others' behavior, although in Lori's case, it was mostly about others' behavior.

"You have something stronger than this seltzer?" She held up the half-empty can.

Hannah brought them each a small glass of tequila, the acrid smell comforting as she brought it up to her lips. Tequila burned all over, and she held that first sip in her mouth enough to swirl every flavor around and spread that numbing burn into all her senses. Of course, tequila reminded her of celebrating with Ben and Mitchell the other night after the Fall Festival, celebrations she'd tried to forget in the intervening days. There was actually nothing there for her to celebrate.

With both of them holding their glasses and the environment suitably settled, Lori let out another sigh and looked across the space between them. "I've been thinking about leaving the paper."

"What? Why? You love the paper."

"Correction. I *used* to love the paper." Lori held up a finger like a teacher giving a word of wisdom, then took another sip of her tequila. "Fuck, that is good."

"How long have you been thinking about this?"

"Just this week. I don't know. I don't want to rush into anything. I've been there for a few years now, and I've got a good gig, but it's so…" Lori made a face, wrinkling her nose, and then waved her hand in some kind of vague gesture. "It's so small-town."

Hannah raised an eyebrow. "You live in Mapleton. We *are* a small town. The *Valley Voice* is a small-town paper." Lori was usually good about moderating her expectations, but damn. She couldn't expect the small town they were in to have a big-city paper. "You've been happy there for years. What's changed?"

"I think it's my thesis." Lori played with the fringe of the couch pillow. "I want to go into relationship coaching, not journalism. I started working at the paper back in undergrad, and I was good at it, so I stuck with it. But it's not what I want to do forever."

"Can you do that sort of thing here in Mapleton?" Suddenly, the thought of losing Lori loomed on the horizon. Hannah had never conceived of life in Mapleton without her best friend.

"I'm doing some volunteer work with the relationship therapy associates on Main Street, but it's not quite what I want." Lori shrugged. "I don't know. It's a long shot. I'm just now starting to think about it."

"It's weird that this would come on you so suddenly. No warning. Just, bam, I want to change jobs and move."

"I didn't say I wanted to change jobs and move. Don't put words in my mouth. Drink your tequila." Lori gestured with her glass, then took her own advice for a long, slow sip. "Our new boss is kind of an ass."

"Oh, right." Lori had told her about the new editor in chief who had taken over for the retiring one. "He's only been there a few weeks, right? Maybe he's just getting used to it. Give him some time."

"I know. I'm impatient." Lori grimaced. "You know me. I like a challenge. I like change. But I also like things to make sense. And I don't know if what this guy's doing is going to make sense for the paper in the long run. Plus, I've got my defense next spring, and that's a big turning point. I finish the defense, maybe I publish, I don't know." She shrugged. "I have friendships, like this one, and I'll miss them, miss you, but I don't know if Mapleton was ever meant to be my forever home. Come spring, I think I might start to look for opportunities elsewhere." She gave Hannah a hesitant smile. "You'll visit."

Hannah's world had upended just at the thought of losing Lori, but she had time to get used to the idea. Lori wasn't going to leave until after her thesis defense in late spring, at least. And Hannah could surely find some other friends. "Shit, Lori, I don't have a lot of friends."

Lori pursed her lips. "Yeah, so, that's another reason I think you should come to the polyam workshop. You should meet some people."

"Ouch." Hannah laughed, but it felt a little forced.

"I'm just saying." Lori shrugged. "You can never have too many friends. It's good to get different perspectives on things. Make connections. Network." She waggled her fingers back and forth like a little person running around. "You never know. Maybe find someone to help you with your business."

Oh, so that was part of it. "I don't need help with my business." Best to shut that down right away. "And if I *do*, I'll get help on my terms."

Lori sighed. "Right. I forget. Miss 'I have to do it myself or it doesn't count.'"

Hannah didn't really have a good response to that, but it stung. She sipped her tequila with a sour expression.

Lori's next words were gentle. "I'm sorry. I know I can be kind of harsh. I just hate to see you struggling when I can't do anything about it."

She really did mean well, and Hannah softened. "I know.

But I don't need you picking on me. And I really don't want to talk about it right now."

"You're right. You're right." Lori swirled the little bit of tequila left in her glass. "I think I'm kind of nervous, thinking about changing things up. But I think it would be good for me, you know? I never put down as many roots here as I wanted."

"I love it here." Mapleton felt like home: the small-town vibe, the Chamber of Commerce meetings, the shops and students and hippie atmosphere, her own business. Well, one of those might not be around forever. "I don't want to leave."

"So don't leave. Nobody's telling you to leave. This is a good place for you." Lori raised her glass in a toast and drank. She looked down at her glass in hand while she swallowed, brow furrowed. "Are you pissed at me for thinking of moving?"

"Of course not." How could Hannah begrudge Lori her happiness? Thinking about their friendship having a time limit, though, made her uneasy. Although it didn't have to have a time limit. They could still be friends even after Lori moved away. "Are you looking far from here?" *Please don't let it be far.*

"Probably Boston or New York. I think I want to be in the city." Lori licked her lips. "Change of pace. Also, the chance to help more people."

"Neither of those is too far away." Hannah shifted on the chair.

"Oh, yeah, piece of cake. You can take the Metro North down out of New Haven into New York. It's only a few hours. Practically a day trip." Lori smiled. "What, you think I'm gonna head out west or something? Fuck that. I hate California. It's a fucking desert."

"California's a big state. The north is really pretty, I hear."

"So now you want me to move to California?"

"No! I'm just saying." Hannah found herself laughing.

Maybe this wouldn't be too bad. She had survived worse.

Unless she lost her business.

With that sobering thought, she picked up her glass of tequila again.

Lori left later that night, a few hours after they had finished the tequila and most of a large pizza between them. In the silence of her house, Hannah stared at her computer for a while. She could call Ben and talk to him about this, and Mitchell, but calling had an air of "this is a big deal," and phone calls were terrible. Nobody liked getting them or making them. Instead, she went into the group chat.

Hey. Weird question. What are the odds I could get you guys to go with me to a polyamory workshop my friend Lori is hosting?

. . .

Ben flipped the switch at the top of the stairs in the restaurant, flooding the room with light. Although they didn't rent out the event space as often as they thought they would back when they were renovating the place, it still brought in a steady stream of income through the occasional gatherings. This place had hosted some corporate mixers, rehearsal dinners, and bachelor/ette parties, but this polyamory workshop would be a first for both the restaurant and for him.

He was pushing a broom when Mitchell's footfall sounded on the stairs. Already, his heart quickened. He and Mitchell hadn't spoken of what happened the night of the Fall Festival. He wasn't sure if Mitchell remembered his drunken confession, but neither of them had brought it up in the intervening time. They had instead settled into the comfortable intimacy that had developed since the threesome with Hannah, closer and more affectionate than before, but with zero conversation about it. Probably not the healthiest system. Now they were only a few hours away from this polyamory workshop and probably some uncomfortable conversations, and Ben couldn't stop his brain from running away with him.

Mitchell looked around at the room. "Hey. You're getting started early."

"Lots to do." Ben gestured around at the cobwebs. "Clean some shit. Don't just stand there."

Mitchell snorted. "You're telling *me* to clean? Did hell freeze over?"

"Shaddup. Lori wants rounds of six with a presentation space up front." He waved his hand. "Move some tables. And then we've gotta check the taps. Lori paid for an open bar."

"You and Hannah both, just keeping me around to move heavy shit." Mitchell threw his head back and gave a mighty martyred sigh.

"And your back muscles look really good doing it." Ben brushed his hair back from his forehead. Ugh, gross. The skin under his palm felt gritty. "I'm covered in dust. Think I have time to run home and shower before tonight?"

"I'm gonna." Mitchell wrinkled his nose. "Don't want to go into tonight smelling like the grill."

After they'd set up the room, Mitchell checked the glassware, frowning meticulously at each pint glass and re-rinsing it in the sink even though each one was perfectly clean. It was a tiny moment, but so clearly Mitchell, who wouldn't accept less than perfection.

Jesus, he was pretty far gone on the guy, wasn't he?

Facing those emotions felt a little daunting right now, though. "I'm going home to catch a shower."

Mitchell nodded without looking up. "Don't use all the hot water. I'll be along soon."

Twenty minutes later, Ben was in the shower when he

heard the door to the bathroom open. He stuck his head out. "Dude, you couldn't wait?"

Mitchell started to pull off his chef jacket. "No. I smell like food, and there isn't time. And I didn't want to wait anymore." He ripped back the curtain and stepped into the shower with Ben.

Ben spluttered, lifting his head out from under the stream of water. What the hell? He did this to Mitchell all the time, but not recently, and Mitchell hadn't done this to him in...damn, such a long time, but there he was, naked and determined, and he backed Ben up against the wall and *kissed* him.

Ben froze up for a moment, surprised at Mitchell's intensity, before yielding and kissing him back. Fuck. With the steamy water, and Mitchell's warm, tight body against him, Ben's senses flooded with heat and desire. Kisses didn't usually make him feel so dizzy, but he couldn't catch his breath, thoughts dissolving down into the press of Mitchell's lips on his. This wasn't like any kisses they'd shared before. And... yeah, this was the first time they'd done this since Mitchell said he loved him. Those words, said affectionately and drunkenly at two in the morning, were framing everything.

Maybe reading something in Ben's response, Mitchell broke away and took a half step back. There wasn't room in this shower to do much else. With his damp hair plastered to his forehead, he looked so lost all of a sudden.

"I don't..." he began, then shook his head.

He kept opening his mouth a bit and closing it again, wanting to talk, obviously, but not saying anything. God, he was vulnerable and sweet and gorgeous, and this swelling emotion in his chest would not, could not be denied, so he stepped Mitchell back up against the cold shower wall and kissed him again.

This wasn't just an "I want to fuck you" kiss, or an "I

think you're hot" kiss. This was so many different kinds of kisses, hurt and comfort and need and longing, fulfillment in the space between their lips where they slanted and tasted and sipped. He cupped Mitchell's jaw, framing it with one hand while the other reached between them and found Mitchell's cock, half hard, stroking it all the way into hardness while the other man moaned into his mouth. He wanted so much here, and there weren't words for all of the need pulsing in his blood. Mitchell reached for him as well, fumbling between their bodies, until they were awkwardly jerking each other off while kissing hard like teenagers. Something desperate laced these motions, not like the fun and flirtatious sex they'd shared in the past, but something deeper and raw.

Something like love.

Ben's orgasm hit like a punch to the gut, sucking the wind out of him with rapturous pleasure. He succumbed to Mitchell's fast, sure strokes, grip faltering on Mitchell's cock as he spasmed in release. *Fuck*. He broke the endless kiss to rest his head against the tile wall, boxing Mitchell in with his larger body, breathing through the climax that swept over him with the suddenness and intensity of an earthquake.

Recovered, he stroked at Mitchell with renewed fervor, their slickness mingling with the water, and ducked back in to kiss him again. Kissing during sex, that came naturally, but kissing in the aftermath felt like comfort, and he sought out the sweetness, to hell with what that might mean.

Mitchell threw his head back when he came, crying out like he was in pain, a noise of intense pleasure that hit straight in the heart. Ben kept stroking while Mitchell spilled over his fist, hot and wet, washed away immediately in the water pounding down on them.

In the aftermath, they stayed close, even though there was no physical need to do so. The need ran deeper. It felt so good to stand pressed against Mitchell under the heavy fall of water and take this kind of comfort. Tonight they were going to talk about polyamory, about feelings and relationships and all those things he had avoided since the end of his marriage. It might be terrible. But it might also be wonderful.

Both possibilities were terrifying.

Mitchell touched his arm. "The water's getting cold."

"You didn't wash."

"I'm clean enough." He smiled. "We've got places to be."

Chapter Thirteen

Mitchell wasn't sure who he expected to be running a polyamory workshop, but it wasn't the over-sixty couple who exited the elevator with Lori. They were like the cover of an AARP magazine, full of exuberant energy, smiling and laughing at some conversation that had started earlier and continued into the room. Lori called all of them over to make introductions.

The older woman, Kate, wore a brown pantsuit with a yellow silk scarf, and when she took off her smart blazer, the blouse underneath was tan and decorated with delicate flowers. She had that polished look—pants creased, shoes sensible but dressy. She was even wearing pearl earrings. Perfect. Her silver hair was neatly bobbed, not a stray strand out of place, her whole persona bubbling with composed sensuality.

Walter, her husband, had a similar air of confidence and decorum. He looked every bit the college professor, complete with tweed jacket and elbow patches. His gray hair was trimmed quite short, and even though it was getting thin on top, he still had most of it, and his small beard and mustache matched the ensemble. In his pocket were wire-rimmed glasses, the kind that had flexible arms on the sides to hook over his ears, because of course he wore glasses like that.

Ben started chatting with them immediately, walking them around to show them the place and answer whatever questions they had about the venue, leaving Mitchell alone with Hannah for a minute. Even though he hadn't seen her in days, her proximity brought up a whole wave of longing. He had missed her, and told her so.

She blinked in surprise, then smiled shyly, averting her gaze. "Thanks. I missed you, too." Clearing her throat, she pushed her glasses back up the bridge of her nose. "Anyway. Thanks again for coming." She bit her lip, looking over at Ben giving the tour. "I know Lori's grateful, and so am I."

"You're welcome. I gotta admit, this isn't really my thing."

"Polyamory?"

"Group events." He grimaced.

"But you go to all those Chamber of Commerce meetings. You take notes." She raised an eyebrow. "You were amazing at the Fall Festival."

"That's different. That's connected to my business. I'm very good with stuff about my business."

Hannah frowned. "Right." She looked around. "This room is nice. I'm glad you could host it here."

"I'm glad there's beer." Beer would make the evening go much more smoothly.

"Definitely." She smoothed her skirt down her thighs. The action made him look her up and down. She wore a black pencil skirt over purple-and-black-striped tights. The sweater paired with that outfit was the same shade of purple, a nice eggplant color. He always paired appearances with food, but then again, that was how he saw the world.

"Damn, you look good enough to eat."

She grinned and blushed at once, fucking adorable. "Thank you."

People were starting to arrive, the steady thumping up the stairs like a harbinger of social interaction, the dinging elevator carrying others, and then Ben's hand at his elbow steered him away to meet the couple running the workshop.

"So you must be Mitchell." Kate extended a hand, and Mitchell shook it. "Ben says you two own this pub. What brings you here tonight?"

Ben was just smiling with an earnest expression, like he was just dying to hear what Mitchell had to say. What a fucker. He should have known Ben wasn't rescuing him from social interaction but dragging him into more.

"I, uh..." He probably couldn't pawn this off on just owning the business. "We've been...sort of trying it recently. Polyamory. Not real polyamory. But something like it. I'm not sure."

"Oh, good, good." Walter nodded. "Lots of stuff to unpack with that, isn't there?"

"Yeah." Some of the tension in Mitchell's chest eased at their casual tone. Nobody was even judging his inability to talk. Maybe this wouldn't be terrible.

"Walter and I are psychologists specializing in relationship therapy," Kate said, putting a hand on her husband's arm. "It's easy for us to get carried away with the therapy part of things sometimes." They smiled warmly at each other. God, they were clearly so in love. When Mitchell thought about polyamory, he didn't think about a happy older couple in an open relationship. Already he was having to shift his expectations.

At his elbow, Lori suddenly joined the conversation, addressing Kate and Walter. "I want to give people about five more minutes to come in, and then we can get started, if that's all right. I'll introduce you?"

"Sure, sure, sounds good." Walter nodded. He turned back to Mitchell and Ben. "Well, I hope you gentlemen get something out of tonight. There's a lot to talk about, and I know it can get a little overwhelming at times." Nodding sagely at his own comment, he then turned to Kate. "Let's get unpacked, hon."

People had started to mingle and make small talk, taking the beer that Mitchell and Ben had poured, until Kate and Walter called everyone to seats.

"If you're here with any partners or friends, please sit with them at one of the tables," Kate directed.

Kate and Walter introduced themselves first. They had been together since high school, and they began experimenting with open relationships when they were in their early thirties, which if Mitchell's math was correct was a bit past the actual free-love era. Kate spoke confidently, with the soothing voice of one comfortable with public speaking.

"We were already psychologists and relationship therapists together, and we both felt the need to get more information about this type of relationship. That has become our calling, to the point where it's taken over most of our regular practice."

"We still take clients," Walter said, "but on a much more limited basis. We give these workshops and help empower communities to develop their own support systems. Discussion groups, book circles—more than just play parties and orgies, which is what people seem to think polyamory is."

There was a bit of nervous laughter in the room. Okay, maybe people were also nervous. That felt like a relief. Kate's attention on their table, though, gave Mitchell another rush of adrenaline.

"If you could please take a minute to tell us your name, and what brings you here tonight, it would be nice to get to know each other."

Fortunately, they started with Ben, who cleared his throat. "Okay. I'm Ben, and I own the pub here with Mitchell. I'm...I guess I'm trying to figure out my feelings."

Well, shit. Ben, being honest and thoughtful rather than deflecting with a joke. Mitchell smiled to himself as he answered next.

"I'm Mitchell. Like Ben said, we own the pub here. I'm the head chef. I'm here because..." There was that question again. "I want to know more about polyamory. I don't know if it's for me. I don't know if we're doing it right." As soon as he said it, a blush stole over him, because shit, he'd just told the room he was fucking these people. He'd never said that out loud to anyone but Hannah before. The smiles from people around him were genuine, though, and he relaxed a bit as Hannah shared.

"I'm Hannah, and I own the sex shop here in town." She folded her hands in her lap. "I'm here because I don't know if one person is ever going to be right for me, but I don't want to take on more than I can handle." She paused. "Emotionally. Not physically." She blushed, and it was adorable. There was a lot of innuendo in that sentence.

The rest of the room shared, one at a time. In general, the group comprised a mix of ages and reasons for being there. A few people identified as openly polyamorous, but several were in the "I'm curious but I don't know what I'm doing" camp. This was very much an intro thing, which was good. Mitchell did a quick head count: there were eighteen people in the room. Most appeared to be with partners, and a few with more than one partner, which was what it must look like with him, Ben, and Hannah. The group seemed more normal than he'd expected, very little "hippie love child" vibe. A place like Mapleton, with five colleges right in the surrounding area, tended to skew liberal and sometimes *very* liberal. With his two moms and his Subaru, Ben was probably one of the more hippieish of the group, which made him chuckle quietly just thinking it, since he'd never thought of Ben that way before.

"To start with," Kate said, "we'd like you all to take out the journals from your folders."

Great. Journaling. He expressed himself through food, not through writing. They were supposed to write about their individual goals for the session. Kate and Walter insisted that no one would read the journals but them, and they would have no obligation to share.

Okay. His goals for the session. Mitchell paused with his pen over the paper.

I don't know why I'm here. That wasn't entirely true. *I don't know if I want to do polyamory. I don't know if I could love two people at the same time without feeling like I was always everybody's last choice.* Yikes. That was probably *too* honest. He stared at the book and swallowed. Well, if he was going to have to express his feelings, that was an okay place to start. At least he didn't *have* to share them. *If I have to pick a goal, and I guess I do, I will say that I want to learn whether or not I'm the kind of person who can do this polyamory thing.* There. That was a suitable goal. If he figured that thing out, he could know at least whether there was any future in anything he was doing, or if he was just going to have to move on.

And leave Ben and Hannah behind.

The thought of that hit hard, and even though he had stopped writing and was just staring at the blank page, a series of emotions cascaded through him, all right after one another. He took a deep breath and steadied himself.

When everyone had mostly stopped writing, Walter asked for more, because why wouldn't he? This was going to be the kind of event where everyone asked for more. "Now, we have another prompt for you. This is the second of three prompts. For this prompt, please write about what qualities you value most in your partner or partners. This can be a romantic or sexual partner. If you do not have any partners right now, you can write about your ideal partner."

Writing about Ben was easy. *Listens to me. Funny. Smart and always looking to learn. Honest. Trustworthy. Compassionate. Can be serious, but not too serious. Team player. Good conversationalist.* If he wanted to, he could probably fill a page with everything he admired about Ben. He loved this man, had probably been in love with him for years. But he'd told him after the Fall Festival, and Ben hadn't responded in kind, so it was easier for both of them to pretend it never happened. If he was brave enough, sometime, he would do it sober.

And then there was Hannah.

He wrote her name on the page. Wow, he had awful handwriting. It was blocky print, not like the loops and scrawls Hannah showed in all her notes. *Nice handwriting.* He snorted aloud after writing that, making her look over with her brow furrowed, and he shook his head dismissively. This task made him want to guard his paper, curling it protectively toward himself so no one else would read it. What a silly thing to start with. *Beautiful. Funny. Quick-witted. Challenges me. Doesn't let me get away with things. Spontaneous. Independent. Brave.* He wrote "brave" and then underlined it, because she was so brave, taking on all of her business alone. *Inquisitive. Curious.* This list was barely a start.

He looked over these lists, trying to see them objectively. He cared about both of these people—maybe loved both of them—and yet they were so different. Ben was a team player and Hannah was fiercely independent. Ben was predictable, but Hannah was spontaneous. He had laughed himself to tears with Ben, but he could also imagine talking seriously through the night with Hannah. He loved Ben. He was falling in love with Hannah. They were different people, different feelings of love, existing simultaneously in this way that confused and overwhelmed him.

And this was just the first part of the evening.

. . .

Kate had given them some time to skim the documents, so Ben leafed through the collection of materials in his folder, his sense of being overwhelmed quickly yielding to fascination. He loved paperwork. The folder included a glossary of terms about polyamory and then a whole page of different types of polyamorous relationships. He hadn't known there were so many. They'd included a *New York Times* article on the subject as well as a list of suggested reading. Finally, there were some polyamory conversation starters, ways to talk to your partners about it, and common issues and resources for managing them. The next task was to practice role-playing conversations.

Walter handed out envelopes with instructions and topics. Hannah and Mitchell watched Ben expectantly as he pulled out a scenario from the envelope and read it. "Okay. The situation is I'm feeling jealous after watching you with someone else, and I want reassurance that you still find me desirable. Who wants to start with this one?"

Mitchell cleared his throat. "Could…uh…could I do that one?"

Ben stared. Shit, he hadn't expected that. He handed over the slip of paper. Mitchell pulled out the list of sentence starters Kate and Walter had included in their folder. He directed his questions to Hannah.

"I like seeing you with Ben." He paused, considering his words, then continued. "I keep thinking that you'd never choose me over him. I would like some reassurance that you aren't going to forget about me."

Hannah's smile dipped, as Mitchell's words seemed more sincere than she'd probably expected. It certainly felt that way to Ben. Hannah's eyes flicked to Ben before she returned to Mitchell, and then she took a minute to look through the same list of sentence starters.

"Thank you for sharing that with me. The things I like about you and Ben are completely different." Hannah paused and seemed to look for her words, but Mitchell took the silence to press on.

"I don't want to feel replaceable." He swallowed visibly. There wasn't any serious emotion in his voice, no tears or sadness, but he seemed as intense as Ben had seen him. "With this kind of relationship, I don't know where the commitment is. I feel like I'm just waiting to be tossed aside. For Ben, for somebody else, whatever."

They hadn't talked about commitment, but their connection had shifted to something different than pure friendship, and even Ben knew it.

Hannah pressed her lips together, her expression thoughtful. "I think...it's not about being together because we don't have another choice, or because we made the choice one time and we're locked in forever. Going forward with this is about choosing to...keep choosing? If that makes sense. I'm choosing you not instead of someone else, but just for you. Because you're you."

Mitchell frowned, contemplative.

Hannah shifted and grabbed Mitchell's hands. "Okay. I'm gonna get real direct here." She exhaled. "Being with you isn't like being with someone else. You're smart, and you're funny, and you're so passionate about the things you care about. I love the way you care about your work, and your friends, and I love to see how much you care about Ben."

Mitchell flushed, color rising into his neck and the tips of his ears, and he shook his head. "It's all right. I don't need a big list of my good qualities. I wasn't fishing for compliments." He started to pull his hands back.

"I'm not just giving you compliments." Hannah took his hands again. "You have to know I'm choosing you because I want to be with you. Not because I think I have to, or because I'm biding time for someone better or something."

Mitchell smiled, something softening in his expression, and then he chuckled. "This is supposed to be hypothetical, isn't it?"

"Meh." Hannah shrugged and let go of his hands. "We might as well be honest, right?" Then she looked over at Ben, sitting beside them and watching the whole interaction. "What about you?"

Ben licked his lips. Okay. If she wanted honesty, he could give her honesty. "Talking about this…scares the shit out of me."

"This particular situation, from the card?" Hannah pointed to Mitchell's slip of paper. "Or polyamory in general?"

"Commitment." He swallowed. "I haven't been in a romantic relationship in a really long time, and I got pretty fucked-up over it. Ever since then, when I start to feel like I might have stronger feelings than just fooling around, I generally leave." He rubbed his hands on his thighs, and the friction was enough sensation to make him feel more grounded in his body. "I know I've lost out on years because of this. And I don't want to lose any more." He looked at both Hannah and Mitchell, these two people who meant more to him than anyone had in a long time. "I don't want to keep running away."

Before they could respond, Walter brought the conversations to a close. Shivers lingered on Ben's skin after his confession, his words more honest than he had been in a long time. Thank goodness the next part of the workshop just involved some sitting and listening to info about polyamory. Then they transitioned to an open conversation piece, where they moved the chairs into a big circle and then were able to ask questions of Kate and Walter themselves.

A few questions in, somebody on the far side of the circle raised her hand. She was a young woman with long blond braids, and while at first glance she didn't seem old enough to be at a workshop like this, on closer look, she was clearly in her midtwenties instead of her midteens.

"So." She sandwiched her hands between her knees. "How do you keep from developing feelings for the people you're sleeping with?"

Kate nodded. "That's a really good question. Do you mind sharing your name?"

"Sloane."

"Thanks, Sloane. So let me ask you a question back, since that's usually how we do things." She smiled gently. "Why don't you want to develop feelings for the people you're sleeping with? What kind of feelings are you trying to avoid?"

Sloane twisted her fingers together. "Well, I know that polyamory is about being in love with lots of people, but I... am really scared of that."

"Okay. Let's unpack that a little." Kate looked very calm and open to the conversation. "Why are you afraid of falling in love with more than one person? Or of falling in love at all?"

Sloane looked baffled. She opened her mouth for a moment but didn't speak for a few full seconds. "Love gets complicated. I don't know if they love me back, or if they want any kind of relationship with me, or if they'll get weirded out by it and just never want to see me again. Sometimes I just want to fuck somebody." She clapped a hand over her mouth. "Can I say 'fuck'?"

Everyone laughed, including Kate and Walter, and it broke the tension.

"Sloane." Walter leaned forward. "Your question isn't a bad one. My answer is going to sound kind of like I'm not answering you, but I'm going to try. If you want to have multiple sexual relationships without any other connection beyond casual sex, that's fine. Have fun and be safe. There's nothing wrong with that. Most people wouldn't consider that polyamory, but that doesn't mean it's unhealthy or morally wrong in the slightest." He smiled warmly. "On the other hand, it's not a bad thing to develop emotional attachment to someone that you're sexually active with. Kate and I, and most other polyam practitioners, ascribe to the belief that there's nothing wrong with falling in love with someone, or many people, even if that person or those people don't love you back in the same way."

Kate picked up. "You can't control your love in the way that you only put yourself out there when you're absolutely sure someone else shares your feelings at the same level and intensity as yours. That's not possible. Somebody has to make the first move and take the risk."

"But it's not even really a risk, because you can't control someone else's response and you're not trying to. Polyamory isn't about that." Walter looked like a sincere British professor giving a thoughtful lecture on his favorite topic. "Loving someone doesn't mean you have to be in a romantic relationship with them, certainly not a monogamous one. You might love them with a deep and abiding friendship kind of love. And even if you become romantically involved with someone, that doesn't mean you have to stay together forever, or that your relationship has to stay the same. If you are okay to let go of some of the expectations of monogamy, you can be free to feel emotions, or not, and accept whatever develops."

A wave of heat and then cold washed over Ben. He had

never thought about it in those terms. If his feelings didn't have to make him do anything, if he could just *have* feelings and they didn't make him beholden to any particular course of action, then maybe he could open himself up to the feelings he'd been putting aside. Maybe love didn't mean risking friendship.

Sloane was nodding as Kate and Walter finished their spiel. "Okay," she said.

"Does that help?"

"Yeah, I think so." She let out a nervous laugh. "It's scary."

"Lots of this is scary." Kate smiled a warm smile at the girl, and then at the rest of the room.

Well, she was definitely right about that.

· · ·

As the questions began to wind down, Hannah finally got up the courage to ask what she'd been wanting to ask. "This all seems good in theory. But...do people really make this last, like, long-term? Can someone love someone else, multiple people, and stay with them, and stay happy? It happens?"

"It does happen." Walter seemed to remember something from his past; he looked up and to the side before adjusting his glasses and coming back to the present. "Sometimes forever, sometimes just for a long time, but the love is real and valid no matter what. It shouldn't be denied. When you love, whether it's one person or many, that love binds you together in ways that are beautiful and multifaceted. Even if you move on from that love, that person will always be a part of who you are."

How could something be both exhilarating and terrifying all at once? Hannah had been playing with this idea of seeing multiple people for weeks now, but she hadn't really believed it had potential. If she didn't believe that love was possible this way, it was easier to move forward with Mitchell and Ben. She'd written off their time together as an experiment, a fling with an eventual expiration date. But...if this could be forever? God, she wanted it, and wanting it felt terrifying. Right now, sitting at the cusp of what could be love, all she had to do was *believe* and she'd be willing to risk it all.

Kate and Walter were right. Loving Ben and Mitchell, both of them, was going to change her in ways that she could never undo. She had been safe. She had been self-sufficient and independent. She hadn't failed any relationships because she hadn't taken the risk. Now she was looking at something different. There was even a fancy term for it—a closed triad, a relationship between three people. To make it work, she would need to do all those things she hated, like being vulnerable and asking for help.

The safest option, the one that wouldn't ask her to risk her heart and her independence and her pride, was to shut off those emotions altogether. Yeah, maybe it wasn't polyamory. Maybe it was just sex. But maybe that was all she could handle. That, at least, wouldn't leave her heartbroken and alone.

She nodded when appropriate throughout the rest of the question-and-answer session, but her thoughts remained on her own best next steps. By the time the meeting finally drew to a close a little while later, she had made up her mind. People stuck around to talk to Kate and Walter, and Lori eventually shuttled everyone out the door, thanked Hannah and Ben and Mitchell profusely for the space rental and the beer, and then everyone was gone except the three of them standing upstairs.

Hannah faced the two men. If she was going to try to have the physical benefits without the emotional risks, she should practice right away. "So I was thinking, maybe you guys could both come back to my place?"

As she drove home, Mitchell and Ben following close behind, her decision settled more comfortably on her shoulders. They would fuck, and she'd make sure she could enjoy the sex without having feelings attached to it. She'd had a lot of meaningless sex in her day; what was another fling? Enough of these long, soul-baring conversations. She didn't want to end up needing Ben and Mitchell for more than friendship and warming her bed. She needed only herself.

The queasiness in her stomach was just from anticipation.

The night was cold, and the wind whipped around Hannah as she found her keys in her coat pocket and unlocked the front door. Her hands were shaking. That was weird. She should be excited about the upcoming sex, not nervous. She'd already made up her mind, and Ben and Mitchell were getting out of their car behind her. The ship had sailed.

She put on a smile as she turned on the lights to her living room. Ben and Mitchell followed in behind her, taking off coats and shoes, doing the regular shuffle of getting into a warm place after being cold outside. This was what it would look like if they lived together: they would each do this same shuffle after work, coming into their home, settling in, the three of them hanging out like a different style of family unit.

The thought made her breath catch in her throat. But no. She was putting those ideas aside. No risk of failure, no risk of depending on someone who would decide she wasn't worth the effort. There were reasons to keep her emotions closed away. Surely she was making these choices for her own good.

Mitchell didn't resist as she stepped in and kissed him. After a second, he stepped back, using a hand on her shoulder to keep her away.

"Wait. Don't you think we should talk, after that workshop?" He looked over at Ben, who gave a slight nod. "That was a lot. I feel like we should talk about this thing between us. Clarify what we want."

"I don't want to talk." Hannah licked her lips. "I think we've been talking too much lately. Can't we just have fun?" A panicked desperation was welling up inside her, that longing to feel instead of think. "Ben? What do you say?" Ben had always been the one who put his emotions aside. He kept his distance. He would be with her in this. She reached out for him, grabbing his wrist and pulling him even closer.

Ben shrugged. "If she doesn't want to talk, Mitchell, she doesn't want to talk."

Mitchell took Hannah's face in his hands, studying her, his eyes only a few inches away from hers, their noses nearly brushing. He had the look like he wanted to say something else, but instead he only kissed her, bruisingly hard, holding her in place. The power he exuded weakened her knees and sent shivers racing down her spine. Yes, this was what she wanted. She reached up to grip his arms for balance.

The kiss ended, and she wanted more. Reaching over to one side, she grabbed Ben instead, dragging his mouth down to hers. Mitchell was so close she could feel him, and she pulled at him as well, her movements awkward as she fumbled both men closer. The need to feel them here, the solidity of their presence, rose like a living thing inside her.

She wanted this. And she wanted it tomorrow, and next week, and forever. Fuck, she was thinking of forever. This desire running rampant through her veins wasn't just for pleasure, for sexual release, but for the intimate closeness, both physical and emotional. Maybe instead, she could lose herself in this moment. Maybe sex would be enough to quiet her brain. Maybe right now, maybe forever, this could be enough.

• • •

Damn, Mitchell should have known this was going to be a bad

idea. Hannah was acting like there was a wall between them. She'd been closed off since the last part of the workshop, and now she was groping them like some kind of lust-filled animal. He didn't want this, or at least, he didn't want to limit their relationship to this, as much as he tried to convince himself that sex was almost as good as love. Worst of all, though, Ben seemed fine with this parody of what they'd shared together before.

Now, as he tumbled into Hannah's bed with her and Ben, his physical desires waned against the empty feeling inside his heart. God, he shouldn't push this. That emptiness represented everything he wanted and couldn't have. The people in his life were giving him something, friendship and sex, and that was more than some people ever got. Wanting something different was selfish. Fuck every single part of him that wanted something other than this. If this was what the other two wanted, he would have to be all right with it.

Hannah was amazing. She was smart, independent, and strong-willed, and she challenged him. He had seen what was possible for all of them today in that workshop. They could have something special, the three of them together. Instead, though, she didn't want to talk. She seemed to want…less than before.

Hannah rolled over and faced him, her eyes bright and her hair loose and wild across the pillow. God, she was beautiful, and her beauty hit him again as though it were the first time. Now, reaching out to kiss her, a thought came to mind that this might be the last time he ever did so. He tasted her lips, opened her mouth with his, delved inside while he held her body against his. Ben moved on the other side of her, his hands skimming over her skin as well.

Could he forget himself in her body like this? If he tried to quiet his mind, maybe he could let go and just give in to his desire to fuck her. His dick could lead the way. Lots of guys let their dicks take over. Ben probably did it most of the time.

The thought about Ben brought him up short, too. His body was still going through the motions of kissing Hannah, but his mind raced with thoughts about Ben kissing Hannah as well, Ben sharing this woman with him. God, he *wanted* that. Why couldn't he be satisfied with what he was getting?

He broke the kiss and slid off the bed all in one motion, because if he didn't do it all at once, he might not do it at all, and he wanted to be done with this.

Hannah gaped up at him, blinking heavy-lidded eyes in confusion, and Ben looked equally baffled by his sudden move.

"I'm sorry." He shook his head. Now that he was out of the bed, he had to get out immediately. At least they were still all fully clothed.

"What's wrong?" Hannah propped herself up on one elbow. "Where are you going? Are you okay?"

"I'm sorry. I can't do this." Mitchell ran a hand through his hair. "Tonight, all that conversation, I need to think. I can't just"—he gestured at them—"do this. Without talking about anything first."

He paused, halfway to the door. Shit. He was Ben's ride home.

Ben seemed to read his mind. "I can call a cab or something."

"I can give you a ride." Hannah touched Ben's arm, and the casual intimacy of her gesture made Mitchell ache. He wanted more, and she barely wanted anything...or at least, maybe not with him.

"Okay. Ben, I'll...see you." It was an awkward exit, and he felt awkward as hell rushing down the stairs like he was fleeing some kind of scene of a crime, or trying to get out of a lover's house before their spouse came home, complete with the wave of shame and guilt. He pulled on shoes and coat at the door, not wanting to linger in case he was stopped, but also...well, also kind of hoping they would stop him. He even paused a moment, keys in hand, just to hear if there were sounds upstairs. If he took his time, they could change their minds and come down and stop them. Was that the sound of someone standing up? A creak of hardwood floor? He waited another second, then one more. No one came to the stairs. No one raced down to beg him to stay.

He left.

The ride home was filled with the silence of the aftermath. He hadn't even been in Hannah's house long enough for the car to cool off. He turned on the heater, and the immediate warmth felt somehow even more humiliating. He hadn't been able to see it through. He hadn't had the strength, or fortitude, or whatever it was to be able to *just have meaningless sex*. Wasn't this what guys did? Weren't his former girlfriends always calling him emotionally unavailable? He had never had a real relationship with a guy, but he'd had plenty of short-term sex with them, and they never seemed interested in more, so he hadn't pursued it. Maybe he would have failed at that, too. Damn him and his needy emotional bullshit.

Mitchell slowed down for a couple of pedestrians in the crosswalk. The couple in the road held hands, bathed in the light from streetlamps, laughing and talking in casual conversation. Past them, more couples walked along the sidewalks. Everywhere, couples—couples on the sidewalk, couples going into bars and shops, pairs of people wherever he looked.

A honk behind him broke his train of thought. Right; he was still sitting at crosswalk, so he pulled forward and drove on into the night. It would be weird for three of them to be together, anyway. This was a world for couples, not triads. Hannah didn't want to date him. And Ben... Whatever Ben might be feeling, he hadn't responded to Mitchell's confession of love.

Right now, Hannah and Ben were probably fucking in ecstasy on the bed he had just vacated, enjoying the casual freedom of sex without consequences. He, the brokenhearted idiot that he was, was driving home alone instead.

. . .

The closing door reverberated all throughout the house. Hannah and Ben had stopped all sexual activity, lying in the same positions they had been in when Mitchell left the room. She was sitting half upright and Ben was sprawled beside her, propped up on his elbows. The silence left behind was deafening. She shifted, and the bed squeaked, but Mitchell didn't come back upstairs. She waited for him to come back. Surely he would do what people did in the movies and run back into the room to kiss her and make love to her.

The thought of that idea, him *making love* to her, shook her as she sat silently in bed.

When the silence became too much, when it was clear that no one was coming back for them, they each moved on some unspoken signal. Ben scooted up to lean back against the headboard, and she joined him.

Ben turned to Hannah. "I know why he's gone." He didn't need to ask if she did, too.

"He shouldn't want something different." Hannah had been very clear to him from the beginning. "He understood what he was getting into. Right? You both knew."

"We all knew." Ben reached out and touched her hand, his large fingers resting lightly on hers. "But shit's changed. You can't pretend everything's the same as it was. And honestly, whatever you're trying to do here, it isn't gonna work for me, either. Mitchell was just braver than me to leave."

Hannah turned her hand over, their palms touching

lightly. She stared at their hands together and finally let out a sigh.

"Is this really what you want?" Ben closed his hand around hers, holding her gently but firmly.

His expression was so earnest, so honest, that she wanted to cry. Emotion clogged her chest, rushing in thick and fast. Her words sounded foggy. "I thought so."

"Do you know how I feel about you?" Ben asked, but she wasn't ready to hear that, and she shook her head.

"Please don't. I can't." She kept shaking her head like the shaking might clear it, as if her brain were an Etch A Sketch. "I thought... This was supposed to be fine." She looked up at Ben, and although she didn't ask it, the question lingered in her mouth. *Why isn't this fine?*

"Maybe this isn't right for us. It's too soon." He squeezed her hand again before releasing it, disentangling their fingers. "We've had a lot going on lately."

Hannah laughed, self-deprecating, her own annoyance coming through. "I can't even do fuck buddies right."

"Some people aren't meant for that." Ben shrugged. "Not everybody enjoys casual sex."

"I've always enjoyed it in the *past*." She could probably name a dozen guys she'd slept with and everything had turned out fine, exactly as casual and fun as she had wanted it to be. Sure, they hadn't exactly known what they were doing, and she hadn't wanted to see any of them a second time, but she had kept her bed warm and she could have orgasms if she wanted them.

"People change."

The simple statement was too trite for her wealth of emotions right now. "So what? We just stop? We leave each other alone?"

"Maybe we just need some distance to sort things out." Ben got to his feet.

Hannah nodded. It would be for the best. She was going to have to put all her attention into finding a job, anyway, when her business went under.

Their goodbye was casual, too casual, impermanent and awkward. In the aftermath, the house was silent.

God, the house was silent.

Chapter Fourteen

The lights were still on when Ben got home. He sat in the driveway looking at the windows of the condo. Mitchell wasn't in bed. It was late, yeah, but the lights were on, and Mitchell didn't leave the lights on when he wasn't awake. Ben had been awash with feelings ever since leaving Hannah's, his brain running through everything he had to say, but now that he was sitting in the taxi waiting to go inside, all his emotions had coalesced into fear.

Now that wasn't going to do at all. He took two deep breaths. *Buck up, soldier.*

Inside, Mitchell was cooking.

Mitchell couldn't have arrived home that long ago, but he was already in the middle of some kind of chili, grinding steak into hamburger, onions sweating down in a saucepan on the stove, mise en place laid out in tiny glass bowls along the kitchen counter. The aroma was fantastic. Those must be tomatoes roasting in the oven.

Mitchell seemed surprised to see him. Not just surprised but shocked, stopping midmince with his hands full of steak.

"Hello?" Ben ducked and tipped his head to the side. "You seem really surprised to see me. You forget I still live here?"

"I thought you would still be at Hannah's." Mitchell went back to his steak, and for a few minutes, the roar of the stand mixer's grinding attachment drowned out any possibility of conversation. Ben pulled up a chair at the table, because he was going to be here for a while.

When the meat had been ground, Ben was finally able to talk and be heard again. "I left."

"I see that. Things not take very long?" Mitchell steadily didn't make eye contact.

Ahh, a bit of passive aggression. "Mitchell, can we talk?"

Mitchell glanced up from the onions he was stirring in their pan. "Sure. Talk to me."

"I mean together. Can you put this all on pause?"

Mitchell stopped stirring the onions and looked hard at Ben, as if sizing up whether this conversation was really a conversation he wanted to have at all. After a minute, he nodded and sighed.

"Okay. I can stop some of it. Give me ten minutes to get the onions off the heat and let the tomatoes finish roasting. Those can rest while we talk."

Ben had nothing to do, then, but watch him cook. This wasn't a luxury he allowed himself very often. Mitchell was so composed, completely in his element right now: stirring the onions, then peeking in at the tomatoes.

Ben really should have figured out his feelings for Mitchell a long time ago. Maybe if he hadn't been so obtuse, this would all have been simpler. But there was no denying what needed to be said.

After washing up, Mitchell flopped down on the couch. Ben came and joined him, making Mitchell move over to make room for him.

"I couldn't stay with Hannah tonight." Ben pressed his palms into his jeans, grounding himself. "Neither could you. It isn't because you don't care about her. Why is it?"

Mitchell made a face. "You said you wanted to talk. I didn't realize you wanted to interrogate me."

"Please, just answer me."

Mitchell sighed. "It feels awful trying to have casual sex with her like I don't care about her."

"I feel the same way." Ben nodded. "I don't want to pretend."

Mitchell hesitated, waiting for more. "Okay."

"But this isn't about Hannah." Ben took a deep breath. He wasn't the kind of guy who read emotions as challenging to his masculinity, but damn, feelings were not helping him get this out. "I was thinking on the way home that it's weird to not be able to have casual sex with Hannah when you and I have been fucking that way for years."

Mitchell nodded. "Yeah. But it's different with guys."

"Why?"

Mitchell hesitated. "I don't know. I just assumed it was."

Ben was going to have to circle around this topic from a different angle. He thought back to their early days together, when he was trying to get himself back on his feet and Mitchell was there, no questions asked, to give support and advice and not judge him. After that were their early restaurateur days and the difficulties of getting started, the way they felt like it was them against the world. Then there was the first time he offered Mitchell some casual sex and the way Mitchell had gone with it, the two of them fitting together in bed as naturally as if they were born for it.

"Mitchell, I'm in love with you."

Mitchell froze. His reaction wasn't laughter, as Ben had feared, or anger, as Ben had also feared, but neither was it tearful realization or obvious joy. Instead, his expression shifted to utter disbelief. Overtalking at this point wouldn't be good, but damn, he had to give Mitchell at least a little bit more.

"I realized today at the polyam workshop that you're the person I'm closest to. It's friendship, but it's also different than friendship. I don't know how long it's been since it was ever just friendship. I think I've been in love with you for years and have been in denial about it. And then you said it last week, and I just wasn't ready to face it."

Mitchell swallowed, then swallowed again. God, Ben could read a lot of emotions in the minutiae of Mitchell's twitches, but this was hard even for him.

Mitchell looked down at his hands. "Why were you in denial?"

"Shit, you know everything with Vivian. She broke my heart. And when things ended with her, I lost one of my best friends."

Mitchell was still looking at him as though dying for more information, more details. So he gave them. "But that isn't all of it. I didn't want to risk what we had. I thought if we call it friendship, if we call ourselves fuck buddies, we're safe. But I can't deny anymore that I love you. I don't want to deny it. And if it's a risk, it's a big fucking risk. But I want to take that risk." Ben took a deep, shuddering breath and released it. "I'm not asking you to be monogamous with me. I'm not asking you to pick only me above everyone. I just thought… maybe you and me could be more official with this."

Mitchell's hands were trembling. Mitchell, who had the steadiest hands, who could mince onions to perfection and shave cloves of garlic into slices as thin as paper and transparent as glass…Mitchell was shaking with his hands pressed onto his knees. He didn't tear up, because that wasn't Mitchell's style, but the emotion welled anyway.

"I've wanted this for a long time, but it's fucking scary."

Mitchell shook his head, kept shaking it as he looked down at his hands, still trembling with all that built-up emotion. "I don't know. I mean. I do. I know." He looked up again, and his eyes were bright, wide, filled with longing and panic, all the mixed emotions that he usually held back flashing through his expression like a kaleidoscope. "Yeah. Completely. I love you. I've loved you for years."

Ben didn't wait. He scooted over the small distance between them and kissed Mitchell on the lips, grabbing his shoulders, holding him in place until Mitchell shifted and welcomed him in with an embrace. It was awkward, their bodies partially reclined on the couch, Ben half kneeling and half sitting, but fuck all of that. Mitchell's mouth was hot and wet, his entire body vibrating.

"Okay. Okay." Mitchell put a hand on Ben's chest, and Ben shifted so he was sitting more evenly next to Mitchell, not quite on top of him but so close he could breathe the same air. "What about the business?"

"The business stays the same. We're the same. We stay partners, we stay friends. Plus love. Plus whatever crazy shit this is." Ben laughed.

Mitchell started laughing as well. "I don't even know what this changes with us. I've loved you for years. I didn't want to admit it. But I don't know if we're going to be any different? Together? Anything?"

"I'll probably hold your hand in public sometimes." Ben smiled. "And kiss you on the mouth."

"Oh god, public physical affection? No." Mitchell held up a hand. "Please, no."

"Listen." Ben took both his hands. This felt good and right, holding Mitchell's hands, showing his love, admitting all of this, but it wasn't complete. "I love you. But I don't think I'm monogamous. I might fall in love with someone else someday. It doesn't mean I'm going to stop loving you."

Mitchell looked into his eyes. "We might both already be in love with someone else."

The silence hung between them. It was the first time either of them had said it out loud, this possible truth, the other truth Ben wasn't willing to admit. "That isn't possible right now."

Mitchell nodded. "I know."

"Can you be with me even if I'm not monogamous?" Ben paused. "This feels like the least romantic thing ever. And I hate romance."

Mitchell smiled, but it was a smile with teeth, not just the tight-lipped smile he usually did. "Yeah. I was thinking about that tonight at the workshop. I just want to feel like you're going to choose me. Not always me, and not always just me, but when you're with me, it's because you want me and not somebody else you can't have."

Ben nodded. The workshop already felt like so long ago. It was hard to believe it was the same night.

"Hey." Mitchell squeezed Ben's hands. "This is pretty fucking gay."

"Still bi." Ben tilted his head. "You got it?"

"I've got it. Still bi. Both of us." Mitchell glanced toward the kitchen. "I've got a chili to finish. But then…" His voice trailed off, and he turned his attention toward the bedroom.

Ben smiled. "I'll wait up."

• • •

Having Ben kissing him like his life depended on it was a new experience. Ben kissed with intensity, passion, love. Mitchell could finally name it for what it was. He had been in love with Ben for years, and even if it wasn't exclusive, even if they were already in love with someone else and just weren't ready to say it out loud, this was beautiful and overwhelming and he wanted all of it.

Ben pushed him down on the bed with ease. Mitchell usually gave the direction and took the lead in these moments, some light domination that made Ben hard as a rock, and he wanted that now as well. But he also wanted something else.

He was strong enough to easily roll Ben off him onto his side, and Ben didn't fight, going willingly and looking over at Mitchell with adoration in his eyes. Mitchell threaded his fingers into Ben's hair, which was just long enough for him to do this, and closed his fist, pulling all of Ben's hair and forcing his head still. Ben's eyes fell half closed and he moaned, this deep rumbling groan that went straight to Mitchell's dick. Mitchell smiled. "You want me to tell you what to do?"

Ben tried to nod, found he couldn't, and smiled. "Oh yeah, I do. You know I love this shit."

"I want you to fuck me."

Ben's eyes widened. "You sure?" They had never done this, for a number of reasons. But damn, Mitchell wanted that cock pressing into him, wanted to feel himself getting stretched open, watch the shaking of Ben's muscles and listen to his whimpers as he tried to hold back. He wanted all of it.

"Definitely." Mitchell smiled. "Now. Take your clothes off."

Mitchell lounged on the bed while Ben undressed, watching the slow reveal, his own clothes already on the floor. Hannah flashed into his mind, a momentary vision of her here beside him, and he got choked up for a second. No, he had to put her aside. This wasn't going to be perfect. This wasn't about her. This was about him, and Ben, and what they had together that couldn't be minimized or duplicated. This was something special all on its own.

While watching Ben strip the last of his clothes off, Mitchell idly stroked his dick. Damn, he loved this man. He rolled the thought through his mind, trying it out, and it fit well.

"Turn around," he ordered. "Let's see that ass." Ben obeyed. These dominance games got both of them hard in no time at all. Ben was so large and powerful, and watching him submit made Mitchell's cock throb.

"You have lube?" Mitchell looked over at the nightstand.

"Obviously." Ben opened a drawer and pulled out a bottle of lube. "Tell me what you want."

Mitchell's heart raced at the thought of it. Excitement overwhelmed any nervousness. "Get me ready."

Ben stretched out on the bed and took Mitchell's cock into his hot mouth. Mitchell's hips bucked up, and Ben held him in place, sucking and licking him, driving Mitchell straight from zero to "oh my god" in no time flat. Fuck, this wasn't good. Well, this was actually *amazing*, but it was also going to get him off too quickly, and he didn't want to come this way. Before he could protest, though, Ben spread his legs and lube-slick fingers pressed against him. Oh Jesus, one finger slipped inside with no resistance at all, and his cock twitched hard in Ben's mouth.

Mitchell closed his eyes and threw an arm over his forehead, momentarily overwhelmed by the dual sensations. He'd had sex with other guys before; usually, the stretch was uncomfortable, but Ben's mouth on his cock was so fucking good, it made everything feel incredible. Then there was more, a deeper stretch from a second finger. That fullness was incredible, his cock leaking against Ben's tongue while his ass clenched around Ben's fingers. Suddenly, a shock of white-hot pleasure jolted him. *Fuck*, that was his prostate.

Ben lifted his head to watch, smiling, fingers still working deep. Mitchell's cock pulsed against his stomach. Ben added more lube, then *another* finger, maybe a bit too soon, and Mitchell couldn't catch his breath. Jesus, every single press against his prostate lit him up from the inside. This was fucking incredible. It had been a long time and he wanted more, now.

Ben slowly slid his fingers out of Mitchell's ass, which felt loose and empty in the absence of contact. Mitchell lifted his head, which felt way too heavy.

"Don't stop," he said, and it didn't sound as much like an order as he wanted it to.

"I want to stretch you out more," Ben said. "Nightstand?"

Hell yes. Mitchell rolled to the side and reached into the nightstand, finding, yes, a blue silicone dildo. Although it couldn't compare to Ben's dick, it was wider and thicker than fingers, and it was going to feel so good inside him.

"Do you fuck yourself with this?" Mitchell asked.

"I do." Ben locked eyes with him. "Sometimes I pretend it's your cock."

God. Mitchell couldn't stop his own groan, the image flashing into his mind of Ben on his back, fucking himself with that fake cock. Ben plucked it out of his hand and reached again for the lube. Mitchell felt the pressure, the initial momentary discomfort, and then flash of hard pleasure as the head slipped inside. Damn, it hadn't seemed that big, but he hadn't done this in a while. Ben waited and, when Mitchell nodded, started to push it in.

He couldn't help the low, guttural noise that slipped out of him as Ben pushed the dick right up to the flared base. Mitchell strained to keep his eyes open to watch Ben's concentration, watch the way Ben's own dick hung heavy and hard and neglected, untouched. He managed to pull together some presence of mind.

"That feels good," he said. "It's gonna feel so good when it's you."

Ben was breathing as heavily as if he was the one getting touched. His arousal was so fucking hot, the sexiness of having him get off on this, too.

"Stroke yourself," Mitchell told him. "Nice and slow. Fuck me at the same pace."

Ben pulled the dick back out, slowly, gripping his cock with his free hand. He slid his lubed hand up over his shaft as he slid the dildo out, then dragged his hand back down as he pressed it back inside. In and out, steady, slow, achingly slow, opening Mitchell up for what was to come. Ben's dick was amazing, Ben was amazing, this entire situation was so fucking hot. Mitchell couldn't touch his cock or he was going to come in no time flat.

He let this continue for a few minutes, this steady stroking and the gentle fucking, watching as Ben's breath got more ragged and his cock darkened, the head nearly purple. Mitchell didn't want to wait anymore.

"That's enough. I want you."

Ben slowly slid the fake cock out and grabbed for a condom. Mitchell rolled over onto his stomach. As much as he'd love to watch Ben's face, this would be an easier position for him to take that massive shaft.

"How much do you want this?" He looked back over his shoulder at Ben, who was lined up to fuck him, his face filled with lust and concentration in equal measures.

"So fucking much." Ben exhaled. "You have no idea."

"Good." Mitchell smiled. "Do it."

The first press of hot cock against his ass, and holy hell, he had to grip the sheets to keep from driving his hips backward on instinct. Ben had always seemed too big, and Mitchell had never felt ready to feel vulnerable to him like this. This was a different kind of intimacy. He wasn't the kind of guy to let his guard down in a situation like this. He was the kind of guy who liked to dominate.

Dominating, though, didn't mean he had to top.

"Nice and slow."

He hung his head, resting there on his hands and knees

against the blunt press of Ben's cock. The pressure felt overwhelming, like it was never going to fit, a moment's sharp stab of sensation, and then the blissful stretched-out feeling of the head of Ben's cock inside him.

"Jesus Christ," Mitchell breathed. There was nothing like this in the world. He might explode just from these first inches.

"You all right?" Ben's voice sounded strained, and Mitchell's ass probably felt tight as hell around Ben's sensitive cock.

"More." Mitchell tried not to wriggle or move. Ben slowly shuffled forward, pressing into him, and every inch was lubed and slow and steady and thick and absolutely gorgeous. He tried not to whimper as that swollen cock head rubbed over his prostate, but when Ben went balls-deep, pressed as far in as he could go, Mitchell made a punched-out noise like some kind of injured animal.

"Fuck." He could barely think; the cock was pushing his brain cells out. "Fuck. I just... Oh. *Ohh*."

Mitchell wanted to keep up the dominant dirty talk, but he needed to get his act together. He took a few deep breaths. "Feel good?"

"So good." Hearing Ben's voice like that, totally wrecked and tense, was a boon. This kind of control turned him on almost as much as the act.

He looked over his shoulder and locked eyes with Ben, who had his hands on Mitchell's hips and was nearly trembling with pleasure. "Fuck me *slow*."

Ben's eyes rolled back, and his mouth fell open. He loved it when Mitchell talked dirty, and Mitchell could talk dirty, at least right now, before the inevitable pleasure overtook him. "Fuck me with that cock. Gonna..." He had to pause as Ben drew back, rubbing over his prostate again, and couldn't help gasping when Ben pushed back in. "Fuck. Yeah. Gonna make you fuck me till I come. Think you can wait?"

"I'll try." Mitchell could hear the smile in Ben's voice, and he loved that smile.

Ben thrust into him, fucking him steadily, as nicely as he could ask for. That thick slide of a hard dick inside him, the deep-seated pleasure—this was just what he was hoping for, just what he had wanted. Even though he couldn't see it, he could picture it, and that was nearly good enough.

Nearly. But not enough.

Mitchell pulled himself off Ben's dick, ignoring Ben's sudden cry of surprise and his own stretched-out feeling, and rolled over onto his back. "Fuck me like this. I want to watch you."

Ben smiled, taking one of Mitchell's legs up onto his shoulder as he moved forward to align himself.

Thank god for yoga. As Ben's hard dick slid into him, Ben simultaneously stretched his leg back, opening him up. Jesus, every inch felt twice as big like this, and Mitchell gasped in lungfuls of air as Ben pushed all the way inside. He was split apart in the best possible way.

He loved this man. He was in love with this man.

The sudden upswell of emotion closed around his heart and stopped his breath. Ben must have noticed it happen and paused halfway through a thrust. "What? What is it?"

"I'm in love with you." Mitchell tried out the words again.

Ben smiled. "Yeah, you are." And thrust all the way home.

With just a few firm strokes of Ben's hand on his cock, Mitchell was lost. Pleasure spiraled inside him, winding tighter and tighter, stealing his breath as he climbed to that precipice. His orgasm came hard, white-hot, blinding, a panoply of color and sound and light and pleasure. He gripped the sheets, the hard length moving inside him, extending his climax. He cried out, wordless at first, and then Ben's name, opening bleary eyes to watch Ben's tense face as he held back his own climax.

"Come," Mitchell begged. "Please. I want to feel it."

Ben gripped Mitchell's hips, every fingertip a sharp indentation, and threw his head back in orgasm. He came undone like a hurricane, a force of nature, and Mitchell's heart swelled in his chest at the privilege of watching.

After the basic cleanup, they both flopped on the mattress, breathing in the silence. Ben turned to Mitchell. "You know, my bed is big enough for both of us."

Maybe that wasn't such a big step, but Mitchell's heart warmed at the invitation. "Gonna give me a break from my spartan room?"

"I figured you could use it." Grinning, Ben reached over to tousle Mitchell's hair. That teasing gesture shifted, and Ben cupped Mitchell's cheek, rubbing a rough thumb over his cheekbone. His expression grew tender. "I want you to know. There isn't anyone new for me right now. I'm not looking for someone else. I have you. And..." He trailed off.

He didn't have to finish. "And Hannah."

"We don't have Hannah."

"But we want her." Mitchell lay next to Ben, the two of them curling together like parentheses. "We both do. Right?"

Ben nodded. "Yeah. But I don't know if we're going to have her, ever. She needs to figure out if she can trust us or not." Ben's hand idly traced Mitchell's back, soothing and sweet. "You know, I want you no matter what happens with Hannah."

"I know. I feel the same." He paused. "But I miss her."

Ben smiled. "Yeah. I miss her, too."

Chapter Fifteen

Making a clean break was pretty damn hard when you left your wallet at someone's house. Mitchell stood on Hannah's doorstep, waiting for her to answer the bell. Her comments this morning on the group chat had been cordial, and she'd found his wallet on the floor below where his coat had been, but it didn't mean he wanted to be here so soon after leaving her house.

Hannah opened the door and gave him a neutral smile, waving his wallet. "Here you go." She paused, maybe considering whether to just shut the door in his face. "You want to come in for a bit? I just made some coffee."

"Sure, maybe just for a minute." He didn't want to stay long, but seeing her in the doorway like this, he had really missed her.

Daylight made everything seem harsh, the events from the night before too fresh for him to deal with. He followed her to the kitchen, where she was already pouring him a cup.

"Thanks." He stirred creamer into his coffee, then looked over at the kitchen table, which was strewn with papers.

"Mind if I sit here?"

She was already headed out of the kitchen. "Sure. I left my phone upstairs. Let me grab it."

These papers looked important. Mitchell started stacking them up to move them aside so he didn't accidentally spill coffee on them or something. There was Hannah's nice handwriting again. Ben's was chicken scratch, and his was utilitarian print, but Hannah wrote in scrolling loops and swirls. Even her numbers were beautiful. He absentmindedly perused a sheet out on top, looking at the patterns and figures. Oh, wait. This was a budget sheet for next year, with months sketched out along the side. The pluses and minuses, the labeled amounts—rent, loan payment, vendor bills with a bunch of companies listed—these were her expenses, and then her income, a much smaller amount. He took it all in within a moment, not even needing to read much more closely, and quickly put the paper aside and stacked a few other documents on top of it. He shouldn't look at that. He shouldn't have seen it at all. He should forget what it was, the way her bills were so much greater than her income, the numbers carefully inked in red with a terrifying figure. Maybe he had flopped his numbers again. He took another look at the sheet, reading it carefully, making sure he wasn't switching figures. Unfortunately, no, he had been correct. He put the document back under the others.

Hannah wasn't making enough money, or at least, she wasn't going to be making enough money next year. Shit. Was she in the red now? How long had it gone on like this? How was she staying in business? Her net sales were strong, but her rent was astronomical.

Now that he had started looking, he couldn't stop, all the papers jumping into his vision. Here, a financial adviser's name on letterhead. Over there, a series of promissory notes from the bank. He glanced at the figures again. She was actually pretty close to breaking even, regardless of that crazy rent. If she had a loan, she could probably turn that around.

"Sorry about that." Hannah reappeared, carrying her phone, just as Mitchell had set the papers back down. "My mom's supposed to be calling this morning, and she'll give me so much shit if I don't pick up."

"You close with your parents?" Anything not to talk about the current subject and the papers he had just seen.

"Yeah, I guess." She shrugged. "Liberal hippies up in Burlington. I love 'em. A little overbearing at times, but they want what's best for me. How's the coffee?"

"Good, good." He looked back down into his mug.

Hannah sipped, holding the mug in one hand while she pushed a few tresses of hair out of her face. All at once, she seemed to notice the state of the table. "Oh god, this is all still out." Grimacing, she swept all the loose papers toward her, piling them messily on the other side of the table. "Sorry about that."

"I said I didn't mind."

"Yeah, but I didn't know what I was asking you not to mind." She sighed. "This is a fucking mess. Nobody should have to deal with that."

"Yeah, so." He had to bring it up. She was on the verge of losing her business, from the looks of things. "Are you doing okay?"

"I'm fine." The words came out automatically, like a reflex. "It's fine. Don't worry about last night. It's okay."

"No, not that." He hesitated. He was crossing a line, but he couldn't just let it be. "Did you get all the money you needed from the festival?"

Hannah looked at him, her eyebrows drawing together, and then all at once seemed to realize what was happening.

"Oh my god." She looked around at the papers. "You went through my shit. What the *fuck*, Mitchell?"

"I didn't mean to see anything! I was just moving papers out of the way. I saw your budget sheet. I couldn't help it." He spread his arms out to the side. "It was an honest mistake."

"Well, it isn't your business, so forget what you saw." Hannah's nostrils flared as she got to her feet, folding her arms. "I'm fine. Things are fine. And even if they weren't, it's not your *business*."

"Maybe I can help." He couldn't leave her like this, not when he had the means to support her. "I'll talk to Ben. We can give you a loan, or a gift, or something. We've had a good year. Really, we'd do it with any of our friends."

Her jaw looked so tight, she was practically shaking. "You should go."

What the hell? On the heels of confusion, anger rushed in. "You're turning down help? You're just going to let your business collapse?"

"It's *my business*, Mitchell!" She was shouting now, trembling, and he wanted to reach out and comfort her, but she was already pressuring him toward the door.

He left his coffee on the table, backing away. "Okay, okay." What the hell was up with her? Why didn't she want his help? Did she really hate him that much?

"How could you think I would say yes to this? I barely know you."

"Barely know me?" Rage and hurt stabbed at him. "I thought we've moved pretty far beyond 'barely knowing' each other."

"Fucking doesn't count. It doesn't mean anything when we fuck. And you don't even want to *fuck* me anymore."

Mitchell pulled back, her words cutting into him like a physical pain.

Hannah crossed her arms tightly across her chest. "I'm not your girlfriend and I'm not your pet project and I'm not your charity case."

Jesus. He couldn't believe he was hearing this. He'd thought they were close. Months of flirting at the restaurant, that first date and the way he'd held her afterward, their threesome, evenings hanging out at the apartment, the Fall Festival, all the in-between times and laughter and friendship.

How could she ignore all that?

"I thought I was being helpful."

"Well, you're not. Thanks." She spit the last word out like a curse.

Throat tight, he walked out and slammed the door behind him.

. . .

Ben was down in their brewery in the basement of the restaurant when footsteps echoed on the stairs. Mitchell usually walked more lightly, so hearing him thundering down, it was obvious something was wrong.

Ben turned in his swivel chair and looked up from his work, waiting with hands folded for Mitchell's arrival. Mitchell was already scowling as he entered the room.

"What's up with you? Get your wallet back?"

Mitchell held it up, then put it back in his pants pocket. "It's Hannah."

"What about Hannah?"

Mitchell hesitated, and Ben was instantly on his guard. Whatever Mitchell had done, it wasn't good, or he wouldn't be giving his guilt face.

Mitchell rubbed the stubble on his chin. "I was trying to help."

"Oh god."

"Hey." Mitchell lifted his chin indignantly. "She had financial paperwork out on the table. Her business is headed deep into the red, and it looks like the festival didn't help her that much at all. I don't know how she's staying in business. Her rent is completely ridiculous."

Ben frowned. It made sense that she had to be paying too much with a storefront on Main Street. "Well, shit, that sucks. No wonder she never wants to talk money."

Mitchell looked over to the side, toward the large, gleaming brewing tanks. He started to pace, walking back and forth across the floor in front of Ben, his black chef shoes squeaking when he turned to make another lap.

"I just don't understand it. She knows me. She knows I care about her and I don't want anything bad for her. I don't get why she won't just let me help."

"How did you try to help?" This could be really bad.

Mitchell paused, hands in his pockets. "I offered her to give her the money."

Aww, shit. "You didn't."

"I don't see what's wrong with that." Mitchell got a little louder. "What am I supposed to do, sit and let her go out of business? I care about her! And I know you do, too."

Too bad he didn't have a beer.

"Clearly, I don't want her to go out of business. But nobody wants to feel like they're getting charity. It's embarrassing." How was he supposed to communicate this to Mitchell? "She's got pride."

"Well, she shouldn't!" Mitchell stopped and threw his arms up. "She's going to let herself go bankrupt because of pride."

"People have done more for less."

Mitchell sighed, the sigh of someone who had just given up. "I don't get it. I thought I was approaching this from a perfectly logical standpoint. But she acted like I insulted her."

"You did insult her!" Ben tried not to explode, suddenly torn between his embarrassment on Hannah's behalf and his irritation with Mitchell. "You told her she needs your charity, like she isn't good enough to do it herself."

"I don't understand why someone isn't going to confront the complete truth of their situation and do whatever they can do to get out of it. You have a friend who wants to help, you swallow your pride and you *take the help*." Mitchell slowed his pacing until he was really just wandering back and forth in ever-dissolving lines, soon making loops and circles in the open space, meandering as he spoke. "She should have been grateful. I didn't have to offer anything."

"You're really caught up on this, aren't you?"

Mitchell looked over. "Caught up on what?"

"Being the one who saves the day. Having her be grateful to you."

Mitchell flushed. There it was, that savior complex, the one that was going to get him in trouble over and over again. He mumbled something and turned his face away.

Ben got up. "I didn't catch that."

Mitchell sighed. "I said, I don't care if she's grateful to me."

That was a crock of shit, so much that Ben didn't even need to argue with him. They both knew it.

"Hey," he said gently, trying to get Mitchell's attention.

Mitchell looked up at him, then away again, his expression sour. "What?"

"You remember back when we decided to open the pub?"

Mitchell nodded.

Ben swallowed, because this was the worst part. "You remember how I had, like no money, because I blew it all at the casino, and was about to lose my apartment? You remember that?"

"Of course I remember that. I don't get what that has to do with anything." Mitchell shifted in discomfort, probably unsure why Ben was bringing this up now.

"You told me you wanted to go into business with me and

open a pub. Move together to western Massachusetts. You said you needed my help."

"I did need your help."

"Bullshit." Ben pointed at him, because dammit, Mitchell needed to understand this. "You had more than enough money to open the pub on your own. You could have paid for everything and hired me on to work on the beer. But instead you waited until I could buy in to it. We even signed a contract to make sure we were each putting in equal shares. Equal shares, equal responsibility."

"Well, yeah." Mitchell shrugged as if it was the most obvious thing. "I didn't want you to feel like you owed me anything. We wouldn't have been equals." He paused, and then his face fell. "Oh."

"Hannah's allowed to have her pride. She's kept that business going for four years."

"So what am I supposed to do? Just sit back and watch her fail?" Mitchell's agonized expression reflected back in the steel of the tanks, distorted by the curved surface.

Ben sighed. "I don't know if there's anything we can do. It's her business. If she doesn't want help, that's her right." He looked up at the ceiling, staring into the distance...and then focused on the ceiling itself, imagining the building above.

"Actually, I might have an idea."

Chapter Sixteen

A full day's work hadn't alleviated Hannah's feelings of embarrassment and anger at all, even though she had managed to distract herself with endless tiny jobs at the shop. Everything she saw reminded her that she had a chance of losing this place, though, and when she finally closed up for the night, she sat behind the counter for a good fifteen minutes trying to pull herself together to drive home.

The meeting with the building owner had been useless. The woman was nice enough, but her own expenses had gone up, and they had a business looking to rent the space who was making a much better offer than what Hannah could pay. Hannah couldn't meet it, so she was going to be out. Strictly business.

Losing this business wasn't just going to mean losing her dream, but it would also put her employees out of work. She could keep things going through the holidays, but she couldn't sign the lease for the new year. She'd have to close. Sitting just this side of Halloween, the next few months felt like a death march.

Once she finally got home, she ate some pasta while standing over the stove and drank half a bottle of wine while sprawled on the couch. Time to text Lori.

Lori showed up in a half hour, already in her pajamas with her hair wrapped in a silk scarf, curls spilling out the top like a pineapple.

"Bitch, this is gonna be about your fucked-up love life, isn't it? I literally got out of bed for this."

"Were you sleeping?" Hannah stepped aside to let her in.

"No, but I was watching a new show on Netflix, so it is *just* as important." Lori flopped down on the couch.

"Thank you, and I love you. And I made popcorn." She retrieved it from the kitchen table and brought it back to the living room along with the rest of the bottle of wine. "I'm a little bit drunk. I already drank half of this bottle."

"Oh, so it's definitely about your love life."

"It's actually not." Hannah paused. "Well, it sort of is. It's related."

"All right." Lori took the entire metal bowl into her lap and patted the spot on the couch beside her, then shoveled a handful of popcorn into her mouth. "Tell me all the stuff you've been hiding."

Hannah sighed, and it sounded pretty dramatic once she had finished sighing.

"Is it about the workshop?"

Shit, the workshop felt like a lifetime ago instead of literally *last night*. "No. It's not about that." She sighed. "I'm about to lose my business."

Lori fumbled the bowl. It slipped out of her hands and crashed down onto the floor, spilling popcorn all over the area rug. She let it lie. "What do you mean, you're about to lose your business? I thought you did really well at the Fall Festival. You said you just needed a boost to pay off the marketing loan."

"They're raising my rent again with the new lease. I can't sign it. I won't be able to break even."

Hannah suddenly felt tears well up in her eyes, and goddamn it, she was *not* going to cry. She tried to will herself to pull it together. *Don't cry, don't cry, don't cry.* She tried to keep her expression neutral, but it wasn't working, given Lori's look of general concern that turned to mild horror.

"Stop doing that with your face. I don't mind if you cry." She got up, walked off to the bathroom, and returned with a box of tissues. "Did you talk to the building owner and try to renegotiate?"

Hannah nodded. Fuck, now she was really going to cry. She grabbed a tissue and let the tears come, hiccuping herself into some wet, gross sobs that normally she'd be mortified to let anyone hear. Her next words came out really muffled and teary.

"Give me another go at that, maybe after a deep breath or two." Lori slid in closer and put her hand on Hannah's back, rubbing it in slow circles. "So I take it that's a no-go with the building owner?"

Hannah nodded. "She's not budging. And I can't find any places for rent in town that are within my price range. I've been looking every day, making calls, nothing." Hannah's lip trembled, but she was not going to cry again. "I just don't see any other options."

"What about investors, or a loan?" Lori asked. "Can you get some financial help from somebody else?"

"I don't fucking want to *do* that!" Hannah saw Lori recoil, and yeah, she'd probably been too harsh there, but seriously, Lori needed to understand this. "I love you. But you've got to know this. All my life, I've been nothing. Nobody. I've been middle of the road, smart but not smart enough. I've done nothing noteworthy until I opened this business. And I did it myself. It was the first fucking thing I've ever done that I've been proud of. If somebody else has to bail me out, I can't even be proud of that."

Lori stared at her without blinking for a couple of moments, sizing her up. The silence in the room felt heavy and Hannah wasn't sure where this was going to go, but she had said her piece and expressed the opinions that she had refrained from expressing out loud for a while.

When Lori did speak, her voice was calm. "Hannah. You know I love you. I've been by your side since college, I've watched you grow up and get this business, and work it, and you've watched me live my life, and we have both been there for each other, and you know. You know I am there for you. Right?"

Hannah nodded, still waiting for it.

"Then please know I speak from a place of love when I say that is the fucking stupidest thing I have ever heard you say."

Hannah's mouth fell open, but Lori wasn't done.

"No, don't talk." She held up a hand. "You've said enough right now. You think you haven't done anything impressive? You think you're mediocre? Shit, you're the least mediocre person I know. You're hilarious, and smart, and kind, and resilient as fuck. You never stay down. And now you're about to lose your goddamned business, and the most important thing to you is your independence? Like you aren't anything if you aren't a business owner alone? What good does it do if you fail?"

Her tears welled up again, a few slipping hot down her face. Lori handed her another tissue. "You think I can do *anything* without help? I've got my friends at the newspaper who edit my articles. I've got the therapists at the relationship center coaching me on my practice. I've got my doctoral adviser on my ass about this dissertation, helping me through it. I've taken loans, I've slept on couches, and I've never done a single damn thing without somebody there to lend me a hand. And am I ashamed of any of that? Fuck no. Because I still did it. Because sometimes the thing to be proudest of is knowing when you're in over your head." She took Hannah by the shoulders. "You need to get some help from somebody instead of trying to do all of this by yourself. What do you need? You need business partners? Maybe you can find a business partner."

"Mitchell offered to give me money." The words came out with the same sense of embarrassment and loathing as when she'd first heard his offer.

Lori pursed her lips. "How did you respond?"

"I said no. He came in all self-righteous, going through my paperwork, offering me a loan, like he's God's gift to business or something." Hannah blew her nose.

"He went through your paperwork?" Lori looked aghast.

"No, not really," Hannah amended. "It was an accident. He was moving some papers on the kitchen table and he saw stuff, I guess. But that doesn't matter. You aren't supposed to do business with people you're close to. And it's not even business. It's just a handout. I don't want to be in debt to them like that." Hannah shuddered.

Lori frowned. "How did he take it when you told him no?"

"He was hurt. Stormed out of here." Hannah sighed. "Told me that maybe we shouldn't see each other at all if I can't trust him."

"Ouch."

"Tell me about it." She didn't like to think about that. "And I was just thinking, hey, maybe there's something here. Some potential for a good friendship." She stared down into her wineglass.

Hannah looked back up to see Lori staring at her. "What?"

Lori wore disbelief on her face, her eyebrows raised and lips slightly parted. "Potential for *friendship*?"

"Yeah?" What was so weird about that? "I went to the polyamory workshop thing. I don't want to get involved with all those feelings and emotions and relationships and bullshit. I want casual sex, no dating, no involvement, just like what we wanted at the beginning."

Lori's nostrils flared in her "God give me strength" expression. "I thought you liked hanging out with them."

"I do like hanging out with them. That isn't the issue."

"But you just said..." Lori trailed off, then shook her head. "Never mind. So you went to this whole workshop on polyamory, which is all about loving more than one person, and decided you don't want to love anyone. Got it."

Hannah opened her mouth, then gave Lori a nasty glare as her brain caught up to the words she had heard. "Fuck you."

Lori waved her hand dismissively. "Consider me fucked. Go on."

"So *anyway*. I thought, hey, I can do emotionless sex. So I asked them back here. For some fun."

"So you came out of the workshop and immediately asked them here for a threesome?" Lori's eyebrow went up, arching loftily. She pursed her lips in what was clearly judgment. "Did you at least tell them your feelings first?"

"Well, sort of." At Lori's even *more* judgmental next expression, Hannah snapped, "What? What are you going to say?"

"Nothing. I am here to listen, not to judge your questionable life choices." Lori took some more popcorn, retrieving the bowl from the floor with whatever was left in it. "At least I have snacks for this."

"You know, you're not being a very compassionate friend."

Lori softened. "Okay. I'm sorry. I'm not going to make fun of you. Tell me more about what happened after you invited them here."

Hannah remembered the way that they had moved together into her bedroom, shifting fluidly onto the bed, their hands on her. "They came over and we started to fool around. But then Mitchell freaked out and left. And then after he left, Ben said he couldn't do it anymore, either, and he left, too. I just let them go. I watched them leave. I didn't say anything."

"And then…Mitchell came back?"

"This morning." She nodded. "He left his wallet here. That's when he saw the papers."

"Right." Lori nodded. "And then you threw him out for trying to give you money." When Hannah opened her mouth to retort, Lori held up a hand. "I know, I know. Your reasons are fair."

"I just feel like everything is a mess right now." Hannah shoved the popcorn bowl over to Lori. "Get this away from me or I'm going to eat all of it."

Lori shifted on the couch, stretching one pajama-clad leg along the front of it so her leg and foot just brushed Hannah's. "You need a bigger couch."

"This couch is fine. I live alone."

"Do you like living alone?"

"Yes." Hannah hated that question. "Why would you ask me that?"

Lori's shrug was maddeningly self-satisfied. "I just thought you might want to have more frequent company."

"Just…" Hannah looked up at the ceiling. "Lori. I love you. But fucking spit it out, okay? I'm not a relationship student of yours. I'm not in therapy. Tell me what you are thinking."

"I think that you have gotten really used to having this emotional connection with these guys, and you've backed off and tried to make it just about sex, and they don't like it and neither do you."

"There is nothing wrong with emotionless sex."

"No, there isn't. But you're not having emotionless sex." Lori raised her eyebrows, daring Hannah to object, which she couldn't do. "You're hanging out with them. You like them, it's intimate, blah, blah. So clearly it's not going to be as fun to back away from that. You were never having emotionless sex, so you're trying to take the fun sex you were *actually* having and take away, what? Half of what was fun about it?"

Hannah shook her head. "I don't want to be in a relationship. I definitely don't want to be in two relationships!" She thought about what Kate and Walter had said, about how being in a triad involved an additional relationship with the three of them together. "Three relationships! If you count the triad, that's an extra third relationship. Going from no relationships to three? That's insane! How am I supposed to manage that?" Hannah pressed her hands to the side of her head. "God, Lori. What if I ruin everything? What if I let them in and they both break my heart? How am I supposed to deal with that?"

She wasn't objecting to the right things anymore. Lori reached over and patted her back. "I'm not about to insult you by telling you what to do."

"Thank you."

"But I *am* gonna tell you that if you get chickenshit about this, you are gonna be unhappy about it for a long time."

Hannah looked up, meeting Lori's dark eyes with her own. She nodded, because Lori was right, like she was almost always right. Sighing, she reached for the bottle of wine.

Chapter Seventeen

Hannah pushed open the jingling door of the teahouse and inhaled the deep, earthy aroma of different teas, which was almost enough to settle her nerves on its own. When Ben had texted her about meeting them for tea, she had almost said no, had sat and stared at the phone for five full minutes contemplating, but in the end, she'd made what Lori would consider the brave decision. She had no idea what they wanted to talk about, but she was going to do her part and show up.

Ben and Mitchell were sitting at a low table in the back corner of the restaurant, one open cushion next to theirs. She cautiously made her way over to them and sat down next to Mitchell. Looking from Mitchell to Ben, a weird melancholy settled over her, a mixed-up kind of longing and sadness and hope. She cleared her throat. Those emotions wouldn't help her in this conversation.

"Sorry I didn't get your text earlier. I had my phone in the back room at work."

"It's okay. We're just glad you could come."

In front of them, a tea set was already steaming. "What

kind is this?" she asked.

Ben flipped the page in the book. "It is...Zheng Shan Xiao Zhong. It's a smoky black tea."

Hannah took a sip, tasting pine and hearth fires, cold winter nights, and—somehow—intense nostalgia for the creature comforts of home. She pressed back the sudden emotion in her throat. "It's good. I like it." Sipping again, she tried to calm herself. "So. You wanted to talk to me about something."

Mitchell and Ben exchanged a glance, and Ben was the one who spoke. "We miss you."

"Both of you? The two of you, as a unit?"

"Each of us, separately, and the two of us together." Ben picked up his cup of tea, which was comically tiny in his gigantic hands. "Can we have that friendship back again? Even without anything else."

"The friendship?" Hannah paused. She hadn't expected them to ask about that. Business, maybe, or possibly sex, but friendship was...unexpected. The thought of being with them again, hanging out, even without the sex, filled some of the ache she had been feeling. "I'd like that."

"There's something else." Mitchell started, and then paused, and then restarted, looking into her eyes with longing in his. "I wanted to apologize. I'm sorry I tried to push money on you. It was condescending. Ben says I have a savior thing with you, and he's probably right. It's not fair to you. So. I'm really sorry."

The tea wouldn't go down easily with her throat so tight. How ironic that now Mitchell was taking back his offer of help when she was finally desperate enough to accept it. She managed to nod, but speaking would be difficult.

"The thing is, though," Ben jumped in, "we like having your business here in Mapleton. So even though you said no to the money, we were wondering if you'd be interested in a more mutual partnership."

"What do you mean?" Hannah shifted on her cushion, tucking one leg under her. The tiny sprig of hope inside her chest bloomed, and fuck, she should not get excited here.

Ben looked to Mitchell, then back to Hannah. "We got an email today from Lori, and she said she's thinking about renting the space for an ongoing polyamory discussion group. We wanted to see if you were interested in partnering up for that and turning it into a mutual marketing opportunity for our businesses."

Hannah furrowed her brow. "What do you mean by partnering up?"

"It would be pretty straightforward to do the marketing for the two businesses together and make it an official promotion." Mitchell gestured between Ben and Hannah. "You sell sex toys at the events, we sell beer, too, and we promote the event at both our shops."

The connection was logical, but her optimism was short-lived. "That wouldn't be enough to keep me open." Saying it out loud left a sour taste in her mouth. "The woman who owns my building is raising my rent for next year if I renew my lease. A few more sales won't cut it. I'll have to close after Christmas."

"Well, that's the other thing." Ben set his teacup down. "We know rent is the biggest part of your problem. We have retail space if you want it. We have that whole office space on the first floor that we aren't using. It would be pretty straightforward to turn it into a storefront."

"There's a second entrance on the side, which you could use as your main entrance," Mitchell added. "Separate entrance, separate parking area, but we'd share the building."

Hannah hesitated. God, that was tempting. "That's a lot of renovation." Prices started stacking up in her mind. Could she afford to take out another loan to renovate the place?

Mitchell put down his cup, too. "Not cheap. Free. No rent. No renovation costs."

"I don't want—" she began, but he cut her off with a wave of his hand.

"It's not charity. Let me finish. In exchange for rent and renovation costs, we want a profit share. Financial investment." Mitchell opened the satchel he always carried and pulled out a document, and she already knew what that was going to be. Heart pounding, she took it. This was her contract, her equivalent of the one Mitchell and Ben had hanging on their wall. "We had our lawyer look into it and draft up some terms that we thought were fair for both of us. We thought you could take it with you, maybe have someone else look it over. It's a place to start."

Hannah's heart and mind tumbled over each other, excitement and fear wrestling with comprehension. "So you're saying you would renovate part of your building and let me operate my business out of it, rent-free, and in exchange, you'd take a cut of my profits?"

"A fair percentage. It's an investment in the success of your business." Ben was talking more quickly now, too, getting caught up in the excitement. "We both believe in it. With this contract, it's in everyone's best interest that you succeed."

There had to be a piece she was missing. Even with the excitement—no, the elation—something nagged at her, and she couldn't put her finger on it. This was too good to be true. "I don't know." She held the papers and tried to read them, numbers and words swimming in her vision as she blinked to focus. The numbers looked good, definitely fair but not charity. Still, though. Fear skittered under her skin, the rabbit-racing heartbeat of anxiety thrumming through her. Her hands were shaking again, and she set them down in her lap to try to settle them. After a moment, Mitchell's hand closed over hers.

"Hannah." Mitchell's gaze was sympathetic, but he wasn't looking at her with pity. "You don't have to do everything alone."

The words opened up something inside her, and tears began welling up, tears she did not want to spill in front of someone else. She blinked them back, pressing her lips tightly together as if that might stop the flood. When she spoke, her voice trembled, and she hated that, but she said it anyway.

"What kind of person am I if I can't do the one thing I set out to do?"

Mitchell didn't shy away from the strong emotion, not letting go of her hands. "What kind of person are you if you'd rather fail alone than succeed with friends?"

Something twisted low in Hannah's stomach. "Are we still friends?"

"Of course we're still friends."

She didn't want to ask the next question, but it was torn out of her. "And you still want to do this for me even though we're not fucking?"

Mitchell and Ben exchanged a dubious look, both of them with eyebrows raised. "Clearly," Ben said. "We told you we want to stay friends."

Hannah held the paper in her hands, her fingers wearing creases into the edges. Her emotions rolled over each other, jumbling together in a whole mixture of confusion and hope all at once that she couldn't parse into any conclusions. "I'm... worked up. How about I take these home and think about it? Is that okay?"

"Sure." Mitchell nodded. "Call us."

Back home, Hannah stood on her back deck looking up at the night stars. The sky was clear with the cold of late October, the way the stars became crisp pinpoints of light when the air hovered around freezing. Her breath fogged in the cold, and she had layered up in a few sweaters to stay warm out here, but something about standing on the back deck in the cold made her feel alive. Not so long ago, she had opened the house after that September Chamber of Commerce meeting, overburdened by heat and the intensity of being face-to-face with Ben. How much had changed in just a few weeks. She wasn't the same person back then. The guys probably weren't the same, either.

There was no good reason not to accept this offer. Mitchell might not have explicitly told her she was too proud, but she wasn't stupid. This was one way out of a bad situation. And she would see Mitchell and Ben every day, probably, and work closely with them, and they wouldn't expect anything more from her than a business relationship. She had seen the contract on their wall. They could mix business and friendship and keep the lines drawn where necessary.

Except she didn't want those lines.

That was the actual problem, the real reason she stood out here breathing her hopes into fog in the stillness of night. The real problem was that she was in love with them.

She was in love with both of them, each of them separately and also somehow with the two of them as a unit, whatever weird triangle they had woven together. She could love either one individually, sure, but that was only a tiny piece of it. This wasn't about choosing one or the other. This was about choosing both of them, for all the weirdness and wonder that entailed.

And hoping they would choose her in return.

They might not. There was something between Mitchell and Ben, whether they had acknowledged it or not, and their intimacy was going to transcend whatever she had with the two of them. There were parts of their relationship that she would never share, no matter how close they all became. She would never be exclusive with one of them, probably.

They were part of a whole team. The thought of that was frightening...and exhilarating.

If she really wanted, she could have the independence and the success. She just had to accept help. And accepting help wasn't really the same as giving up her independence.

Indecision was its own kind of decision, and she had never been one who was okay with indecision. She was more likely to make the wrong decision but decide quickly rather than sit on uncertainty for any length of time. Right now, though, the enormity of yes and no weighed on her. What would it mean to say yes to everything? To say yes to the business partnership, the relationship, the future? She had not imagined a future where she was in a relationship. She'd pictured friends, acquaintances, casual sexual partners, but not love. Yet now she was imagining it, and longing pressed against her heart from the inside.

All of it, though, was contingent upon Ben and Mitchell.

If she told them, and they weren't interested in the relationship after all, they would probably still make the business offer. It might be really awkward, but they would be able to make it okay. But she would have to live with that awkwardness, as well as the knowledge that they didn't want her in the same way. She could always *not* tell them about her feelings, just live with the friendship as it was, and she wouldn't have to be vulnerable.

Mitchell wanted her to swallow her pride. Lori wanted her to be vulnerable and open. For the first time in her life, she was afraid of everything, and she didn't want to be afraid anymore.

Hannah rested her arms on the railing and looked out into the night, watching her breath fog up in the cold air and then dissipate, the way worries sometimes did. Not these, though. These lingered like frost, gathering slick on all the surfaces. There was so much yet to come.

Chapter Eighteen

The last time Mitchell had been standing on Hannah's doorstep, she had thrown him out for offering money. It hadn't been that many days, and now he was here again, this time with Ben, and he had no idea what to expect. At least this time she'd invited them. They'd driven over here together after work in the darkness, the two of them silent but both probably remembering the last time they'd made this drive together. Hopefully tonight would go differently.

Hannah opened the door, smiling tentatively, her hands thrust in the pockets of an oversize hoodie. "You want to come in? I haven't cleaned."

Seeing her like this reminded him again how much he missed her, how much he wanted her back in his life, in whatever capacity. He noticed her beauty every time, the way she was soft and warm and luminous, her skin glowing as though she were lit from within. With her long, wavy hair and those color-changing eyes, maybe he would always see her as some ephemeral fairy creature, more lovely than any person had any right to be, and damn, he was so in love with her. He and Ben hung up their coats and slipped off their shoes, then sat together on the couch, across from where she took her spot on a chair.

"So." Hannah looked between the two of them. "I know it's been a few days. I've been thinking about the offer you guys made me. Been thinking about it pretty much nonstop, honestly." She smiled, looking down at her hands. "This is hard for me. I'm not gonna lie. I don't take help easily and I never have. I think that's always going to be a struggle for me. I don't want someone to give me charity, and I don't want to feel like I'm in somebody's debt." She shifted in her chair.

Mitchell could get that, and told her so. "I'm proud of what I've managed to do," he added, "but I never could have done it all without help. Ben balances me. We make a good team."

"You do." There was something wistful in Hannah's gaze. "The two of you complete each other, don't you?"

Mitchell glanced at the man next to him. "We complement each other. But we're not halves of a whole."

"But you make good partners."

"We decided to get more serious." Mitchell blurted it out into the room and then looked at Ben, who nodded.

"Yeah. Turns out I love him." Ben smiled. "Who knew?"

Hannah smiled. "Me, for weeks now. I can't believe you two took this long to figure it out."

Mitchell fiddled with the hem of his shirt. "Yeah, she was trying to tell me this since the Fall Festival."

Ben shrugged. "I guess we figured it out eventually."

Hannah shifted on the chair, tucking a leg underneath herself, her large hoodie making her look small. "I don't know if what I have to say is relevant anymore. But is the offer still open? For business partners?"

"Of course it is." Mitchell didn't even have to look at Ben to confirm.

Hannah got up again, went into the kitchen, and came back with the single sheet of paper they had given her, a contract written in eight-point font to match the one on their wall. "I signed it." She set it down on the table between them and stayed standing, her hands clenched at her sides. "I'm in. And I'm scared, and I hate being vulnerable like this, but I'm in."

God, he'd been hoping this was her answer. Overcome with emotion, Mitchell got to his feet and swept her into his arms. She returned the hug, but her body was still stiff with tension.

"It's good," Mitchell said, holding her against him. "This is good."

"Better than good." Ben beamed up at the two of them, getting to his feet. "We can do this together."

"There's something else." Hannah disengaged herself from Mitchell's embrace, holding him at arm's length, and then took another full step backward. "The business thing, that's no matter what. I want to do that regardless of what comes next. But I think I need you both to know..." She took a deep breath and let it out. "Ooh. Man. This is hard. Okay." She looked up at the ceiling and rubbed her hands together. "Shit. Maybe I should have just texted this."

And just like that, Mitchell knew. He knew with the certainty he had felt when he went to culinary school, and when he opened the pub, and when he first took Ben to bed. He knew what she was going to say even as she struggled to find the words, looking at him with longing in her eyes.

"I'm in love with you." She looked from Mitchell to Ben. "Both of you."

Mitchell couldn't answer, his heart beating so fast it might come out of his chest, and fuck, this was what he wanted, and he knew it was what Ben wanted, and he wanted to answer for them. Instead, he looked to Ben, who was staring at her with the same expression, dumbfounded and hopeful.

"I love you," Mitchell said, because someone had to say it into the silence. "I think I've loved you for a long time. I didn't...say anything."

"Because I told you I didn't want it," Hannah finished.

"We both thought that," Ben echoed. "Of course I love you. We love you. We love you back."

"I didn't want to want this." She was laughing, the kind of upset, emotional laughing when someone was so strung out with fear and hope and longing that all their feelings tumbled out in a wave of cathartic release. "I wanted to be fine with just friendship, or sex, or business partners, but I want all of it. I want this messy, weird-ass triad. I love you both, I love the three of us together, and I don't know how it's going to work, but I want it to work."

"It's going to be a mess." Ben walked up to Hannah and took her into his arms. She hugged him back, resting her head on his chest. As one, Hannah and Ben looked over at Mitchell. "Well?" she asked.

"Well, what?"

"Are you coming over here or not?"

Mitchell joined them in their awkward three-person embrace, and when Hannah turned to kiss him, his heart swelled like it might burst right away from joy. This was going to be a mess, sure, but he couldn't think of any better mess he'd rather have.

Hannah pulled back and put her hand on Mitchell's cheek, then turned to Ben. "This feels too good to be true."

"Yeah." Ben huffed out a laugh. "I can't really make sense of it, either."

She bit her lip. "I'm probably rushing back into things but...can I please take you both to bed?"

• • •

Hannah's bed wasn't as big as Ben's, but it was plenty big enough for all of them. It gave underneath Hannah as she climbed onto it, letting her body sink into the soft memory-foam surface, and watched the two men approach. Her men. Something warm settled in her heart at the thought, something emotional and not as lustful as she usually felt in this exact same situation—at least until she saw them start stripping off their clothing. Then that love turned way more directly to lust.

As soon as Mitchell was down to his boxers, the shift came over him, the way he transitioned into dominance with the look that she absolutely adored. She let him tug off her clothes, blinded by the dizzying speed with which he got her naked in moments, all in the time it took Ben to get out of his jeans.

Mitchell pushed her back on the bed with a firm hand in the middle of her chest, then stretched out alongside her and began to nibble his way down her neck. Hannah closed her eyes. God, there were the sparks under her skin, those tingles of pleasure running through her body with each brush of his teeth or his lips. The bed dipped on her other side, and then Ben was there, too, his mouth working her over as well.

Each of them found her breasts at the same time, and at the sensation of mouths closing over her nipples simultaneously, Hannah arched up off the bed. Fuck, she hoped she never got used to that intensity. With the tight, sucking pull, the scrape of teeth, the warmth of their mouths, her pussy throbbed with need. She hadn't thought she'd get this again. She hadn't thought she'd be lucky enough to have this more than once. Gratitude overwhelmed her, momentarily taking her out of the moment, before sharp teeth on her nipple slammed her back into the experience of her body.

Mitchell pulled away first, moving back up so he could whisper in her ear, but his fingers tugged and twisted the nipple his mouth had just left. "I want to watch you suck Ben's cock." He traced the shell of her ear with his tongue. "I want to see you take that giant dick in your mouth. Do you want to do that?"

Hannah nodded, her breathing coming in gasps. Mitchell's hand had strayed to the V at the juncture of her thighs, teasing the curls there, but he wasn't touching her, not yet, even though she spread her legs to give him access. She shifted her hips up, because come on, this was not the time for teasing. "Eager?" he asked, smiling.

"Yes." Desperate was more like it.

"Good. Do a nice job on Ben and maybe I'll touch you."

She shivered, because his words hit exactly the right nerves inside her. She loved seeing this shift in him, the duality between the calm, reserved chef and this naughty, confident Dom. Ben lifted his head from her breast, and Hannah immediately took the chance to push him over onto his back.

She loved his cock, loved sucking it, loved the way he was nearly too big for her mouth. Ben lay back, breathing heavily, as she dragged her tongue across the head. She kept her eyes on him as she wrapped her lips around him and began to suck.

Mitchell moved to sit right beside her and gathered a fistful of her hair in his hand. He tugged, just a bit, testing it out, and she moaned her approval, because this was good every single time. She relaxed her mouth as he forced her down farther onto Ben's cock. His grip on her hair became merciless, tight, painful, exactly what she wanted. She used her fist on the part of Ben's cock she couldn't reach, squeezing and twisting while she sucked the head and top of the shaft.

Ben tensed up beneath her, but Mitchell's voice was right there.

"Don't come," he ordered, and Ben wouldn't, because

he would hold off forever to keep from disobeying Mitchell. Mitchell used his grip to pull her all the way off Ben's cock, and she wiped her mouth with the back of her hand, her lips sore and swollen, hoping she looked as fantastically slutty as she felt.

She wanted to taste Mitchell, too. He shifted on the bed for a better angle, and she stretched out to swallow him down. She could take more of him into her mouth, but he still stretched her out, was too big to deep throat. He made perfect little groaning noises as she sucked him. Damn, this was so fucking hot, so perfect, decadently wicked. Slickness coated her thighs.

"Stop." His voice was sharp, commanding, and she pulled away, seeing the tension in his body. None of them wanted this to be over too soon. Mitchell spoke to Ben, dragging his tongue across his lower lip. "I want to fuck her with you."

Ben nodded, talking about Hannah like she wasn't even there, and fuck, that was always going to be one of her favorite kinks. "God, yeah."

Hannah shivered at the thought. She'd never done this before, and she knew they hadn't, either. But she'd spend many nights with her fingers and toys between her thighs, thinking about this very fantasy.

Mitchell finally addressed Hannah. "Do you want that?" His voice sounded low and husky, hot like a lit match brushing her skin. "Do you want both our cocks inside you at the same time?"

She nodded, whole body trembling with a mixture of arousal and excitement and apprehension. At her trembling, Mitchell moved forward, cupping the back of her head and bringing her closer for a kiss. She'd expected a bruising, intense kiss, but instead his kiss was sweet and caring. "Do you want to feel stuffed full?" he asked against her lips.

"Oh god," she breathed. Yes, she wanted that, if her body

would handle it.

"You're not nearly warmed up enough for this." Mitchell pushed her down on her back and then looked over at Ben. "Come help."

Ben grinned. "Absolutely." Ben kissed her, his beard brushing her skin, lips moving over hers. Ben's large hand on her breast, tweaking her nipple, took her into this moment so deeply she lost track of everything else. Dimly, she felt Mitchell spreading her legs apart, then his mouth firm and wet against her clit.

Hannah jerked in Ben's arms and cried out, breaking the kiss at the sudden surprise of Mitchell between her legs. Fuck, she couldn't breathe. He was attacking her clit with steady sucks and pulls, sharp pleasure slicing into her, and she couldn't get enough air. She could come like this if he continued, but did she want to come so soon? She might not be able to resist; her climax bore down on her, inexorable, consuming her in the steady build.

At the last minute, though, Mitchell pulled away, leaving Hannah twitching and clenching at the near edge of an orgasm. She moaned, flopping her head back on the pillow as her climax faded away to a dull ache. What the *fuck*. That tease was horrible, and delicious, and perfect.

"There's no rush." Mitchell smiled up at her and stepped out from between her legs. She twitched, wanting him to continue, not wanting him to leave her like this. But then he opened the doors of her toy cabinet. "Ben, do you want to help me find something good?"

Jesus. Watching the two of them inspect her collection was incredibly hot, the moment filled with immense potential and the perfect mix of excitement and apprehension. Ben emerged with lube and two dildos, one rather thin, and the other quite a bit thicker...each with flared bases, and this was headed someplace wonderful.

"Here we go." Mitchell smiled and sat down on the bed next to her torso. "Why don't you lie back for us?"

It was more tempting to look down at what was happening as Ben sat between her legs, spreading them, but Mitchell lightly touched her under the chin.

"Eyes on me." He began to pinch her nipples lightly, then harder, making her gasp and bringing all her attention to this pleasure-pain. She almost didn't notice the first moment of pressure at her ass, but then, *ohh*. The dildo slipped inside, slicked by lube, that sudden stretched-out feeling jolting her like a shock to her nerves. Ben began to work her clit in slow circles with his other hand, taking time to slip the dildo deeper and deeper inside her. Jesus, that was fantastic, that delightful combination of forbidden and illicit, enough to make her shift her hips up and meet his thrusts. Her vision went fuzzy as Ben rubbed her clit harder, taking her back to that peak as he fucked her back and forth with that dildo. Damn, she was on the edge fast.

Before she could warn him, Ben had already stopped and slid the dildo out. *Fuck*. Her body clenched at nothing, hole probably gaping, seeking more. Then he pressed the other dildo against her, the larger one, the one almost as large as Mitchell's dick.

The toy popped inside with little resistance, an electric shock of sensation. Hannah gasped as her body clenched around the toy, spasming in arousal even though she hadn't yet come. He slid the toy the whole rest of the way in one long, smooth slide, and she moaned long and loud at the white-hot pleasure.

"Feels good, doesn't it?" Mitchell leaned down to kiss her. "I had Ben open me up just like this last week before he fucked me."

Hannah couldn't help but picture it, Mitchell letting Ben press that giant cock into him, and she focused on the sensations as Ben worked the fake dick into her ass, opening her up the same way he had opened up Mitchell. She could fall apart just like this and never be put back together, and right now, that sounded perfect.

"I think she's ready." Ben's voice sounded husky with want. He set both dildos aside, leaving Hannah soaked and empty and needy for more. They had better hurry up or she was going to combust.

Mitchell stretched out in the middle of the bed. He had already slipped a condom on and was rubbing a lube-slick hand over its length. "Come lie down on me, faceup."

She paused. "Um. Aren't I..." She gestured to herself.

"You're not too heavy. Come on." He stroked himself again, closing his eyes in pleasure. Fuck, he was gorgeous.

Hannah let him guide her as she lay back on top of him, her legs to either side of his. His cock pressed against her from below. Holy shit. She'd never done anything in this position before. Mitchell moved her around easily, guiding her hips. Gently, steadily, he pressed her down onto his cock.

Hannah moaned at that first harsh stretch as the thick head slipped inside. In this position, he could use her however he wanted, and damn if that defenselessness wasn't almost as hot as the sex itself. Mitchell shifted his hips and pushed deeper and deeper into her ass. She was getting impaled, unable to do much more than take whatever he wanted to give her. Inch after inch, he kept going, moving her body to slide her farther onto him until, finally, he was nestled snugly all the way inside.

She was already so full. With Mitchell stretched out beneath her, he was able to whisper right in her ear.

"You're so tight around me. You feel that? Does it feel good?"

Better than good, it felt *incredible*. She squirmed, not really wanting to get away, but wanting to feel how much she couldn't get away even if she wanted to. His cock pulsed steadily in her ass and her clit ached, absolutely ached to be touched. "God. Yes. More."

She reached for her clit, but Mitchell grabbed her wrists from each side.

"Not yet." His voice was rough and low, sexy just in its tone, and his words lit her up. "Gotta wait for that. You want to feel Ben inside you, too? Want to feel him stretch you so wide? Are you ready for that?"

"Ahh, *fuck*." Her curse was a high-pitched whimper. "Fuck. I don't know." She wanted it, but she was nervous, her whole body vibrating.

"Well, you'd better decide." She could hear his smile in his voice.

Ben knelt between her legs, straddling Mitchell's knees below her, and brushed his large fingers against her clit that was so aching to be touched. She swore again at the piercing stab of pleasure, her ass clenching hard around Mitchell's thick cock and making him swear as well. She'd been on the edge twice already, and as Ben touched her, that tension built again. Fuck, she wasn't ready to come like this, not yet, not before the best part, and her body trembled with the effort of holding back.

"Good girl," Mitchell whispered in her ear, and she whimpered brokenly. "You want him to fuck you?"

More of this would kill her. "Yes," she sobbed. "God, yes, please."

Ben's expression was pure lust. He let go of her clit and slipped a finger into her wet pussy, and damn, that one digit felt *huge* when she already had a cock inside her. When she moaned again, he wrapped his free hand around his latex-covered shaft and started giving it slow, steady strokes.

"You want me?" Ben asked. "Say it again."

She nodded. "Please," she begged, throat tight. "God,

please, Ben. Please fuck me."

Mitchell let go of Hannah's wrists and, instead, turned his hands palm up to twine his fingers with hers. She let her head drop back against his collarbone, and his firm, muscled body beneath her was the only solid thing in the world as Ben slowly, carefully pressed his giant cock against her slick folds.

The moment he slipped inside, Hannah's breath caught. She literally froze up, every muscle in her body clenching down, including around Mitchell's cock in her ass. He gripped her hands more tightly and swore into her ear. It burned, it stung, it stretched her impossibly, and it felt absolutely amazing.

Ben, too, looked like he might fall apart. "Damn." He closed his eyes for a moment, one of his hands splayed out on Hannah's belly as he gathered himself. "You okay?"

She nodded, throat still tight. "Yeah. God, don't *stop*."

Every inch he pushed into her was going to make her shatter apart. How could her body handle this? There was no pain, only blinding pleasure, the whiteout overwhelming sensation of being completely filled, and she could do nothing but lie back and take it.

Mitchell's voice was soothing in her ear as he whispered to her. "I can feel him inside you. Do you feel us filling you up?"

"Yes." She didn't know if he could even hear her; she was barely breathing at all.

Ben kept inching forward, pressing into her, bracing himself on her body as he slid forward. He went on *forever*. Finally, *finally*, he stopped, his hips flush with hers. This was impossible. She had no words, nothing to articulate that fucked-full feeling, her body pressed beyond its limits, stuffed totally full.

Mitchell let go of her hands to grab her hips and, oh, began to move. In this position, he could thrust shallowly, sliding back and forth just enough to emphasize how stretched she was. Ben had more range of movement, and as he began to move as well, her body lit up from the inside.

Every movement sent off fireworks, and she couldn't hold out. Damn, she wanted this to last; she wanted to delay her orgasm and savor this experience, but she had been on the edge for so long, her body was already shaking apart. "Fuck," she whimpered. "Oh. I'm gonna *come*." Ben took her breasts in his hands, catching both her nipples between his fingers, a whip crack of sudden pain, and she was lost.

This wasn't like any orgasm she'd had before, this climax with its waves of pleasure, its intensity, its painful beauty; this rapture was going to kill her and rend her apart. The ecstasy was never going to end. Hannah couldn't focus on anything but the way her body tensed up over and over around the fullness inside her, the twisting fierceness of Ben's fingers on her nipples, the sensation of Mitchell moving in short strokes inside her. She was just one nerve ending, no thought, just feeling, the world dissolving into shards of touch and sound.

She had only just begun to come back to herself when Ben began to thrust harder, and with those thrusts, she tumbled over the edge into another climax right on the edge of the first, or maybe it was still the first, and she knew she was crying out. Ben came, pulsing inside her, and then Mitchell, the hot swell of their cocks stretching her minutely farther, mutual thrusts changing in the moment of climax. Then she collapsed weakly, all pleasure and intensity fading away, leaving her limp in Mitchell's arms as everything dissolved around her.

"Hey."

Ben's voice in her ear brought her back, and she dimly opened her eyes, groggy and stretched out and sloppy-loose with sated comfort. "Hmm?"

"Don't fall asleep on us." Mitchell's voice came from

behind her, clearly smiling. "We're a mess."

Hannah laughed. They had already pulled out of her, and everyone was slick with sweat and lube and fluids.

"We didn't kill you?" Ben brushed her hair back. "I thought we'd lost you for a little while there."

"What a way to go. Death by fucking." She managed to push herself up to a sitting position. "Shower?"

Next to her, Mitchell sat up as well, sweat-slick and mussed, but smiling. "Shower."

Hannah had never slept between two people before, definitely not in her queen-size bed. In the future, they'd have to do this in Ben's king-size monstrosity. She could allow those thoughts now. A new sensation settled in her chest: hope.

On either side of her, the two men curled close, Ben spooned along her back and Mitchell facing her. In the darkness, she could just see the glint of his eyes. He was looking at her. She traced a hand through his soft hair.

I love you still felt weird in her mouth, but she said it, quietly into the stillness. Mitchell smiled.

"I didn't think we'd end up here." He tangled his legs with hers and slid an arm over her side.

Ben kissed her cheek from behind. "I don't think anybody knew."

Hannah closed her eyes and reveled in their warmth. This was not anything like what she had expected. And yet, somehow, it was exactly what she needed. Tomorrow would bring new challenges, surely, and new questions and introspection that she couldn't foresee. But now, she no longer had to face tomorrow alone. She could face it side by side with Ben and Mitchell. For now, tonight, in their arms, she was content.

Epilogue

"Wow, look at this place."

At the sound of Mitchell's voice, Ben looked up from the shelves he was stocking. Mitchell stood in the doorway in his chef jacket, rubbing his palms briskly as he stepped in from the November chill. Hannah looked up, too, from where she was arranging dildos on a shelf.

"It's pretty good, right?" Hannah looked around the space. "We should be able to open by Black Friday, right on schedule."

Ben stepped back and surveyed their progress as well. They had been working hard on setup for the last three days, getting everything moved over from her shop so she could open as quickly as possible for the holiday rush.

"I can't believe it's happening so fast." Hannah exhaled. "I don't think I ever really thanked you for this. For getting the construction work done so fast, getting me in here within three weeks."

"Yeah, well, it's what business partners do for each other." Ben smiled. He couldn't help being happy that he was able to help. He looked over at Mitchell. "Why don't you have a coat?"

Mitchell rubbed his arms briskly again. "Coats are a weakness. It's so hot in the kitchen. I'm just on break before dinner prep. Wanted to see how everything was turning out."

Hannah laughed, leaving the dildo rack and walking over to him. She wrapped her arms around him. "You smell like the kitchen."

Mitchell grimaced. "Ugh, don't remind me."

"I like it. Smells like food." She nibbled up to his neck, and Mitchell ducked, ticklish. Ben smiled. Watching the two of them flirt like this warmed his heart. He hadn't expected this kind of casual intimacy from polyamory, the joy of watching people he loved loving each other.

Mitchell pulled away, but he was smiling back. "You two going to come up for dinner tonight?"

"We might be able to make a late meal." Ben gestured to the room. "I think we can finish most of the setup tonight if we hustle."

"And then tomorrow I'm going to help him bottle the next set of winter lagers." Hannah walked back over to Ben. When Ben went to protest, she held up a hand. "Come on. It's the least I can do."

"I won't mind the help." Bottling was always a pain in the ass. "And you've got the grand opening info going out in an email blast?"

"Marketing folks got me all set up." Hannah smiled. "I keep waiting for the other shoe to drop. When does the shitty stuff start?"

"Maybe when we start this polyamory discussion group after Thanksgiving?" Mitchell offered. "And we have to talk about our feelings with strangers?"

"It's going to be good marketing." Hannah didn't sound convinced. "At least, that's what Lori keeps telling me."

"It's our next adventure." Ben looked between the two people in the room with him, the ones who had stolen his heart. "I think we're due for one, don't you?"

Hannah laughed. "I don't think we need any more adventures for a long time."

"But we're going to get them." Mitchell seemed apprehensive but confident, and it was a good look for him. "We're going to have a lot of them in the future."

That may be true, but for Ben, for now, having these two in his life was all the adventure he needed.

Acknowledgments

It seems fitting that a book about polyamory would take so many people to bring it to life. First off, I'd like to thank my agent, the indefatigable Saritza Hernandez, for standing by my side throughout this process. This has been the most challenging book I've ever written, and she talked me off the figurative ledge several times when I wanted to give up. Her steadfast coaching, shrewd business mind, and talented mentorship have helped me in ways that transcend my writing career. Every Hufflepuff should be so lucky to have a Slytherin like her on their side.

I'd also like to thank Entangled Publishing for believing in this trilogy, especially Tera Cuskaden, my editor. Her ruthless edits challenged me to push this book as far as it could go, deep-diving into character, conflict, and structure. Her high standards have pushed me to become a better writer, and I will be forever grateful.

I am blessed with a number of close friends who have encouraged me throughout this book's creation. Thanks to the Sanctuary, my Kik chat group, for having unwavering faith in me. A huge thanks to my bestie Kysmet for co-hosting the Come and Play podcast and for letting me vent over Memories of Prague at the Dobra Tea House. And finally, this book wouldn't be what it is if it weren't for my own experiences with polyamory. To my intimate network—you loved ones who have been in my head and in my bed over these past two years— thank you for the conversations, the cuddles, the challenges, and for expanding my understanding of love.

About the Author

Stay informed about Elia Winters! Receive bonus content and subscriber-only specials, plus info on new releases and personal appearances. http://eliawinters.com/newsletter

If you love erotica, one-click these hot Scorched releases...

GOOD GIRLS LIKE IT DIRTY
a *Dirty Debts* novel by Carmen Falcone

Monique Drummond needs to focus on studying, but right now she can't get her mind off her sexy boss. Her desire for him has some seriously racy fantasies rising to the surface and she can't concentrate on anything other than being a hot distraction for him too. Monique isn't sticking around much longer, and she's all too willing to make a sinfully wicked deal with the man who wants nothing more than a thirty-day, all-access pass to her body.

A NEW ORLEANS THREESOME
a *The Vampire, the Witch, and the Werewolf* novel by Louisa Bacio

Haunted by paranormal abilities she can't control and plagued by nightmares about a demon that seeks her soul, Lily Anima travels to New Orleans in search of salvation. She enlists the help of an unlikely couple: a vampire, Lawrence Justice, and a werewolf, Trevor Pack. The attraction is immediate and fierce. There's only one problem. Lily's a virgin. And whatever paranormal problem she's having is what has kept her that way.

Improper Proposal
a *Dossier* novella by Cathryn Fox

Billionaire Will Thomas is back in England for a big surprise. Could Harper be it? One thing he is sure of...he wants her for himself. It's been a long time since he's been attracted to a woman like this. Harper takes one look at Will and her body burns. He's tall, hot, and looks at her with hunger in his eyes. But giving in to their desires means all kinds of complications for them both...

Fight Twice for Me:

Two Stepbrothers are Better than One
a *Fight for Me* novel by C.C. Wylde

The last place I wanted to be is at my ex's MMA club, especially since I've sworn off fighters. I never anticipated meeting the De La Cruz twins there. Could *anyone* resist a chance at a night of mind-blowing sex with them? It felt good to forget the rules... until I woke up to find out they were my new stepbrothers. It's about to get complicated.

9 781724 687715